ANTONY

Also by Allan Massie

Novels

Change and Decay in All Around I See
The Last Peacock
The Death of Men
One Night in Winter
Augustus
A Question of Loyalties
Tiberius
The Sins of the Father
Caesar
The Ragged Lion
These Enchanted Woods
King David
Shadows of Empire

Non-Fiction

Muriel Spark
Ill-Met by Gaslight
The Caesars
Portrait of Scottish Rugby
Colette
101 Great Scots
Byron's Travels
Glasgow: Portrait of a City
The Novel Today 1970–89
Edinburgh

ALLAN MASSIE
ANTONY

SCEPTRE

Copyright © 1997 Allan Massie

First published in 1997 by Hodder and Stoughton
A division of Hodder Headline PLC
A Sceptre Book

The right of Allan Massie to be identified as the Author of
the Work has been asserted by him in accordance with the
Copyright, Designs and Patents Act 1988.

10 9 8 7 6 5 4 3 2 1

A CIP catalogue record for this book is
available from the British Library

ISBN 0 340 55604 8

Typeset by Palimpsest Book Production Limited,
Polmont, Stirlingshire
Printed and bound in Great Britain by
Clays Ltd, St Ives plc, Bungay, Suffolk.

Hodder and Stoughton
A division of Hodder Headline PLC
338 Euston Road
London NW1 3BH

For Alison as ever

LIST OF PRINCIPAL CHARACTERS

Marcus Antonius (Mark Antony)	Triumvir
Gaius Julius Caesar Octavianus (Octavian)	Triumvir
Marcus Aemilius Lepidus	Triumvir

ANTONY'S WIVES, FAMILY AND FRIENDS

Fulvia	wife
Octavia	wife
Cleopatra	wife
Cytheris	mistress
Glaphyra	mistress
Antyllus	son
Scribonius Curio	stepson
Gaius Scribonius Curio	friend
Publius Clodius Pulcher	friend
Publius Canidius Crassus	General
Publius Ventidius Bassus	General
Cnaeus Domitius Ahenobarbus	General
Critias	secretary

RIVALS

Marcus Vipsanius Agrippa	friend of Octavian
Caius Cilnius Maecenas	friend of Octavian
Marcus Junius Brutus	conspirator and assassin
Gaius Longinus Cassius	conspirator and assassin
Decimus Junius Brutus Albunes ('Mouse')	conspirator and assassin

MISCELLANEOUS

Sextus Pompeianus (Pompey)	warlord
Artavasdes	King of Armenia
Herod	King of Judaea
Caesarion	son of Cleopatra and Julius Caesar
Alexas	servant to Cleopatra, lover of Critias

CHRONOLOGY

BC

82	Birth of Antony.
63	Catiline's Conspiracy.
58	Caesar begins Gallic War. Antony in the East.
57	Antony fighting in Egypt.
54	Antony joins Caesar in Gaul.
49	Caesar crosses Rubicon, begins Civil War.
44	Antony consul. Caesar murdered. Antony named 'imperator'. Fights against Decimus Brutus. Octavian claims to be Caesar's heir. Cicero delivers speeches against Antony.
43	Triumvirate of Antony, Octavian and Lepidus formed. Proscriptions.
42	Antony defeats Brutus and Cassius at Philippi.
41–40	Siege of Perusia. Pact of Brundisium. Antony marries Octavia and makes his last visit to Rome.
39	Treaty made between Triumvirs and Sextus Pompeius.
36	Antony's Parthian War. Antony goes through a form of marriage with Cleopatra.
34	Antony conquers Armenia.
32	Octavian prepares war against Antony and Cleopatra.
31	Battle of Actium.
30	Last battles of Alexandria. Suicide of Antony and Cleopatra.

I

The gale of the night had blown itself out, but the wind from the mountains still struck cold in little gusts. Trebonius had drawn me out of the theatre and held me in the portico with some tale – of dire import, he insisted – which was so long in its rambling telling that I grew bored, stopped listening, and instead amused myself with eyeing up a pretty whore plying her trade even so early in the day. It is one of my minor regrets that in the tumult that followed, I lost the chance of enjoying her. She was a Syrian, I think, with a dark liquid bold gaze. – You don't need to take that down, Critias.

But I have, as you see. Actually I have learned to ignore this sort of request when he is dictating his memoirs, of which he has already completed three substantial volumes, the last some while back when his fortune was happier. I stopped obeying such commands one day when I was very tired and when my pen seemed to run on without the consent of my will. If that seems odd, I can't help it. It's how it was. Then later, transcribing my notes, for I use a sort of shorthand of my own devising, I judged that what he had not intended me to take down was as interesting and perhaps more revealing than what he wished me to record. So from that day I have trusted my own judgement in deciding what I should write and what not. And I have formed the habit, as you see, of adding my own comments. This can be confusing because I am not always certain subsequently whether I thought something or he said it. Moreover our affairs are now in so wretched a state that ... but he's ready to begin again. No ... he's still pacing the

1

room like a lion in a cage. He still looks like a lion, he still has a noble presence.

Of course Trebonius had been put on me by the conspirators – the self-styled Liberators. I realised that as soon as the cry went up and he grabbed me and assured me that I was in no danger myself. I couldn't believe that, and broke loose from his grip and ducked into the crowd. I'm not going to describe the confusions – you can work that up, later, Critias. You've heard me speak of it often enough and read enough accounts to be able to make something dramatic of it.

Shan't bother. This is at least the third time that he has approached the awful Ides of March, and on previous occasions found himself unable to go on.

All right then, to be quite honest, I couldn't give a description of it myself. I saw nothing, the way you remember nothing of a battle except the odd flash. Violent action is like a dream, more vivid than waking experience. Yet only a few fragments may lodge and be recalled, while the dream itself escapes you. It was like that. In passing, let me say that I've always thought people who claim to remember their dreams in exact detail – Himself was one of course – to be liars. Of course we all lie in our different ways and for different reasons. Octavian lies because he's naturally so crooked he shits in spirals. He might as well be a Cretan like you, Critias.

If my lord says so.

They should have killed me too, then and there. I've never understood why they didn't. Mouse Brutus – that is, Decimus, not Marcus Junius Worthy Descendant of the Noble Brutus – told me later that Cassius had argued for me to be chopped along with Caesar, but that Cousin Markie, as Mouse who loathed him always called the Liberator, nobly said they were killing the tyrant, not his jackals. "Thanks a lot," I said. "Me a jackal?"

"That's how Markie put it," Mouse replied, grinning.

"And what about you, Mouse? Whose side were you on in this debate?"

"Well," Mouse said, "you know I've always been fond of you, and

I even tried to get you on our side, but you were drunk and I don't think took in what I was saying. But now, well, I have to admit that I agreed with Cassius. Entirely, my dear, on account of the respect I have for your abilities."

Well, he was quite right, Mouse was no fool, even if he wasn't as clever as he supposed. They would have been wise to bump me off along with Himself. I soon gave them cause to regret they hadn't. But there was never such an addle-pated business as their conspiracy. They took no measures to seize power or secure control of the city. They really seemed to suppose that with Himself out of the way, the Republic would naturally return to its old equilibrium. I can understand Marcus Brutus thinking that, but Cassius? He was after all no fool.

Himself . . . I think I should say something about Caesar here.

"You have said quite a lot about him already in your previous volumes, my lord. Mind you, it was all rather contradictory. Do you think you can get it straight this time?"

He smacked my head.

"Don't be pert, child."

Child! I'm nearly thirty, and have lived in his household for at least fifteen years, but he still calls me that sometimes, when he is in a good mood, and occasionally when he is perplexed and wandering. The truth is that he's a sentimentalist, like so many Romans, though they would all rather have their tongues drawn than admit it. Intellectually, I despise such soft emotion, but I confess that this is one of the reasons why, in spite of everything – he'd better never see this – I love him. In a way.

Caesar, he said, and threw himself on the couch and drained a goblet of wine, which he then continued to hold, empty, between his hands. Nobody who ever had anything to do with him has ever escaped him. He was a twister – every woman's husband and every man's wife. That's what he was called, on the floor of the Senate. I can't remember who by – you can find out later, Critias. It was true, but not the way it was meant. He loved to exert his charm to take control of you, and then he twisted what he inspired in his conquest. But what was that? Love isn't the right word. I don't think anyone ever really loved Caesar. A few women perhaps, Servilia, Markie's mother, maybe? Not Cleopatra, she played him at his own game. No man who knew him loved him, that wasn't the feeling he inspired. The common soldiers? Perhaps. Certainly he set himself to win their love. He got their devotion. But love? I don't think so. There was something cold in Caesar which denied love. Perhaps he really was a god? After all, Critias, nobody can really love a god, can they? Fear, adore, yes, but love, no.

I was of his party. I served him faithfully. In battle I acted as his lieutenant, and won honour and glory at his side. Yet I was not distressed by his murder, felt no sense of personal loss, could even understand why others whom Caesar trusted and regarded as loyal adherents could have brought themselves to the point of killing him. But if I was not distressed, I was alarmed. I sniffed danger for myself. Excluded from the conspiracy, I was at risk of being excluded from public life. All Rome was in turmoil. I stood at the foot of a landslide that threatened to crush me. And yet, even that first moment, while Caesar's body still lay heaving in its blood, I caught sight of new opportunity. While Caesar lived I was condemned to be subordinate. Now, in the crash of the world, what might I not make of myself?

Fleeing the scene of the crime, uncertain of what was to follow, I repaired first to my own house, and gave orders that preparations should be made for its defence. Then I sent out to discover what was happening in the city. You were among those I sent, weren't you, Critias?

"Indeed I was, my lord," I replied.

After the murder, conscious of the danger to my master, I could not yield to my natural impulse to applaud the deed – for, as a Greek, let me say that I have always viewed these tyrannicides with greater sympathy and, I would claim, more understanding than my master has, tyrannicide being according to our way of thinking an honourable act, approved by all philosophy and deserving of admiration. Following the crowd to the Capitol, I heard Marcus Brutus justify their action and proclaim that the Republic had been restored. He spoke lamely. It would have been very different, men said later, if Cicero had spoken in his place, but the conspirators had not elected to make him privy to their plot. Therefore the opportunity was lost.

As for the mob, it displayed a sullen disapproval. The truth is that the Roman plebs are a degenerate lot. They live for pleasure and have acquired the mentality that seeks a master to fawn on. Incapable of intelligence or reflection, their nature appears to justify the perpetual dictatorship that Caesar had established. Consequently I was able to report to my lord that there was no danger to be feared from the populace.

Calpurnia. Caesar's wife. A bitch of the first order, neurotic, demanding, and with a vile tongue.

"I warned him," she shrieked at me. "If he had listened to me, he would never have gone to the Senate. I had such awful dreams. But he scoffed at them. He must know best. I was only a woman, only his wife. He never would listen to me. So he's dead. Well, I hope he learns his lesson."

It was agreeable to find her in no need of comfort. I wouldn't have known how to set about it. As it was, her indignation quite overcame any grief she may have felt. So I did not waste much time on her. I assured her that she need not be concerned for her personal safety which I would guarantee, and I promptly took possession of Caesar's private papers and cabinet. I told her that I acted both as Caesar's friend, and in my official capacity as consul. I had as it happens no idea whether, as consul, I possessed any authority to act as I did, but I was certain Calpurnia would have no notion herself. In any case she did not care. She had only two requests, she said: first, that I would see Caesar's murderers punished, and, second, that I would get "that Egyptian whore" – which was the disrespectful manner in which she referred to the Queen of Egypt – out of Rome immediately. I didn't argue or tell her that I was in no position to do either of these things, and didn't anyway know whether it would be in my interest to attempt them. She wasn't a woman with whom you could reason. As I left, she asked, "How many dagger wounds were there?"

"I'm afraid I don't know precisely."

"Twenty-three they tell me. It all comes from not listening to what I told him."

I had sent message to some of Caesar's friends, or rather adherents, to meet me at my house. Three attended me on my return. The first was Balbus, banker and one of the few whom Caesar trusted in his heart. He used to say that he had been borrowing from Balbus for so long that it would be absurd to try to keep any secrets from him. Now the banker sat and looked at me with the reserved expression of a man who already knows the worst.

Second was Aulus Hirtius, already designated, along with Vibius Pansa Caetronianus, as next year's consul. Both were *novi homines*, of the type that Caesar's aristocratic assassins most resented and hated. That, rather than their loyalty to Caesar's memory, ensured that they would follow me. I had already decided that I would force the Senate to consent to allowing Caesar's nominations to the offices of state to stand, but I knew that Hirtius would be uncertain whether he would be allowed to enjoy his promised consulship, which was indeed the summit of his ambition, and which would of course ennoble his family.

The third person waiting for me was personally the least consider-able, but, by reason of his position, the one whom I had most need to attach to my side. (I was already thinking, some of the time, at least, in those terms.) This was Marcus Aemilius Lepidus. Well-born, handsome, no fool, Lepidus had it in him to be awkward. This was because he was conscious both of his distinguished birth, and of his inability to live up to the highest standards of his ancestors. For, though he was no fool, he suffered from an habitual lack of confidence in his own judgement, which was itself corrupted by his inability to see any event except as far as it concerned him. Yet at that point, Lepidus was of the utmost importance, for, as Caesar's Master of the Horse, he commanded the only body of troops in the vicinity of the city.

I said to him: "I must congratulate you on your loyalty, Lepidus. I have no doubt that the conspirators made every effort to attach such a man as yourself to them, in view of your own distinction and the importance of the post you hold."

"Nothing of the kind," he said. "Do you think Caesar would lie with fifty gashes in his body if I had had the slightest hint that such a monstrous crime was being planned?"

Though I saw Balbus raise an eyebrow, I refrained from saying that Lepidus must have been the only man in Rome – including Caesar himself – to have had no inkling, or suspected nothing. Instead I remarked that his ignorance was a further tribute to his integrity, for it showed that the conspirators had known better than to approach him.

"I should think not indeed," he said. "And let me add this. When I heard of this most horrible murder, my first inclination was to march my troops to the Senate House and order them to seize the villains. I wish I had yielded to that impulse, for I burn to avenge Caesar."

"The desire does credit to your noble heart," I said.

But not to your common sense, I thought.

Of course I flattered Lepidus, but let me add that, though I did so, and often mocked him also, I had a certain respect for him. He was so perfectly the old-fashioned Roman nobleman, confident, as few of us can now be, that his every action was directed towards the good of the Republic. If he had been other than he was, he would have done as he said, marched his troops to the Capitol and made away with Caesar's murderers. That would have put him in a position of power equal to Caesar's or Sulla's.

So, in a brief hour, I had assured myself of money, troops, and, most important, respectability. As consul, I could exercise power; the support of Hirtius and Lepidus brought me additional authority. Whether I chose to move against Caesar's murderers or to attempt conciliation, I knew now that I would be able to act from a position of strength. Yes, I thought to myself, they blundered when they let me live. At the very least they should have arrested me; and this recognition of their lack of foresight was wonderfully buoying. Alone, I could do no more than defy them; having secured support as I had now done, I could treat with them as an equal, and might prove myself their master.

He has broken off now, and called for the slave to bring more wine. That almost certainly means the end of coherent dictation for today. He won't admit it, but he can't hold his liquor as he used to. It's interesting what he says about Lepidus. The truth is that he and Octavian made use of that noble booby, and then cast him aside when he had fulfilled his purpose. My lord has always felt guilty about this treatment of Lepidus. I don't imagine that Octavian has felt the least little twinge.

II

I think it's perhaps a good idea to say something of these momentous events as they appeared to me. After all, I have lived in Antony's household throughout these years, and acted as his secretary for much of the time. There are few people who know more about the seamy side of Roman politics than I do, and it is proper that I record what I have learned and judged. I can't suppose after all that I have any future. Indeed I have already made arrangements to disappear into obscurity. I certainly, insignificant though I am, don't intend to trust myself to Octavian.

You may be curious about me. The story has gone around that I am, or rather was, one of those two beautiful boys whom Antony notoriously bought for eight talents to serve at his parties. This is a libel or slander, even though it is perfectly true that as a boy, adolescent, and young man, I was generally judged to be of unusual beauty. (I am still extremely handsome.) But I was never a slave. My father was a freedman who served in the secretariate of my lord's stepfather, the dashing, if dissolute, Publius Cornelius Lentulus Sura, who rashly engaged himself in the so-called Conspiracy of Catiline (from which Caesar himself was not far distant) and who was put to death (by strangling) without trial, by orders of Cicero, that year's consul. My lord was fond of his stepfather, who provided him indeed with an attractive model, for young noblemen are drawn to dissipation as naturally as wasps to a honey-pot, and he never forgave Cicero for the illegal and unconstitutional manner in which he had had him summarily executed as a public enemy. Indeed, I have often heard him dilate on this whenever Cicero presented

9

himself as the defender of constitutional legality, legitimacy, liberty, and virtue.

On account of his regard for his murdered stepfather, it was natural that my lord should extend his youthful generosity and patronage to members of Lentulus' household; and so my father entered his service, and I myself, growing up there, naturally followed, especially as I soon commended myself to my lord by reason of the evidence I soon offered of intelligence and good sense. (The two are not always, or indeed often, found in the same person – and even more rarely when combined with the beauty and grace which I possessed.) So I became as a child my lord's pet – though not, whatever has been said, his catamite – and then his trusted confidential secretary.

That should be enough to establish my credentials.

Romans are obsessed, to a degree that seems bizarre to us Greeks, with lineage and family connections. My lord's family was distinguished; though the Antonii were of plebeian origin they had been noble for many generations. My lord's grandfather, also Marcus Antonius, was granted a Triumph – that most glorious honour that can be accorded a Roman – some seventy years ago. He won a high reputation as orator and pleader as well as military commander, before his devotion to the Republic cost him his life during the civil war between Marius and Sulla. That at least was the approved family view. In my opinion he miscalculated and found himself in the wrong place on the wrong side at the wrong time.

My lord's uncle, Gaius Antonius, was also, I have been told, implicated in Catiline's conspiracy, but I confess I do not know the details. He kept, it is said, in the shadows, and prudently developed an attack of gout at a crucial moment. Subsequently – I believe as the result of some deal with Cicero – he was made governor of Macedonia, where his (illegal) exactions aroused the anger of the provincials who protested to Rome. Gaius Antonius also failed to defend the province against the barbarian tribes of the North. Consequently his career ended in disgrace and banishment to the island of Cephalonia. But I have heard my lord speak well of him. He was known as Quadrigarius, because he drove a four-in-hand chariot in Sulla's triumph. Apparently he always liked to attract attention, and, if he was also charged earlier with peculation in the province of Achaea – that sadly exploited and beautiful land – it is said that he justified himself on the grounds that his debts were such that he had no choice. Be that as it may, he was for a time expelled from the Senate.

I have dwelled on his career because this Gaius Antonius resembled my lord in his vices, while possessing none of his virtues. Yet my lord admired him, perhaps on account of his perfect selfishness.

Of more importance however was my lord's mother, Julia, daughter of Lucius Julius Caesar. She was a third or fourth cousin of the Dictator. Romans pay heed to such connections which we Greeks, more careless and self-confident, more light-hearted and individualistic, would think too distant to be of any significance. Her father, Lucius Julius Caesar, was a man of some prominence. After the so-called Social War, fought against Rome's traditional Italian allies (*socii*), he devised a law, named after him, which granted them full citizenship, though he did so in such a manner that few were able to make much use of it, their votes being rendered ineffectual – a typical piece of Roman chicanery, if you want my opinion.

Julia was formidable, and I believe my lord was always somewhat in awe of her. There is no doubt she held the family and the household together. Well, she had to. Both her husbands were improvident and careless, men of lamentable judgement. That my lord grew up as he did is a tribute surely to his mother's rock-like strength in the chaotic – I would say, criminal – world of civil wars, proscriptions, and moral degeneracy. But I am not sure that he has ever properly escaped her: witness his unfortunate tendency to attach himself to strong-willed women – the terrible Fulvia, his second wife, of whom more (and nothing agreeable) later, and of course the Queen herself who has undoubtedly been my poor lord's evil genius.

Yet, though my lord respected – and feared – his mother, he had too much vitality, was of too exuberant a nature, to be subservient to her, as Marcus Brutus was to the austere Servilia. (Not that even she was always so austere – witness her long affair with the Dictator. That was so well known that many said Brutus was Caesar's son. If he was, the idea that the son inherits characteristics from the father looks absurd!)

But my lord in his glorious youth certainly acted as his mother would not have wished him too – kicked over the traces, as the Romans say. He associated with the wildest set of young aristocrats who clustered round the beautiful and violent Publius Clodius

Pulcher. Clodius was clearly magnetic. Among those he attracted, besides my lord, were the poet C. Valerius Catullus (with whom he shared his sister Clodia), C. Sallustius Crispus, who has subsequently "reformed" and now writes bitter moralistic history, and Gaius Scribonius Curio, later the tribune whose attempted arrest precipitated, perhaps, the civil war which began with Caesar's invasion of Italy.

This Curio was my lord's dearest friend, and, I have no doubt, at some point his lover. They were certainly inseparable companions, sharing a taste for wild nights, drinking bouts, loose women, and boys. It was not long before both were heavily in debt, and Curio's father, old-fashioned, pompous, disapproving, forbade their continued association. The ban of course provoked them to further excesses, and on at least one occasion my lord, evading the guards, climbed through the roof of Curio's house, and doubtless into his bed. But of course all this happened years before I entered my lord's service, and therefore I speak of these matters without the personal knowledge that I can bring to my account of later events.

I do know however that when Clodius contrived to have Cicero exiled on the charge of having illegally put the Catiline conspirators, including my lord's stepfather, to death, my lord and Curio were among the band of enthusiasts who burned down Cicero's house. This should be remembered when the vile attacks which Cicero in the last year of his life made on my lord are considered.

Yet the remarkable thing about these young Roman aristocrats – or at least of my lord's generation among them, for I fancy things may be different in the future that Octavian is preparing for the city – is that their addiction to dissipation doesn't, didn't, preclude them from equally intense political activity.

Take Clodius for example. You would have said he lived entirely for pleasure. I doubt for instance if he ever spent a night even before he came of age and donned the *toga virilis* without a bed-companion: if his lovers, male and female, had been laid end to end they'd have stretched the length of the Circus Maximus. (I've no doubt my lord was one of them.) Moreover, Clodius was, as I have on good authority, almost never sober, even if he was also one of those fortunates who are rarely thoroughly mastered by wine. Some of his escapades were such that no sober man would have embarked on them: the occasion for instance when he disguised himself as a woman and penetrated the sacred rites of the Great Goddess, from which men were jealously excluded. (Penetrated some of the celebrants too, as I've heard. Caesar's first wife among them actually.) And yet this wild boy, who not only committed incest with his sister but actually buggered her, became the master of street politics, adored by the mob, and so powerful that he not only drove Cicero from the city, but made the mighty Pompey tremble. And when he was killed in a street brawl by a gang led by T. Annius Milo, the son-in-law of the dictator Sulla, the mob was stirred to such fury that they made Clodius' funeral the occasion for a riot in which the Curia was burned down.

My lord has often talked of the relish he had for street politics. Sometimes I think he has these days no greater pleasure than looking back on his wild youth. But he had too keen an intelligence and ambition – that quality which motivates Romans more than any other – to be content with such. He knew he was destined for greater things and so he aspired to make himself worthy of his destiny. When he was twenty-five he withdrew from Rome to study oratory at the best schools in Greece. Then he accepted an invitation from Aulus Gabinius, proconsul of Syria, to join his staff. Gabinius, though Cicero described him with his usual delicacy as "a filthy vulture", was a man of merit and dignity. At first a partisan of Pompey, he adhered to Caesar in the civil war, being killed at Illyricum. My lord has always spoken well of him.

As his lieutenant, commanding the cavalry, my lord suppressed a rebellion in Judaea, and was then engaged in war in Egypt. It is ironical that Egypt should be the alpha and omega of his glory! Ptolemy XI Auletes ("The Flute-Player"), who had been granted the title of "Friend and Ally of the Roman People", was dislodged as the result of a revolt in Alexandria which saw one of his daughters, Berenice, made queen. Ptolemy naturally appealed to the Senate for help, but that august body was afraid to trust any general with a command which might yield him the power and wealth of Egypt – so corrupt and decadent had the Republic become, so deficient in public spirit its nobility! Indeed, it was even announced that a prophecy had been discovered in the ancient Sibylline Books, forbidding the restoration of the Egyptian king by force of arms. Ptolemy, grinding his teeth, as they say, therefore appealed to Gabinius as the Roman proconsul in command of troops nearest Egypt.

Gabinius had the good sense to disregard the ridiculous and certainly fraudulent prophecy. He looked with more favour on the ten thousand talents which Ptolemy promised him. His inclination to the war was further strengthened by my lord's urging.

The march from Judaea was notoriously difficult and dangerous, for it was necessary to cross a waterless desert, wherein many armies had perished, and then pass through the filthy marshland of Serbonis, whose stench and stagnant ooze is said by the superstitious Egyptians to be the exhalations of Set, which is the name given by them to the Greek Typhon, the author of all evil, that terrible monster with a hundred serpents' heads, fiery eyes, and an awful voice, whom mighty Zeus hurled into Tartarus. I have been there myself however and consider that the smell, which is certainly unpleasant, is occasioned by nothing more remarkable than the drainings of the Red Sea which is there separated from the Mediterranean by only a small neck of land.

My lord forced the land bridge and took Pelesium. Ptolemy wished the citizens to be slaughtered in punishment of their complicity in the revolt against him. But my lord refused. Thus, from his first incursion into Egypt he won the regard of the people by his nobility and clemency. Soon Alexandria was taken also, after an action in which my lord again distinguished himself by his audacity and intelligence, and then, though he was unable to prevent Ptolemy from having Berenice's husband Archelaus executed, he gave the victim so splendid a funeral that he further endeared himself to the citizens.

Did my lord meet Berenice's younger sister Cleopatra at that time?

It has been said that he did, that indeed she seduced him, though she was only twelve years old. But I question it, if only because the authority for the tale is dubious, it having been first circulated, I believe, by my lord's second wife, Fulvia, when they were at odds with each other. Everyone knows that Fulvia had a tongue like a viper's kiss.

From Egypt my lord joined Caesar's staff and served in Gaul, all of which along with the history of the civil war against Pompey and the Optimates, and the events leading up to Caesar's murder, I have faithfully recorded in the last volume of the memoirs which he, more coherently than now, dictated to me.

III

He looks so tired, and his eyes are bloodshot. His hand trembles and will do so till he has downed two beakers of wine. But he is in the dictating mood again. I suppose it is a species of escape.

Cicero said in the Senate, "Was there anyone except Antony who regretted Caesar's death?" Old fool – what made him think I did so?

The immediate necessity was to come to some sort of accommodation with his murderers. It took me some time to get that idea into Lepidus' head.

My first step was to instruct Lepidus to station three cohorts of legionaries in the Forum, and reinforce the guards at the city gates. The Liberators, I remarked, would find Rome had become their prison. Then I had him send the leaders of their conspiracy missives explaining that he was acting in this way only to guard against disorder, and prevent riots. As a matter of fact, this wasn't entirely untrue. There was a danger of rioting. In a day or two I would receive reports that some fellow was going about proclaiming himself the grandson of the old Popular leader Caius Marius, and calling for the citizens to rise and avenge Caesar by killing the aristocratic parasites who had murdered him. I couldn't allow that. The time might come when I would need the mob, but they should rise only on my bidding. In any case like any sensible man I have a horror of riot. You never know how it will turn out. That was something Clodius never understood, which was the occasion of my breaking with him.

15

So, to avert trouble, I had this impertinent imposter put to death. I suppose he really was an imposter.

(I've heard, by the way, a different version of my lord's quarrel with Clodius, which was only of brief duration. It is that he was having an affair with Fulvia who was then married to Clodius. I have to say that I don't believe this – not the affair, that's credible enough – but that it should be the occasion for a quarrel. Nothing I have learned of Clodius persuades me he would give a damn who was lying with his wife, as long as he had a bed-companion of his own. And when was he without one?)

Then, as consul, I issued instructions that the Senate should convene the following day (17 March – check that, child) in the Temple of Tellus. The Senate House itself was of course out of commission, and I thought it tactful not to use the Theatre of Pompey again. Though I was tempted – I won't deny that It would have been amusing to see Marcus Brutus proclaim his virtue on the spot where he had struck down Caesar.

And then I sent an invitation to Mouse Brutus and his father-in-law Cassius to dine with me, arranging that Lepidus should extend a similar invitation to Markie and Metellus Cimber. "It is necessary," I said, "that things be arranged in an orderly and legal manner."

Mouse arrived first, as I had thought he would, since he is a born intriguer. I began by twisting his tail, saying I hadn't thought he could be such a fool.

"I thought from the tone of your letter that we were to be spared recriminations," he said.

"Mouse, Mouse," I sighed, "do you really suppose actions can be free of consequences?"

He flushed and, sorry for him, I pinched his cheek.

"You were always jealous of him of course," I said, "and Cassius felt himself diminished by him. All the same, I'm surprised that you allowed yourself to be inveigled by him into such a ham-fisted affair. Surely you know that envy such as Cassius feels is an enemy to judgement. I'd have thought you had more sense."

"Thank you," he said, "things would have been better managed if my advice had been heeded."

"Meaning I'd have gone too."

"Meaning, my dear, that you'd have been removed from the scene."

Then Cassius arrived, lean, suspicious, prickly, only a little appeased to see Hirtius there too. The sight of Mouse Brutus had absurdly reduced Hirtius to tears.

"How could you?" he kept saying, very boringly. "Caesar loved you more than anyone."

Indeed Caesar lay like a funeral pall over the gathering. Both Cassius and Mouse were abstemious.

I said, to stir them up, "You do know you're in my hands, don't you? I could have you chucked over the Tarpeian Rock and the mob would howl with glee. Don't think it's beyond me. And remember, as consul, I command the armies."

"With your colleague Dolabella," Cassius said.

I smiled at that. We all knew Dolabella wasn't worth a fart. (Dress that line up a bit, child.)

"And there's Lepidus," Cassius said. "I know now he's proclaiming his devotion to Caesar and I'm sure he's swearing revenge, but I think I could get him to sing a different song."

"I'm sure you could," I said. "All the same, you've botched it."

"Not exactly. Caesar is dead."

"And your lives are in my hands." I smiled, pressed wine on them, which they refused. "I'm tempted," I said, filling my own glass and downing it. "But what's the point? Mouse here is a dear friend from years gone by, that counts for something. I value friendship." I cracked a walnut. "Of course I could do it, just like that, but you know, there's one point on which I'm in complete agreement with the late lamented General. I've no wish to copy Sulla. His example was detestable. So: no proscriptions. There has been too much blood shed in our generation. And I'll let you into a secret. I was worried myself about the direction Caesar was heading in. This Parthian war he was planning – I'm happy to be spared that. But I stuck to him. Unlike you. Tyranny is bad, civil war's worse. Well, you've rid us of the tyrant, since you think of him like that. The question now is how we avoid civil war. Have you any answer?"

Cassius shifted. He couldn't keep in one position for long, his buttocks were too thin. He sniffed – he was the sort of man who always had a cold and a drip at the end of his nose. "You're plausible," he said. "I can't believe you're sincere. I find it hard to trust you."

17

"You may have to," I said. "Matter of fact, you have no choice."

Then he brought up the question of the Lupercal when I had offered Caesar the crown. I was ready for him to do so, and ready with an explanation: that it was Caesar's idea, and I had gone along with it, because why not? He had no answer to that, which was just as well because I couldn't really explain it myself. It is one of the few acts in my life of which I am ashamed. It was unworthy of one descended from Herakles. Of course, as I told Mouse, I was drunk. All the same . . . it was one of the occasions when I was altogether subservient to Caesar, which is why I got drunk. I couldn't face what his will compelled me to do. So I brushed the matter aside, though conscious they both knew that I had made myself ridiculous on that occasion. Well, I could put that to use. If the memory of my performance on the day of the Lupercal led Cassius to think of me with contempt, he should pay for it. As I have since painfully discovered myself, there is nothing more dangerous than underestimating your enemies.

Then, before they left, I outlined my intentions for the State.

"They'll do," Mouse said, "if you're sincere."

"Trust me."

The Senate met in an atmosphere of unease. It was raining in the streets, and there were rumbles of thunder.

Tiberius Claudius Nero, heir of innumerable consulars (though I suppose he could in fact enumerate them, for he certainly listed an unconscionable number of names to justify his rising first to address the Conscript Fathers) proposed "Public and exemplary honours for the noble tyrannicides". A shiver of apprehension ran through the assembly; they couldn't forget that Caesar's legionaries were still drawn up in the Forum. There was some nervous cheering and a number of catcalls from Caesar's friends, or from those alert enough to realise that it was wise to be a Caesarian. I restrained my amusement.

Then, since it wasn't my intention that the meeting should break up in discord or that partisan quarrels should be provoked, I rose to calm the House. "Neither honours nor punishment," I said, and looked first Cassius, then Cicero, in the eye. Cicero's shifted away.

I said: "Conscript Fathers, we must have the courage to look reality in the face. Caesar is dead. The manner of his death may be considered good or bad, fortunate or disastrous. That is a matter of opinion, and

I would urge you all to keep your opinion private. For what will be served by expressing views that can only set senator against senator? We have had enough of such quarrels in our generation, and we know that they lead, inexorably, terribly, to civil war. Our purpose today is to secure the stability of the Republic. Therefore I propose first that the office of dictator be abolished, that no man may again be tempted by the opportunity it promises, and none may be oppressed by the power it puts in the hands of a single Roman. Our ancestors in their wisdom removed the name of king from the Republic; let us do the same with the name of dictator."

As I spoke I felt the House warm towards me. This was not what many had expected, but it was what pleased them. They did not in their enthusiasm realise that "dictator" was a mere word, but that Caesar's power had been a reality.

Then, I said: "Since our intention is speedily to restore order and stability to the Republic I propose that all magistrates should be formally confirmed in their offices, both actual and designate."

I knew that this would be carried; after all, there were several among his murderers who had been allocated provincial commands, which they undoubtedly feared, and in many cases could not afford, to lose.

"Finally," I said, "though we acknowledge that Caesar has been slain by honourable and patriotic citizens, alarmed by the course his policies seemed to be taking – and it is not my intention to argue whether the deed was justified or not – nevertheless, as consul, I propose that all his acts should continue to have the force of law. I warn you, friends, that we shall be in the devil of a legal mess if you decide otherwise."

There was of course little more to be said, and I had considered ordering that proceedings be brought to an end after my own speech. But it was better, I thought, to indulge the senators, to let them have the illusion that they were coming to a free and independent decision, rather than merely bowing to the cogency of my argument.

So, I sat back, no doubt with a quiet smile playing on my lips, as first Marcus Brutus and then Cicero himself rose to speak. Markie of course could do no more than justify the action they had taken, superfluous since I had made it so clear that even Caesar's followers accepted that the Liberators were to be free of criticism. But I daresay Markie had prepared his speech in advance, and lacked the dexterity to change it. He would have done better to keep silent, for I could see his fellow-murderers look gloomy as they listened.

As for Cicero, he had the audacity to propose a general amnesty which should include even Sextus Pompeius, the most able son of the Dynast, who was defying the authority of the Republic from Spain where he still commanded six legions. However this plea met with no positive response even from old adherents of the Great Pompey. Cicero then lent his authority in support of what I had proposed, though not deigning to mention my name, and even giving the impression that my proposals were in reality his. There was no end to the old man's vanity, which was indeed the cause of his failure as a politician. It made him distrusted, for you can never be certain how the vain man will act since you cannot tell just what will prick his vanity.

Finally, Caesar's father-in-law, L. Calpurnius Piso rose to propose that Caesar should be granted a public funeral and his will be published. We had had some discussion as to whether we dared suggest this, and it had been agreed that Piso should do so only if I gave him the signal. Cicero's speech convinced me we could get away with it, and the old man even got to his feet again to support Piso.

"We must create a new concord in the Republic, commencing here, Conscript Fathers," he said.

It was his old tune, a good one of course, for we should all have liked to see concord. What he never realised is that this is possible only when men are in substantial agreement already about how the State should be ordered and power shared. Since such agreement had been lacking in Rome all our lives and for some years previously, concord was impossible. Thirty years of political life had taught Cicero nothing.

Caesar's funeral . . .

He has paused, closed his eyes, and, yes, drifted off to sleep, perhaps to dream, of that day in his life when for the first time he found himself Master of Rome and controller of the mood of the Roman People. Once, in a rare flash of insight – not my dear lord's strong point – he remarked that that day he had felt himself the vehicle by which the populace found words for what it collectively felt.

The funeral was held on a gusty day with heavy rain-laden clouds scudding across the sky on a wind from the hills. The mob was in an ugly, unstable mood. Gaius Trebonius, old lieutenant of Caesar, a man who had distinguished himself in the terrible battle at Alesia, and who had attached himself to the conspiracy from motive of pique and slighted ambition, dared to put in an appearance, declaring to all who would listen that while Republican duty had compelled him to consent to Caesar's death, he had not been among those who struck him down. (His role you will remember, had been to detain my lord.) Much good his protestations did him! The mob pelted him with mud and one brawny fellow, a butcher in a blood-streaked smock, seized his toga and tore it. His life was in danger, till my lord ordered some of Lepidus' guardsmen to break up this incipient riot, and carry the blubbering Trebonius to safety.

My lord rose to speak. On the rostrum he stood, god-like in majesty, with the beautiful serenity of Apollo, as he stretched out his hands and silently willed the crowd to silence. It fell, absolutely, and then he spoke, honeyed words, full of pain and grief. The speech, which he had rehearsed all morning with the help of, or rather under the direction of, the celebrated tragedian Tirogenes, was magical.

He called them friends, Romans, countrymen. He declared, modestly, that he had come, unworthy as he was, merely to bury Caesar, who had been slain, sadly slain, by honourable men, from great families that had done Rome much service, from honourable motives. Who was he to judge them? They had said Caesar was ambitious. So indeed he was. There had never been a man so ambitious as Caesar, ambitious for the greatness of Rome and the welfare of the Roman People. He had added Gaul to the Empire, restored peace, and bestowed riches on the people, whom he had dearly loved. Yes, he was ambitious, and for this reason these honourable men had killed him.

Then, brushing tears from his eyes – it had taken half an hour's rehearsal before Tirogenes was happy with that gesture – he displayed Caesar's bloody toga.

"This was the gash the noble Brutus made . . ."

The mob howled in fury, and again he silenced them.

"We are here only to bury Caesar," he said, and paused, to let his words hang on the air, "to bury – Caesar . . ." he repeated with a long gap between the words, so that all felt their grave finality. Then he lowered his head, and held the crowd a long minute watching him. When he spoke next, his voice was slow and halting.

"I had intended," he said, "to read his will. It is right that you should hear it, as you are entitled to do. And yet I hesitate, for I read your mood. I see the pain and anger which the death of Caesar, on account of his ambition, has brought you. If I read his will, you will learn how he loved you, and then your anguish will be insupportable and may turn to anger. Would I be right to tell you how Caesar loved you?"

The cries convinced him that he would.

So he read the will, with its gift of money to each citizen and of Caesar's private gardens to their common good. He read it very quietly, and the mob burst out in wails, acclamations, and cries of fury. They surged forward, tore up the benches and tables in the Forum, and made a pyre for the body.

I believe that at that moment they would one and all have thrown the noble Brutus on the fire, and given the crown to my lord, such was the magic of his oratory.

For a little afterwards he even convinced himself he had spoken truth.

IV

I was sincere when I abolished the dictatorship. Though I followed Caesar in recognising that Rome and the Empire required that one man be in a position of authority, I also saw that the office of dictator was an irritant. And I believed I could secure my position by other means.

Nevertheless my authority was precarious. The city itself was no great problem. The populace remained hostile to the conspirators. Marcus Brutus, who held the office of urban praetor, came to me in great agitation requesting my consular permission to withdraw to his estates. His life, he said, was in danger. Naturally I granted permission, only remarking that this was a strange position for the man who had restored liberty to Rome to find himself in.

My priority was to secure the support of the legions. That meant I had to find farms for the veterans. I entrusted my brother Lucius with this charge. I had taken possession of Caesar's Treasury, and also of the treasure which he had accumulated in the Temple of Ops for his planned campaign against Parthia. I dispersed some to the legions, thus combining prudence with generosity. Meanwhile, on account of the disturbances in the city, I summoned one legion from Campania.

I had no desire to disturb the allocation of provinces which Caesar had already made. On the other hand it was necessary to safeguard my own position, and I therefore resolved that I must displace Mouse Brutus from Cisalpine Gaul, which had been allotted to him, and take it over myself, extending at the same time my proconsular imperium there from two to six years. It was the ideal province, since any army based there was in a position to overawe Rome, and control political developments in the city.

Mouse protested, slipped out of the city, and made ready for war. But I was confident that he would get little support, and that I could master him. For one thing, though not without ability in a subordinate role, he had no successful experience of an independent command. Nor was he popular with the troops.

And then things started to go wrong. It has been my experience all my life that just when everything is going swimmingly, when Fortune and the gods seem to smile upon you, something nasty comes along to trip you up, and it is always something unexpected.

What made it more annoying this time was that the something nasty was the boy Octavian, whom I had once thought rather attractive.

Octavian: Caesar's great-nephew, and grandson of a municipal money-lender.

He had been studying somewhere in Greece when Caesar was murdered. He was eighteen and arrived at Brundisium with two friends of his own age – Maecenas, an effeminate fop such as every legionary would like to kick in the arse, and Agrippa, who looked and sounded like a wooden-headed peasant.

I confess I had given no thought to him. Even when word was brought that he was returning to Italy, I thought nothing of it. He was a mere boy.

Next I heard that he had seduced a legion and was marching on Rome, proclaiming himself Caesar's heir.

Certainly he was named such in Caesar's will, and had been adopted by him, so that he could legitimately style the dead dictator "Father". But it had not occurred to me that he could have the audacity to regard himself as Caesar's political heir also. It was absurd, at eighteen.

I was amused, but the impertinence had to be brought to a halt. I invited him to come to see me.

Will people understand how insignificant I thought the boy? Should I be blamed for that? Everyone else misjudged him too. Only old Cicero saw that he might play a part – and he got it wrong himself.

He looked so demure, almost timid. The line of his jaw was firm, but his lips were soft and his eyes were those of a lovely girl. His arms were soft too, and rounded like a girl's, and you could see that he had never known what it was to be so weary that you could scarcely lift your sword or support your shield. His body had never stunk and sweated under armour, and he had never been so parched with thirst that he would drink from a stream in which men had bled to death.

I let him settle himself on a couch after my greeting, and he smoothed his thighs, and his tongue flickered over his lips. I can see him waiting for me to speak, waiting like a little cat.

"You're making trouble, dear boy," I said. "I've no doubt you don't intend to, but that's the result.

He didn't reply, but waited while the cries of the Forum cut through the May morning.

"I'm grateful to you, however, for having secured the south," I said. "That was well done. But the stories which you are allowing to be circulated can help only our enemies."

"What stories?" he said. "What enemies?"

"You know what stories, and if you don't know what enemies, the worse for you. They'll cut you in collops, dear boy. You've been in correspondence with Cicero."

"A distinguished man," he said, "and an old friend of my father."

"Your father? Do you mean Himself? Keep that for those who'll be impressed by it. And as for Cicero, remember this. No one has ever trusted him and been the better for it. Now, you're breaking the law."

"Is there any law?" he said.

I kept my temper.

"Don't be insolent, dear boy," I said. "I am the consul of the Republic in which you have no position. You are commanding troops, and have no authority to do so. By marching them to Rome, you are legally guilty of making war on the Republic. I could have you put on trial for that, and if you were put on trial, sentenced to death."

He smiled, but said nothing.

"However, I'm prepared to overlook it. You're only a kid. I'm ready to take your word for it that you don't realise the enormity of what you've done."

"Enormity," he said, pausing on the word as if he relished it.

"Partly also," I said, "because I've always liked you."

25

That caught him for the first time, and he blushed.

"But I want these soldiers you have. How many is it? A legion? Half a legion? As consul they are mine to command. Not only do you have no official position, but at your age, kid, you can't have one. Besides, what makes you think you are capable of commanding an army? That takes years of experience. I need those men. Decimus Brutus – you know, Mouse, you used to be close to him, I think – is loose in Cisalpine Gaul, and stirring up trouble. As for the other buggers, they are already raising armies the other side of the Adriatic, though they don't yet know I am aware of that."

"And what will you offer me?" he said, and opened his eyes wide and looked candid.

"A place on my staff. A consulship years before you are legally qualified. Safety, to see you don't go the same way as Himself and end up with your throat cut. Get one thing straight, kid, I need these troops, but you need me even more. If I fail, you're done for."

"I'm not so sure of that," he said, but smiled as if he agreed and drank the wine I called for. But he took only a couple of sips and laid his cup aside.

Then he listened attentively while I outlined the strategic situation. He was a good listener. It was one of the ways he had commended himself to Caesar.

"Yes," he said, "it's complicated, but you make it admirably clear. I'm grateful. I understand it better now."

"And you'll do as I say."

Again, he smiled, but this time warmly and without the cat-like reservation.

"By the way," he said, "you will make arrangements, won't you, to let me have my inheritance by Caesar's will."

"Of course," I said, "you come from good banking stock. You'd better speak to Balbus. He understands these matters. I'm only a plain soldier."

And then he left. A couple of days later I heard he had gone straight to Cicero.

Again, he's worn out. He was animated while dictating, but he's now exhausted. He sits brooding, and has called for more wine, though the present flask isn't empty. He'll drink himself into a stupor, that's certain, almost as if I wasn't here. There's no mirth in his drinking now.

That mention of Octavian blushing. Well, there are two stories that have gone the rounds. Some say my lord raped Octavian one night when he was drunk during the Spanish campaign. The other has it that Octavian tried to seduce him and failed. I expect the truth is betwixt and between.

Cicero was of course delighted to receive young Octavian. Though he was over sixty, and it was twenty years since his famous consulship, when in his view he saved the Republic, and in a more balanced one, violated the Constitution, he still itched to control affairs of state. In truth he was incompetent to do so. Ever since Gaius Marius and Sulla had vied for supremacy, the secret was out: to control the Republic, first find yourself a sword. Cicero, with the naivety of a philosopher, supposed that a man with a sword would put himself at his disposal.

I have always been an easygoing fellow – haven't I, Critias? (Well, yes, in some respects, my lord.) I've never been able to believe that I can arouse hatred in others. Perhaps that's a weakness? Perhaps that's why my affairs are in their present lamentable condition?

My relations with Cicero had never been easy, that's true. There was too much between us – the blood of my family and my friendship with Clodius who had so delighted in twisting his tail. But in recent years we had seemed to put this behind us. When we met on formal occasions we were agreeably complimentary to each other. If we found ourselves at the same dinner-table, I yielded to him and delighted in the elegance of his conversation. He really was a wonderful talker, even if the next day you couldn't actually recall anything he had said.

It was Fulvia who told me he hated me.

Have I said anything about Fulvia, Critias?

No, my lord.

He certainly hasn't, and I'll tell you why, because I doubt if he will care to do so himself.

She was the most terrible of my lord's wives. Beautiful certainly, as beautiful, men said, as her first husband Clodius, as beautiful even as his sister Clodia, whom the poet Catullus loved and loathed. I don't think anyone loved Fulvia, and I'm not sure my lord didn't loathe her. He did so eventually. But, though I've heard him swear and curse her in her absence, she had only to enter a room for him to roll over with his paws in the air. Yet she didn't look formidable. Her eyes didn't flash and her voice was soft. Indeed you had to strain your ears to hear what she said. All the staff feared her, and everyone knew that she had a keener grasp of the political situation than most men.

Fulvia said: "Don't underestimate that little rat Octavian. Cicero thinks he will use the boy to destroy you by luring Caesar's old supporters away from you. He will try to do that, and will succeed unless you act quickly, and then . . . he will discard Cicero. I know his mother, she's a calculating bitch, and he's a whey-faced mother's boy who takes after her."

It's a measure of the power Fulvia had over my lord that when they married three years before Caesar's murder he immediately broke off his liaison with the actress Cytheris, which had been going on even while he was married to his first wife Antonia. That was a shame. Cytheris was the most delightful of women, a poor girl from the Suburra, slim, even skinny, with a wide mouth and black eyes. She could never speak grammatical Latin except when using a dramatist's words. In ordinary conversation she scattered verbs wherever she chose, and if she ever made an adjective agree with its noun it can only have been by chance. Even the chorus-boys adored her, and I don't need to tell you how uncommon that is, because they're mostly little bitches. But she would giggle with them about anything. She really loved my lord, though she at least once had to pay his debts, and I have never heard of another actress who would do so much for an aristocratic lover. Of course people said that she was a bad influence on him, even degrading, and the cause of the wild parties which did such harm to his reputation among sober men. They exaggerated; it's not as if there have been no wild parties in recent years, is it? No, he never met anyone as sweet as Cytheris. And yet, you know, she was always a little frightened of him. "Is he really in a good mood, Critias?" she would say, and kiss me fresh as morning roses if I said he was no worse than a bear with a sore head. We had a lot of fun when she was about, and everyone in his household was sorry when Fulvia took over and expelled her. She actually told poor Cytheris that if she saw her again in the same room as my lord, she would have her flogged as a common prostitute. Can you imagine?

This from a woman who had been married not only to Clodius but to Scribonius Curio, so that actually all three of her husbands had been to bed with each other. That didn't stop her from inveighing against the depravity of the Greeks.

But I admit that she had a good mind.

Here's a letter she wrote after that conversation with my lord:

For an intelligent man you can be awfully obtuse. It's partly because you don't give enough attention to business, and partly because you are too trusting. I've told you before, you must never take things at face-value.

You gave me several reasons why you have nothing to fear from little Octavian, and none of them does credit to your intelligence.

You say, first, that the soldiers will never follow him into battle, because they won't trust a boy with no experience.

I say, they will follow him as long as he pays them, and if he attracts enough, he won't need to fight a battle.

You say, Cicero is using the boy as a cat's paw.

I say, that's what the old man thinks he is doing. But when did he last judge wisely? He is corrupted by vanity, you ought to know that.

You say, Cicero's a back number anyway.

I say, he still has influence. More than that, he has a venomous tongue. He can destroy with words as surely as other men can with the thrust of a dagger. I appreciate that, since I have the same ability myself.

You say, in any case the real battle is still between the party of Caesar and those who follow the self-styled Liberators.

I say, Cassius is intelligent enough to seek to divide Caesar's party and it's already happening.

The truth is that you are too easy and complacent. You underestimate Octavian. I can't stand the little rat, but I can appreciate that he has nerve and judgement. Of course I've heard Cicero's boast, that the boy must be praised, employed and discarded. We'll see who does the discarding.

In short, you have to get him back on our side.

Or cut him down now.

Your complacency infuriates me. It prevents you from realising your abilities. The truth is you have gone through life
assuming that you are a favourite of the gods, and that someone
will always smooth your way and spread roses before you.

Well, you have no patron now. You are exposed. You must
depend on your own wits, your own energy, and your own
nerve.

Be the man you are capable of being. It was he whom I chose
to marry. Prove to me that you are worthy of me.

Your wife, Fulvia.

Really, bitch and virago though she was, you couldn't help admiring
the woman.

V

I had no wish to renew war against fellow-citizens. I never have had, whatever lies have been told against me. So that summer I made no move. There was no reason why I should. Though the boy Octavian had ignored my advice, and continued to collect an army, drawing both raw recruits and retired veterans to his colours, I could not consider him to be in any serious degree a threat to my interests. Likewise, while Mouse Brutus still refused to surrender his province, as it had been decreed he should, I had no doubt that I could eventually compel his obedience without the use of force. Mouse had his virtues, and I was fond of him in a way, but he lacked nerve.

So I passed the summer pleasantly.

Then, late in August, while I was enjoying sea-bathing on the Adriatic coast, word came that Cicero had returned from his villa on the Bay of Naples, and fiercely attacked me in the Senate. His trawl through my alleged misdeeds was the usual bag of wind, and I couldn't suppose that anyone would pay much attention to it. I lay under the olive trees and laughed.

It was my brother Lucius who roused me. He came to my house at Tibur wide-eyed with indignation. Cicero's speech was having an effect, he said. Already it was being muttered that true Caesarians would be wiser to follow young Octavian.

"They say Antony drowns himself in wine, and is sunk in lethargy. Looking at you, brother, I'd say there is something in the charge."

"It's summer," I said, "and the sun is still shining."

31

It was however necessary to answer Cicero. It was also a pleasure. I addressed the Senate in the third week of September. Cicero absented himself. Later he said that I had forces to hand ready to murder him if he put in an appearance. That was absurd. I should have preferred him to be there. It would have added spice to a day that was already highly-seasoned.

I said: "I am told that Cicero attacked me in this house recently and I'm sorry I wasn't here to answer him on that occasion. But it's a curious thing; the people Cicero attacks are almost never there when he speaks out. I wonder why that is. And he's not here today either, I observe, though I made a special point of inviting him.

"Of course he used to speak out against Caesar – when Caesar was in Gaul. And then he joined Pompey in the civil war, if you remember, and scuttled back to Italy when Pompey was defeated. Now I come to think of it, I arrested him myself, then, at Brundisium. He asked me if I was going to have him put to death. Dear me, no, I said, you're an ornament of Latin literature, and I gave him a cavalry escort to see him safely home to his country-house. I forget which one it was, he has so many, but then he seems to have forgotten that I saved his life. Well, old men forget, we all know that, though Cicero has remembered certain episodes in his long life, quite brilliantly, with advantages and embellishments.

"One thing he has forgotten, it seems, is how he used to write to Caesar – this was when Caesar had supreme power in the State. I have one of his letters here, and I only wish he was present himself to listen to it.

"But, if I read it, I daresay some kind friend will remind him of how he fawned on Caesar, thanked him for all his many kindnesses and told him he was proud to call Caesar 'friend'. Listen:

"From Cicero to Caesar:

Greetings: you did me great honour by visiting me at home, and so I shall treasure the memory of your too brief stay and our agreeable conversation in my heart and memory as long as I live. It was pleasing that your achievement has not taught you to neglect old friends and that, engaged as you are in great affairs of state, you should still have the inclination to converse, with such admirable point and wit, on matters of literature with which a 'back-number' like myself contents his old age. Truly, our dialogue was so pleasing that I recollected that, greatly daring, I once wrote to tell you that I was persuaded that you are indeed my *alter ego*.

You have, my old friend, onerous responsibilities now, and none can bear them more gracefully, nor dispatch them more felicitously. The prayers of all good Romans go with you.

I ask only that you should take care of your health, on which Rome so greatly depends, and that in your characteristic goodwill and generosity, you will continue to keep a warm corner in your heart for your old admirer and friend who is proud to style himself such. Cicero."

I remarked: If Cicero wasn't so immensely distinguished, I would say he was grovelling before Caesar.

"And then a few weeks later he came here, Conscript Fathers, and announced that he was delighted Caesar had been murdered.

"What can you do with a man like that?

"Can you believe a word he says?"

My lord was delighted with that speech. He still is. But I have always wondered if it was wise to cover a man with a tongue like Cicero's with such mockery.

In any case, as everyone knows, Cicero subsequently embarked on a violent course. He wrote a pamphlet and circulated it, though he did not dare to publish it openly. He railed against my lord's private and public life. Antony was, he said, a drunkard, brawler, ruffian, debauchee, homosexual; a tyrant, corrupt, brutal, and unmanageable; a wild beast who must be cut down before his madness infected others and destroyed the State.

Invective convinces only when it contains a germ of truth, and then only those who wish to be persuaded. Cicero's charges were absurdly exaggerated. Nevertheless people had seen my lord reel drunk through the public streets. Stories of his love affairs had gone the rounds. He had often offended the conventional and strait-laced. There were many ready to believe the worst of him. Cicero made it easy for them to do so. He poisoned the air, and, though my lord brushed off the slanders with contempt, some of the mud stuck. There were men indifferent to him previously, who never quite trusted him – on account of what Cicero had said. Others granted him ability, but began to question his character. They saw him as a man who might do anything, and feared him accordingly.

VI

This then was the position. My lord was languishing at his villa near Frascati, uncertain of his next move. (Fulvia had gone to the seaside for her health. Or so she said.) Marcus Brutus and Cassius had left Italy, ostensibly for their assigned provinces, Crete and Cyrene, neither important. But no one knew whether they had arrived there, or were forgathering in some more dangerous place. There was for instance a rumour that Cassius was expected in Egypt, where the legions were reported mutinous. Mouse Brutus still refused to surrender his province of Cisalpine Gaul. Cicero was said to be preparing new attacks on my lord, and it was clear that many were willing to believe the gross slanders he had already retailed.

Most sinister of all, the boy Octavian was recruiting in Campania from the lands where Caesar's veterans had been settled. With unparalleled cynicism he gave each man he suborned a gift of five hundred denarii – the equivalent of two years' pay for a serving legionary.

Buying a man is one thing however. Ensuring that he stays bought may prove more difficult. Octavian overplayed his hand. He should have stood off, demonstrated his strength to my lord, and come to an agreement with him. Instead he marched on Rome, occupying the Forum with his legions in the second week of November. His move alarmed even those who favoured him. They could not be certain he was as strong as he appeared to be. So they held back. The Tribune Titus Cannutius was an exception. He made a speech to the People in praise of Octavian in which he supported the boy's claim to the honours and position of his "father" Caesar. That was

35

more than most people had bargained for. It made them nervous. Even those who still expressed admiration for Caesar had no wish to find a successor spring up.

News of the boy's doings stirred my lord into action. Casting aside his luxurious lethargy, he was himself again. That at least is how he would have put it. For my part, I know him to be equally himself in the hours devoted to debauchery.

He had summoned legions from Macedonia, and hurried south to meet them at Brindisi. He found them disturbed, seditious, on the point even of mutiny, their ears flattered by Octavian's propaganda. He acted with that power of decision which – ah! till recent weeks alas – a crisis has always evoked from him: he ordered summary execution of the loud-voiced ringleaders. Then, order restored, he distributed bounty, and turned his face to the north.

Word of his movements reached Rome, spreading alarm. Octavian's soldiers were dismayed. The veterans among them had served under my lord, knew his quality. It was one thing to have taken the boy's bribes and played a part in his charade; quite another, to brave Antony's wrath and stand to meet the lion in battle. Octavian soon found his legions weakened by the desertion of the prudent. He had overreached himself. Rome was untenable. He fled north, to Maecenas' home town of Arretium.

My lord summoned the Senate. It was in his mind to have Octavian arraigned for treason, outlawed as a public enemy. Legally, there could be no question: the boy was guilty. He had brought arms into the city. Without holding any public position, he had attempted to usurp the powers of the State.

I have reproached myself since. Men say my nerve failed. They don't dare tell me that to my face, but the whispers couldn't be kept from me.

Yet it wasn't a question of nerve. I have dared greater things.

The truth was that the desirable course was impossible. Had I tried to outlaw Octavian, guilty as he was, a tribune would have interposed his veto; and, unlike the high-minded self-styled Optimates who had opposed Caesar in the year of the Rubicon, I was not prepared to break the law and lay violent and sacrilegious hands on the person of a tribune. My enemies have condemned me as adventurer and tyrant, but I have had more respect for law than they.

And yet, and yet, there were other reasons . . .

Is it yet night, Critias?

Or do the rays of an unwelcome sun cast shadows on the sands?

How I loathe Egypt now.

Where was I? I wander. More wine!

The boy was not only boy. He was inhabited by Caesar's ghost that guided his footsteps. When the veterans looked at him, they did not see this slim effeminate figure. They saw the shade of Caesar . . .

I was powerless against it.

His troops would not stand against me. They dared not. But mine trembled at the name of Caesar.

Now things turned against me. I could see the omens. My enemies were gathering. I would soon be no longer consul. Now I can scarce remember details of the dangerous months that followed. I left Rome, in a hurry, yes; but not in flight. It was time to assume control of the province I had allotted myself: Cisalpine Gaul which Mouse Brutus refused to relinquish. Very well, I would drive him out. My men might not fight Caesar's heir; they would fight his murderers.

Or so I hoped.

We forced Mouse into Mutina, and invested him there. The ground froze, the snows covered the mountains, the dead did not decay between the camps.

Meanwhile in Rome, the new consuls, Pansa and Hirtius, whom I thought my friends, proved feeble in my defence. So feeble indeed that they were soon mouthing in the ranks of my enemies. Cicero, clever-silly as ever, held out a bribe to Octavian. He would have all laws set aside – by the agency of Cicero, archpriest of legality – and be named a pro-praetor, in defiance of custom and reason. The boy had got authority to add ballast to the power he had seized.

We attempted conciliation. Why should Romans fight again against Romans? Were there no enemies of Rome on the frontiers? Lepidus, loyal, for even he could see that if I was destroyed, they would turn against him next, slicing through the Caesarian party salami-style, urged an accommodation, protesting loyalty to the Republic, devotion to the principle of concord. It was a good letter, better than Lepidus could have composed himself.

Servilius spoke against it in the Senate. Cicero rose to second him. He praised Lepidus, in honeyed words, false as a lover's pledge of eternal fidelity. Then he produced a letter I had written to Octavian and Hirtius. The letter was just. I told them clearly that they were being used by Caesar's enemies to destroy me, his loyal follower. When they had served their purpose, they would be tossed aside. Can anyone believe I did not speak truth?

Then Cicero wrote to Lepidus. I can remember his exact words: "In my opinion you will be wiser not to make meddling proposals for peace with Antony; neither the Senate nor the People approves of them; nor does any patriotic citizen . . ."

Lepidus could boast of a line of consular ancestors stretching back to the springtime of the Republic; he would not take lessons in patriotism from a New Man like Cicero, a jumped-up lawyer from a small municipality.

That letter would cost Cicero dear. It would cost him his life.

Strategically, the danger was great. My army besieging Mouse Brutus in Mutina was soon itself invested. Octavian marched up from Bononia, linking with Hirtius. They did not yet dare to attack, but waited for Pansa to come up with four legions. My one hope was to prevent their merger. Feinting against Octavian, who, deceived, promptly withdrew, I then turned to confront Pansa at Forum Gallorum some seven miles south-east of Mutina.

The battle was a battle like others. There was neither time nor space to manoeuvre. I hit hard. Hand-to-hand fighting, ankle-deep in icy mud. It was the way Romans fight each other, silently, without war-cries like barbarians – hack, thrust – with ground gained or yielded by the foot . . .

When he remembers war, his voice is low, darkness shades his face. He walks about the room, and the words come out staccato. I realise that I have never killed a man; he has killed many and been responsible for the deaths of thousands.

Battle is where you lose your virginity. Octavian never felt that. He commands without a sword in his hand.

By evening Pansa's legions were giving ground. We pushed them back yard by brutal yard. They were on the point of breaking. There is a moment in every decisive battle when you see that about to happen.

Then, a cry rose on our left. I sent a legate to see what had caused it, but, before he could return, the word ran through the ranks that fresh legions were appearing on that flank. An officer of our cavalry auxiliaries, his brow gashed and streaming blood, galloped up to report that a new army was pressing in on our wing.

At that moment Pansa's legions wavered. I cried to halt the pursuit which was about to pour through their broken ranks. With that discipline of which only veterans are capable, the order was obeyed. But there was no time to re-form to confront this new enemy face to face. Instead I ordered the retreat to be sounded while our left wing swung into position to fight a holding action.

None but veteran troops could have effected that withdrawal to the mountains. Night fell, we crouched round cooking-pots and tended wounds.

A battle is but an incident, something amateur soldiers do not understand. You can lose battle after battle, without cause to abandon hope. The campaign's the thing.

(So all is not lost, even now.)

But we were pressed hard, compelled to give battle again seven days later, beyond Mutina. Outnumbered, we were pushed back. On their side Hirtius fell, just reward for the treachery he had shown me. Yet what but treachery is to be expected in civil war? I knew that well and held it against no man.

We headed north-west, up the Via Aemilia, making for Gallia Narbonensis. Lepidus and Plancus lurked there with their legions. I could not be certain of their mood. Defeat is costly in more than lives; friends are shed in its shadows.

Lepidus was in a dilemma. Whatever friendship he felt for me, he had a still more tender regard for his own skin. Moreover, there were old enemies on his staff, stern self-admiring Republicans and old supporters of Pompey. Lepidus himself, I knew, had written to the Senate proposing that he act as mediator between the warring parties. In appearance he would have suited the role; in character not at all.

We encamped with a river between my men and his. I sent a missive to Lepidus urging him to remain loyal to the cause with which we had been for so long associated. While I attended a reply, word was brought from Rome that I had been declared a public enemy. Cicero boasted that Caesar's cause was doomed. Legions that had followed him ardently would not fight for the degenerate Antony. He should have seen how my men died for me outside Mutina, where raw recruits choked their guts out when they looked upon the grim and silent sword-work of my veterans. But Cicero always preferred words to reality.

While I waited for Lepidus' reply, I wrote to the boy Octavian.

I grant you, you have surprised me. I didn't think you capable of so much. You've proved your point, kid. You deserve to be treated as my equal.

Of course this won't interest you now.

Just remember what I'm saying in a couple of weeks.

Let me tell you precisely what is going to happen.

You will be granted an ovation (though some old fogeys in the Senate will vote to deny you even that – since you have served your turn). A triumph, supreme command of the direction of the war and of the legions which were commanded by the late lamented Pansa and Hirtius – consuls forever linked together as if they were a comedy duo – will be granted to one of the self-styled Liberators – Mouse Brutus, I expect.

The point is, kid, now that they think I am defeated – which by the way, I'm not – they have no use for you. You are dispensable – so will be disposed of, so that things may revert to the old corruption and rule of the Senate.

If you don't believe me, try looking over your shoulder.

Meanwhile, take it from me, the war is only just beginning, and I think it's time we were on the same side. Let's arrange to meet.

Lepidus still hesitated. In retrospect I cannot blame him, though I did so then, prudently however concealing my irritation. Prudence is not a virtue my detractors have ever been willing to grant me, but I have possessed it, on occasion.

Don't smirk, Critias.

(Curious: I had thought him lost in a dream of words, oblivious of my presence even.)

I can't blame Lepidus now because, lacking insight, he could see things only as they seemed to be. And they wore a grim aspect. The

Senate, acting with a precipitancy which I swore they would come to regret, had consigned all legions and provinces in the East to Marcus Brutus and Cassius. They had even welcomed the proffered aid of Sextus Pompeius, little considering how he had sunk from the proper station of a Roman nobleman.

But I had one assurance: that I could always overawe Lepidus. So, without warning, I crossed the river and entered his camp. When word of my arrival spread, the soldiers rushed to greet me. Men of the Tenth Legion remembered the glories they had won under my command, and crowded round, clamouring to touch me. Then they raised me on their shields and carried me, as if in triumph, to Lepidus' headquarters. It must have seemed to him that his own legions had surrendered themselves to me.

As, in fact, they had.

A nerve in his face twitched. He didn't know what to expect.

I commanded the soldiers to allow me to descend. Then, looking him in the face, I advanced towards Lepidus. I placed my hands on his shoulders, and felt him twitch. I embraced him and smelled sweat.

"My old comrade in arms," I said, "it's time we had a chat."

Do you know, my arrival had come as a relief to him. It absolved him of the responsibility of making a decision.

At my suggestion he drafted a letter to the Senate. I let him choose his own words – Lepidus was a stylist of some note – so long as their sense was mine. He explained that his soldiers had been unwilling to take the lives of their fellow-citizens. It amused me to have him say that, for I knew how soon they would be required to do just that in earnest.

Lepidus lay on the couch after supper, and said: "But, my dear, I still fear young Octavian."

"Octavian," I said, "has no choice but to ally himself with us in the end. Otherwise, he will be crushed between two forces, neither of which he can comprehend. He still thinks he can trust Cicero, he doesn't know the depths of the old man's malignancy."

There remained the question of Plancus, governor of Gallia Comata, an old comrade, who had however assured Cicero that no considerations of personal differences would prevent him from allying himself with even his bitterest enemy in order to save the Republic.

Lepidus reminded me of these words. He feared that Plancus would join himself to Mouse Brutus, still the general most trusted by the Senate.

I laughed: "Plancus is a politician, he blows with the wind, and now that we have reconciled our difference, that wind favours our cause."

"I do hope so, my dear," he said.

"Trust me," I said; and Lepidus, whose vanity nevertheless could never sufficiently fortify him to trust in his own judgement, sighed with what? Pleasure? Relief? The assurance that I brought to him, which he could not find in himself. Poor Lepidus.

"What do we do now?" he said.

"We wait. Our allies are patience and time."

Meanwhile, unbeknownst to Lepidus, I sent an emissary to Plancus. He carried a letter from me.

Plancus, old comrade-in-arms:
     Believe me, I understand your position.
     You are consul-designate for next year, an honour all noble Romans seek, and you wish to do nothing to imperil it.
     That is honourable.
     But consider this:
     After the battles by Mutina, there are, by my calculation, some forty-five legions serving in the West.
     Octavian has eleven, Mouse Brutus ten (but badly savaged), Lepidus seven, Pollio in Spain two, you have (I think) four, there are another four or five in Gaul and Spain, and I have only four.
     You may say the game is against me. But now I am allied with Lepidus. The eleven legions we command are made up of veterans. They know me, and they know what I am made of. Moreover, Pollio is an old friend. That makes thirteen. If you join with us we approach the ascendant.
     As for Octavian's, his strength is greater in appearance than reality. Believe me, I know. Few of his men will choose to stand against me in battle, or against their old comrades in my legions.
     The boy Octavian owes everything to his name, but veterans know that names don't win battles.

Join me and we have only Mouse Brutus to dispose of.
Stand against me, and what do you stand for?
Cicero and the Senate?
Or do you suppose that the men who murdered Caesar will
ever trust you who served him loyally . . .

Plancus was convinced, as I knew he would be. Mouse Brutus tried
to negotiate with him. Plancus led him on, suborned his soldiers, and
then the contemplation of the forces arrayed against him broke his
nerve. He fled to the north, into mountainous Gaul, where he was
captured by a native chieftain. This man, who knew me from Caesar's
Gallic wars, sent to know what I wished him to do with his illustrious
captive. I replied that it would please me to hear no more of him.

That left Octavian, who at last was made aware of the treachery of
the Senate. He demanded a consulship. It was refused. Persuaded by
my epistles, Octavian marched again on Rome; it was necessary that
he should do so. Only thus could I be certain that he had committed
himself against my enemies. He created himself consul – though not
yet twenty. He had his adoption by Caesar retrospectively ratified,
and passed a law decreeing the death penalty for the Liberators, with
whom, by way of Cicero, he had flirted for so many months.
    It was time for us to act together.

VII

My lord has never been willing to give his version of that meeting on the island in the river downstream from Bononia. Lepidus, in his loose-mouthed way, soon gave his account, or more than one of them. Fulvia did so later too, but, since she was not present, hers cannot be trusted. Octavian like my lord has kept silent. No wonder; he had most reason for shame. What I write now is authentic. I was there, acting as my lord's secretary. (I have tried to urge him to tell in his own words what happened, but he shies away.)

There was apprehension as we boarded the punt that would carry us to the island. The soldiers knew that if the generals could not sustain agreement, there could be fighting the next day. My lord sat in the bow of the punt wrapped in a cloak in the chill mist of the dawn.

Lepidus and Octavian were already in the tent when we arrived, Lepidus chattering from nerves. It was my first sight of Octavian, and I don't mind confessing now that I was eager to see him. My lord had spoken so much about him, and of the mystery of his character and his physical attractions. He had often said that Octavian had been the lover of both Caesar and Decimus Brutus, and I knew that his closest friend was Maecenas, who happened also to be a special friend of a dancer called Cleon for whom, I may as well admit it, I had lusted – hopelessly, alas – myself. So I was excited to see this boy who appeared to combine a rather delicious effeminacy with the ability to win the loyalty of soldiers. I couldn't believe by the way that my lord was right when he said that that was only due to his name.

I must confess I was disappointed. He looked peaky. His face was thin, and his complexion had a sallow tinge. He was also shaking, but whether from a touch of fever or nerves, I couldn't tell. When he spoke, his voice had a harsh note, as if he couldn't trust it.

My lord at once took charge. Octavian tried to insist that they should first discuss matters alone, but my lord insisted that I remain as secretary.

"If we don't have a record of everything that's said and agreed, there's no point to this meeting."

Then he acknowledged Octavian's achievement.

"You've made things tough for me, kid," he said. "And your own rope-dance has had its moments of danger. I like the way you kept your nerve. So, here you are, no longer kid but Caesar."

He hugged the youth, and for a moment I even thought he was going to kiss him.

Then still holding him, he said:

"All the same, for me, you will always be kid as well as Caesar. Do you remember – 'course you don't, you weren't there, but you must have heard, when the mob called out to Himself, that he was planning to make himself king, and he quipped, "my name ain't king, it's Caesar . . .""

He settled himself again.

"So," he said, "the West is ours, as long as we hold together. I don't say there's no disaffection left in Italy, but we can soon clear that up. The high-minded skunks and word-masters are on the run . . ."

"What about Sextus Pompey?" Octavian said. "He's a force to be reckoned with."

My lord laughed.

"Pompey can wait. His father was always good at that. In his last years, all he could do. Pompey will ponce and posture, but we needn't fear he'll move against us."

Lepidus cleared his throat. It was a habit he had whenever he had something to say, as if without this preliminary nobody would bother to attend to him.

"My information is," he said, "that Marcus Brutus and Caius Cassius have raised forty legions and plan to land at Brundisium in the spring."

"They won't," my lord said.

"Allied to Pompey they would have a fleet."

"Pompey wouldn't trust them. Anyway they won't move that fast.

Cassius might, he has nerve. But they're a committee. Markie Brutus is a one-man committee."

"They moved fast enough on the Ides of March," Octavian said, as if somehow offering a reproof.

"Murder's easy, over and done with, not like war." My lord paused. "War's a long haul. You need staying power for war. Have you got it yourself, kid?"

Octavian said: "Don't try to rile me. Not now . . ."

My lord beamed on him.

"That's my boy."

I think Octavian blushed. He wriggled his shoulders and smoothed his hands over his thighs, which were hairless; I'd heard he shaved them with red-hot walnut shells.

"You've got spunk," my lord said, still smiling. "Tell me, kid, you've just come from Rome. How's the Treasury?"

"I paid my troops out of it," Octavian said. "As consul, you understand."

"Oh yes, as consul."

"Perfectly correct," Lepidus said, "perfectly correct though of course the consulship itself, but we needn't go into that now. Certainly not. I wonder whether you might sanction a payment of arrears, arrears, you understand . . ."

"That'll do. Nobody, kid, is questioning what you have done. You were there. So was the Treasury: open to you. So you took the cash. I'm thirsty. Critias, go and tell the boy to bring wine. A flask of white for the generals."

There was silence while they waited. Lepidus twitched and his fingers played a little tune on the table. Antony dismissed the boy, and winked at me.

"All right," he said, "I reckon we have forty-two or forty-three legions between us. Yours are a bit understrength, like mine. So let's say we have an army of two hundred thousand men. Well, the boys love us, of course, but their love will sicken without pay. So how's the Treasury, kid. Did you empty it?"

For a moment I thought he wasn't going to answer. He kept his gaze fixed on the table. I guessed that he hated having to disclose information. But he had to say something, if the meeting was to go ahead. When he spoke, it was as if the words were being dragged from his mouth.

"I don't know exactly, but it is certain it won't support such a force for long. Furthermore, and I'm sure you are already aware of this, we'll get no tax revenues from Asia while our enemies hold Greece and command the seas."

"How true. And that Egyptian bint isn't going to disgorge either. I'd a note from her, saying that while of course she was entirely friendly and eager to avenge Caesar's murder, she couldn't entrust her precious tax money to the seas while Pompey's fleet was ready to snatch it. Quite so. A bloody good excuse. Did you ever meet her, kid?"

Octavian nodded as if offended by the thought of Cleopatra. You really are a tight-arsed little thing, I said to myself.

"The old boy was crazy about her. Silly. Usually it was the other way about, you know. Easy come, easy go. Perhaps he had a premonition she was his last lay. The boys thought she'd bewitched him. Didn't they, Lepidus?"

"She certainly made a remarkable impression."

"He nearly got our throats cut in Alexandria while she teased his cock."

I wonder if my lord remembers speaking like that. He had better not see what I have written. On the other hand he might now agree. With himself again. But it doesn't matter because he no longer has the concentration required to read over my version of events. He's asleep now, actually, with his mouth open, and snoring.

"So," my lord said, "money is going to be a problem. Like I say, my boys dote on me but they won't fight for love. Can't blame them."

He paused again. Of course he knew what was going to be the answer, but he wanted Octavian to propose it.

The boy hesitated, then smiled. When he did so, you saw his charm. His beauty, which I had doubted, emerged. He smiled too as if he knew that what he was about to say was poison. And he liked the thought. Like a cat, he was. Reclining in front of the fire and flexing his claws.

"There's a precedent," he said. "Others have been in our case. Sulla, for example."

He sipped his wine and looked my lord in the eyes over the rim of the cup.

"Sulla?" Lepidus said. "Not a happy precedent . . ."

The memory of Sulla made the Romans of my lord's generation nervous. L. Cornelius Sulla was not only the first Roman general to seize the city by force of arms, but, though rich in consequence of his victories in the Asian wars, then published lists of his enemies whose property was to be confiscated and whose lives were forfeit. It is said that Julius Caesar himself was one of those proscribed, only saved by the intervention of a female relative who had enjoyed Sulla's favours.

"Sulla?" my lord said, as if the name surprised him, though I knew better. "Sulla? Your father" – he dwelled mockingly on the word – "the night before we crossed the Rubicon said to me that he would never imitate Sulla. Sulla's conduct had been hated and deplored by all good men. In a civil war, Caesar said, clemency to the defeated was imperative . . ."

"A noble sentiment," Lepidus said. "We are all Romans of good birth. Let's not forget that."

"Your ancestors," my lord said, "do you credit, Lepidus. Of course, my own pedigree, though distinguished, is in its origins plebeian, and our young friend here . . . well, kid, what do you say now?"

"Sulla died in his bed. You yourself, Antony, have handled Caesar's bloody toga."

"How right you are. And just by chance I have here a list – give it me, Critias – a list of the thirty richest senators and the hundred and fifty best-heeled equestrians who have been rash enough to declare their friendship for the self-styled Liberators."

Octavian said:

"It would be folly, when we march to Greece, to leave enemies here in Italy . . ."

It was the next day they started naming names.

First, though, they were delayed by Lepidus. He sought reassurance. Everything must be in order before he dared give his consent to what my lord and Octavian knew had to be done. On what sort of authority, he kept asking, did they propose to act? Of course Octavian was for the time being consul, but must relinquish that office at the year's end. He and Antony, he said, had proconsular commands, but these granted no imperium outside their provinces.

"We have more than forty legions," my lord said. "What more authority do you look for?"

Octavian said:

"Lepidus has a point."

Was he already trying to separate Lepidus from my lord? I think so. He understood that in any group of three, one must from time to time be isolated.

"Yes," he said, "there is a distinction which I'm sure we all recognise between power and authority. Our legions give us power, but if we are to be respected rather than merely feared we must seek lawful authority for our actions. It is such a pity that you abolished the office of dictator, Antony. Otherwise I would suggest you assume it yourself."

"Sure," said my lord. "Well it won't surprise you to know that I have little time for legalistic formalities. I'm old enough to remember how the boss and Pompey and that gross moneybags Marcus Crassus carved up the State at Lucca. That's precedent enough for me."

"But," Lepidus said, "that was condemned by all good men as sheer gangsterism."

"So what?"

Octavian said, "Well of course I'm too young to remember that, though I have naturally read about it. But I think I see a way out. Let us indeed establish a Triumvirate, as they did, but let us do so by legal process. Let us get a tribune – I know just the man – to introduce an emergency law into the Assembly, empowering us for a period of – what? – five years to order the Republic. He can spout any manner of stuff in justification, so long as it is sufficiently high-minded to permit people to vote for the measure with a good conscience. Such a law would grant us full imperium, and it would mean that if any of us subsequently chooses to retire into private life, which I am sure we shall all wish to do some day, there could be no legal challenge to our acts. We would also be able to control all elections to offices by nominating sole candidates even for years in advance."

My lord said: "I go along with that. One thing however. So that we start on terms of equality as we mean to continue, you kid, will have to surrender your consulship."

That shook the little blighter (as my lord later remarked).

"Of course," he said, "just what I was about to propose myself. You anticipated me, took the words from my mouth."

I began to respect him then. Such a smart and immediate recovery.

Then they got to work. Besides my lord's list, Octavian and Lepidus had each provided themselves, or rather been provided by their staffs, with names of senators and equestrians known to be, as Octavian delicately put it, "disaffected". A great many names were common to all three lists, and many of them had already fled Italy and were to be found in the camp or entourage of the "Liberators". As their wealth was estimated, Lepidus warmed to the task, his previous inhibitions now apparently forgotten. Octavian showed no emotion. Whether he had had any scruples as to the nature of the work on which they were engaged, I do not know. He evinced neither enthusiasm nor repugnance.

As the discussion proceeded, it was however inevitable that disputes arose. All three realised that they were engaged on what must inspire good men with hatred. There is something terrible in such sentencing. In any case, some of those proposed for proscription were friends or relatives of one or other of the self-constituted judges. I noticed that as the argument wore on my lord drank faster. Octavian sipped only at well-watered wine.

"Lepidus," the boy said, "you must sacrifice your brother Paullus."

"My brother?"

"Consider his record, consider his wealth. Can you trust him who betrayed my father who spared him. Antony, I appeal to you."

My lord made no reply. He poured himself more wine and sighed.

"No friend of mine," he said at last.

"Prick him down," Octavian said.

"Very well," Lepidus said. "I consent with tears in my eyes for the sake of the Republic. But, tit for tat, you know, call me, call thee, as they say, in return Antony must agree to yield his mother's brother L. Julius Caesar, a notable Pompeian. I insist. He is connected to both of you. I insist you join me equally in blood-guilt."

My lord drank again. His eye would not meet Octavian's. Did I then feel a premonition? Did a shudder alert me to the boy's force, the fierce strength of will with which he would in time assail my lord? I suppose not. One imagines these things in retrospect.

"Why not?" Octavian said. Then, horribly, sniggered. "He cannot have long to live in any case. He has outworn his welcome in this world. Dispatch him to the next. To sacrifice such a man, a Julian and a Caesar, will convince the doubters that our wills are

51

hard as Etruscan marble. From such proscriptions, there can be no way back."

"Atticus," Lepidus said. "No one will spill more gold than that fat banker."

"Not Atticus," my lord muttered.

"I insist," Lepidus said.

I thought: for the first time perhaps in his life he tastes the drug of absolute power, and it has maddened him.

"There are good reasons for proscribing Atticus," Octavian said. "His wealth for a start. His friendship with Marcus Brutus. The effect his death would have on others. I understand you perfectly my dear colleague. Yet perhaps we should pause. It may be a long war. When we have dealt with Brutus and Cassius we shall still have Sextus Pompey against us. It will take time and money, much money. And proscriptions of this scale cannot be repeated. They are a sort of capital levy, once and for all. But afterwards, we shall still need to raise more money, and no one is better at finding funds than Atticus and his fellow banker Balbus. Would it not be wise to bind them to us by manifest obligation? By all means, let them feel they were near to death. They will be all the happier to live. But we shall get more in the long run if we leave them off our list."

"Atticus lives," my lord said. "Balbus too. There's no question. But Cicero must die."

Now that announcement should have occasioned a chill. Cicero was after all, whatever his faults of character and misjudgement, the most illustrious living Roman. Of course he had insulted my lord unforgivably. But Caesar himself had called him "an ornament of Roman culture"; and he had spared him. To do more mischief, as my lord had often remarked. Moreover, the fact that Octavian was now in a position to weigh Cicero's life in the balance, was indubitably due to the old man's sponsorship of his cause in the weeks after the Ides of March. If there was any kindness, if there was any gratitude, hovering in the air of that cold tent on the river island, Octavian should have spoken then in defence of Cicero.

"As you wish, Antony," he said.

I heard Lepidus catch his breath. My lord looked at Octavian and I could not read his face.

"'The boy,'" Octavian said, "'must be flattered, decorated, and disposed of.' You remember his words. You told them me yourself,

Antony. Cicero has had flattery enough for a lifetime; he will be honoured by generations to come, generations perhaps that have forgotten us. What more can he wish from life? Let the old man die."

That night my lord was maudlin drunk. I helped him to bed and he clung to me, sobbing. His breath stank of wine, and his nails dug into my shoulder.

"Critias," he mumbled, "what manner of boy is that?"

VIII

The treachery of the Senate, Cicero's attempts to play Octavian off against me, hadn't prevented the conjunction of the Caesarian forces. But their machinations had bought time for Brutus and Cassius.

In Greece Brutus had been greeted as a hero. Statues were raised to Caesar's murderer. My brother Gaius was unable to stand against him. He was captured and would be put to death, described as a traitor. Brutus issued coins that showed the dagger of the "Liberators" and his own image on the obverse: a fine display of Republican virtue.

Cassius defeated my former colleague Dolabella in Syria. The East, except for Egypt, was in their hands. Cleopatra wrote to me protesting that she had sent troops to help Dolabella, but her fleet had been intercepted by a storm. It may have been true, though I have never found evidence that it was. Now she asked for recognition of her child whom she called Caesarion as Caesar's son. Octavian was indignant. He alone, he insisted, could boast that title. But I persuaded him that the risk of Cleopatra lending support and the wealth of Egypt to our enemies was so great that we would be wise to humour her. What does it matter? I asked; and he had no answer but a sullen frown.

Even without Egypt's wealth, our enemies had the resources of Asia at their command. The Eastern provinces were accustomed to pay at least fifty million denarii in tax and tribute every year. Not a penny had reached Rome since Caesar's murder. It had all found its way into the Treasury of the "Liberators". They became now still more exigent. Cities in Asia were compelled to provide in one year the tribute normally exacted in ten. And they received no promise of remission the next year. It was as if wolves had descended on the hapless provincials. But they dared not resist.

So the noble Liberators drove their preparations on, even to the extent of making a treaty of alliance with Rome's desperate enemy, Orodes, Emperor of Parthia, who promised aid in men and money. To crush me they would put the Republic itself at risk.

All things moved towards the deciding struggle. The armies converged at Philippi, north of the Aegean in windy Thrace. We had a hard time getting there, for our enemies controlled the sea, and Octavian wasted time and resources in a feeble attempt to subdue Sextus Pompey, despite my advice. It was true that Pompey's fleet hampered our efforts, but it was still a strategic blunder to waste time on him. It is a good rule of war to concentrate your force when it is at its strongest on the most redoubtable of your enemies. But Octavian was a novice, and his friends Agrippa and Maecenas, neither of them with any experience, and Maecenas temperamentally unsuited for warfare, fed his conceit.

Weakened by his delay I had a hard job breaking out of Brundisium, blockaded by Cassius' admiral, Murcus. I lost three legions in doing so, and for the rest of the campaign was troubled by Murcus' continuing ability to block my supply route from Italy.

Indeed supplies were my chief problem throughout the campaign. There's nothing unusual in that.

But it meant that I was compelled to bring the enemy to battle. I could not sustain a long campaign.

Conversely, it was in their interest to delay. Cassius, I have since learned, was in favour of avoiding battle, of giving ground and drawing me further from my base into the inhospitable terrain of Thrace. But Brutus would have none of it. Certain of his virtue, he overestimated his ability.

Yet the position in which they stood to arms was strong. Their armies lay across the Egnatian Way, and their flanks were protected landward by mountains, seaward by marshes. Their supply lines were short and secure.

"It's a bugger," I said; there was no way to turn their flanks. The battle would be hard slogging.

Octavian lingered at Dyrrachium. He sent word that he had fallen sick. Perhaps he had. In my view the cause was nerves. So far, he had succeeded without the need to prove himself in battle.

Now that he was faced with this necessity, he lay shivering in his tent.

I could not afford to wait. We even had to dig wells, for there was no running water near our camp. Every day we were threatened by the breakdown of our supply chain.

Cassius was on their left, Brutus on the right, protected by the mountain spur. I smiled when I learned that, smiled in admiration of Cassius, whose distrust of Brutus' abilities was at least as great as mine of Octavian's. At last the boy's forces moved into position. He followed two days later, whimpering. Again I smiled: ambition had suppressed, if not conquered, fear; he could not afford to allow me credit for a victory, and he was lost if I was defeated.

I found him in his tent, alone with Agrippa. (Maecenas had, predictably, preferred to steer clear of battle, and was exploring and enjoying the bagnios and brothels of Dyrrachium – those that offered boys, of course. Or so I supposed.)

I was brief. Though I addressed myself to Octavian, my words were really directed at Agrippa, who had, I fancied, and subsequent events have alas confirmed my judgement, the makings of a soldier. All they had to do, I said, was stand firm. My own troops would engage Cassius.

"We have already begun to work our way through the marshes, digging a dyke."

"In your letters," Octavian said, "you talked of the necessity of a frontal assault."

"So I did, kid, but it's too hazardous."

"Isn't forcing a way through a swamp equally so?"

"It would be with other troops than mine."

My confidence was of course assumed. I was well aware that even Caesar himself might have hesitated to adopt so bold a strategy. But I had convinced myself that I had no other intelligent choice; and my men trusted my decision.

The battle in the swamp began before first light. For a general the first stages of a battle hold an excitement equal to nothing else in life, not even to the first embraces of a new lover. As I watched my legionaries march, in the silence I had ordained, into the mist, and heard the only sound of feet splashing in the shallows, I drew cold fingers across my neck, and thought briefly of death and dishonour.

Then I put myself at the head of the reserve and gave the order to advance.

The hills over Brutus' camp were touched with rose-pink when word came back down the line that our first troops had come upon Cassius' outposts and overwhelmed them. Soon distant cries told me the alarm was sounded in the enemy camp. I pushed forward, through the marshland that echoed with the cry of waterfowl disturbed by war. In a little while I attained firm ground. There was perhaps half a mile of it between me and the camp, and already I saw that we had gained the surprise we sought and the legions were able to deploy in line ready for the assault. The danger was that now they would move too soon, and I sent word to hold their ground. Many a time the advantage gained by surprise has been lost because commanders think that it itself has ensured victory.

The sun was climbing before all was ready for the general advance. To my relief the enemy were still in process of deployment. We charged; they were swept away, and we were in the camp. The battle itself was a matter of minutes. The victory lay in our preparation, and the combination of boldness and caution with which we had executed our plan. Now, it was up to Octavian. If his men held their ground, the campaign would be over that morning.

But that didn't happen. Whether Brutus (or more probably his staff) were alerted by some movement that had escaped Cassius, or whether our planned assault merely anticipated theirs by a matter of a few hours, I have never been able to establish. But, even as we secured Cassius' camp, and I held my men an instant before ordering a general pursuit – the essential act which turns defeat into rout – word came that Brutus had not only moved against Octavian, but that the boy's army was in headlong flight. Moreover, one of Brutus' officers had had the wit to deploy part of his army in a defensive position ranged against us.

All was confusion, the cup of victory dashed from my lips. It was necessary to consolidate. Myself, I hurried back to the rear, having given orders to my lieutenants to hold their ground.

It was nightfall before the position was clear. Octavian had indeed been routed. The boy himself had fled; he was later found, towards evening, lurking in a wildfowler's hut two miles to the rear. But Brutus, alarmed by news of my success, and perhaps lacking in the confidence to push his own to the utmost, had himself precipitately withdrawn in confusion. Men were to say that in this first battle at Philippi there had been one victorious commander and three vanquished ones. The jest was as true as such jests ever are.

That night I called a council, but first I sought to see Octavian alone.

I found him being massaged by two slaves. He lay face-down on a couch with only a towel spread across his loins. I placed my hand on his shoulder. His skin was hot and quivered at my touch. Then he sat up, told the slaves to give me wine, and dismissed them.

"I don't know what to say."

"Courage isn't constant," I replied. "When you are my age, you'll know that."

I had arrived angry, but he looked so young, so wretched, so ashamed, that the tenderness I had felt for him when Caesar was still alive, came flooding back. I put my arms round him and hugged him and felt him relax . . .

When the council, nervous, despondent, heavy-eyed with fatigue, gathered that evening in my tent, I said:

"Through no one's fault, we're worse off than we were this morning, worse off because we need a victory more than they do. They've only to hold their ground, and the longer this campaign drags on, the more the advantage shifts in their favour."

This was not the word they were hoping to hear, but we had to look reality in the face. Before I could elaborate, a young officer, Salvidienus Rufus, one of Octavian's most capable lieutenants, pushed his way past the sentries and called out that he had great news . . .

"Cassius is dead."

For a moment no one spoke or moved. All were stunned by this reversal of fortune. Then they leaped to their feet, crowding round the young man and clamouring for details. It was some time before order was restored and he could speak. For my part, I experienced a wave of relief; I had not realised how dark our prospects were till these words caused the clouds to roll away.

"A captured prisoner," he said, "whom I have been interrogating, assures me he fell on his sword. I am convinced that he speaks the truth. It seems that Cassius believed that Brutus too had been defeated, and that their cause was lost."

I didn't stop to enquire how it came about that one of Octavian's men should have been interrogating one of my prisoners. I merely said:

"Gentlemen, I was mistaken. We are better off than we were this morning."

Then I called for wine.

Nevertheless our position was still dangerous. Supplies were running short. Brutus had only to delay, to hold his ground, and we would be compelled either to attack, however unfavourable the ground, or withdraw; itself perilous.

For two weeks we fenced, trying to lure Brutus from his impregnable position. Then either his nerve gave way or, provoked by the demands of his officers and men, he committed the supreme folly of attacking us. I could have cried for joy.

By evening I wept real tears. They were not just tears of relief, though that too was cause for weeping. While Octavian's legions this time had held their ground, mine, swinging on to Brutus' foolishly exposed flank, had swept all before them.

Our victory was complete, devastating, and irreversible. The army of our enemies ceased to exist.

Brutus followed Cassius into the shades, in the same noble manner. I looked down on his corpse, and ordered that it be covered with a purple cloth.

"Virtue," I said, "an empty word."

But when I looked on him, the past years slid away. I forgot Caesar's murderer. I forgot the tiresome pedant. I even forgot his responsibility for the death of my brother Gaius. I remembered instead the young Marcus, in the days when we had been close friends. I recalled him in the gardens of the Palatine, speaking of the great things he would do for Rome, and of the nobility of Republican ideals. I recalled too how in those salad days of youth I had admired him, felt his goodness a reproach to my own wild and unruly life, and yet a goodness expressed with such gentleness that I did not feel resentment but admiration and the wish to emulate him; or felt that in my better moments.

Once, when I had been engaged in a debauch lasting several days with Clodius and Curio, we encountered Brutus as we staggered through the Forum knocking against, and sometimes over, the stalls of the market-sellers. When one brawny fellow protested and I would have drawn a dagger on him, Brutus laid his hand on my arm to restrain me, and looked on me with such fond reproof that I turned away, and left my friends and went home. The next day he called on me before I was up and spoke at length with such tenderness and concern, and without shadow of reproach about the need for me to reform my life if I was not to waste the extraordinary talents of which he believed me to be possessed that I resolved to amend my ways, and did indeed so, for several weeks.

"You have it in you," he said then, "to be the leader of our generation. There is no honour open to us which you are not capable of winning. I have a fair idea of my own worth and abilities, but I feel myself insignificant when measured against you. And my love for Rome is such that if I thought this necessary to enable you to serve the Republic as it is within your power to serve it, I would lay aside my own ambition and retire into private life."

These memories flooded back uncontrollable and terrible as Tiber in spate when I looked on his corpse, with an expression of the utmost peace on its worn face; and I wept . . .

He can still after all these years astonish me. I have seldom heard him speak of Marcus Brutus without mockery. No wonder many thought him insincere when in his funeral oration he described him as "the noblest Roman of them all". Yet he is perfectly sincere now. His face is blank with the sense of waste, and even though I am certain that in mourning Brutus anew as his own ruin nakedly confronts him, he is mourning what he has made and failed to make of himself, yet this tenderness is real, and really for the memory of Brutus too. The truth is, I never come to the end of him.

The last letter he wrote to me – you've never seen that, Critias, have you? I've kept it locked in my secret Cabinet, that is, my heart. I can recite it word-perfectly. He sent it to me three days before his world broke at Philippi . . .

Antony: no doubt it is malignant fate that pitches us now against each other, and we are bound to courses from which neither can turn back. Yet it grieves me to think of what might have been.

We both felt the power of Caesar's will and the seductive influence of his charm.

61

But I saw that Caesar was bent on the destruction of all that had been great and noble in the soul and spirit of Rome. I do not think he intended that. He was driven by a daemon against which he was powerless, which perhaps he but imperfectly understood.

What saddens me is that you – so magnanimous and generous of yourself – should have been enslaved by him.

You might have joined with Cassius and my other friends in our attempt to liberate the Republic. Even after our sacrifice of Caesar, I wished to be your friend, and restore the State in concord with you.

Alas, we have been swept apart by the savage course of events, and you are now thirled to the boy Octavian who has all Caesar's ambition and none of his nobility. You have surrendered your will to his, and you will pay for this folly in the end.

Don't you understand yet that the government of a single person means the destruction of Liberty, which no good man yields but with his life?

Oh Antony, old companion of my youth, I grieve for you, my brother.

It may be I shall die in the battle to which we are now bound, and Liberty with me. It would be happier for you if you fell on this field of Philippi. For your victory, if the gods permit it, will bring forth bitter fruit, the poison of which will corrupt and destroy you. Then in your last days you may remember Brutus who loved you and would have saved you from yourself, had you been willing to be saved.

Don't you understand, my dear?

Monarchy is a cruel frost killing whatever has true vitality. Under the government of a single person, all men are slaves

If I die, I shall escape. If you conquer, you will be crushed by that boy's terrible and iron will. You cannot defeat him, for your humanity will be subject to his inhumanity . . .

It's strange that I never thought him possessed of insight.

Philippi was more terrible than any of Caesar's battles. There was never one in which so many distinguished men of noble families perished.

At Octavian's insistence, to which I weakly assented, the slaughter did not end there. Those who had escaped Italy to join themselves to Brutus and Cassius were, many of them, executed.

"Reason of State," Octavian said, "we agreed: no more clemency."

When the defeated were compelled to parade past us, they saluted me as "Imperator" but howled insults at Octavian. Perhaps this accounted for his zeal for blood; but I have long observed that civilians such as he essentially was and is, are always keener for executions after the battle than soldiers are. When Quintus Ligarius, one of Caesar's assassins, looked my colleague in the eye and demanded honourable burial, Octavian said "that is a matter for the vultures". A father and son – I forget their names – pleaded that one at least should be spared; he told them to cast dice. He even ordered that Brutus should have his head struck from his corpse that it might be thrown against Caesar's statue in Rome.

I managed to save the life of Brutus' close friend Lucilius; he is with me even now.

Yet, a paradox: while Octavian, perhaps driven to such despicable cruelty by the consciousness of his own cowardice in the first battle (as if he could expunge the memory of his flight in streams of blood), showed himself harsh as an Alpine winter and merciless as Sulla himself, in our private communications he recovered his boyish charm. He acknowledged frankly how much he owed to me and implored me to forgive him for not having been well enough to bear a greater share of the burden. It was as if, when we were alone, the fears and tensions of the two years since Caesar's murder had thrust him into public life (or given him the opportunity to enter it) had fallen away from him. He joked, smiled, and showed himself delightfully affectionate. He also made it clear that our settlement of the world would be amicable and that he was ready to fall in with whatever I recommended.

"For," he said, "you have borne the heat of the battle, and it is only just that you now wear the palm of triumph."

I could not respond fully. The image of that boy standing on the dais and dealing death came between me and his smiles. I found it difficult to think of him as I had, with that affection that had lingered even as it seemed as if he was bent on my destruction. I couldn't think of him any longer as "kid".

IX

Could we have settled the Republic after Philippi? I had every intention of doing so, and I realised that unless Octavian and I were to engage in war to the death, then concord between us must be firmly established. Since my intentions were good I trusted his.

It was essential to define responsibilities. We met together alone to do so. Lepidus, poor thing, was forgotten. He had had no share in our victory at Philippi and mouldered in Spain, where he had proved himself inept at controlling Sextus Pompey who then, from his base in Sicily, dominated the Western Sea.

We had two priorities: to disband those legionaries who had served their time, and having paid them the promised donations, settle them in colonies; it was unfortunate, as it proved, that we had promised them the finest farmland in Italy. Second, in order to pay off the troops, it was necessary to restore the finances of the Eastern provinces, so ravaged by Cassius' greed, and at the same time prepare for the war against Parthia, which Julius had planned. I had then been sceptical of his determination, believing that he saw this war as a means of enhancing his glory, and evading the task of reforming the Republic. But now the insolence and incursions of the Parthians, encouraged by our internal divisions, had made it necessary, indeed urgent, to engage them.

At first Octavian shrank from the prospect of such a war, on such a scale. But when I had argued its necessity, and convinced him that it was inescapable, he declared himself eager to take the lead; and command our army. It was ridiculous.

The legions, wary of a Parthian war, on account of memories of the disaster suffered by Marcus Crassus a dozen years before, would never have followed on such a dangerous enterprise the young man who had hidden from Brutus' troops in that wildfowler's hut. But of course I didn't state the objection so bluntly. I had, you understand, no wish to wound the boy; and in any case, being certain that the security of the State and the restoration of peace within the Roman world depended on our continued friendship, I was careful to phrase my objection delicately.

So at last it was agreed: Octavian would return to Italy to settle the veterans, but Italy should be regarded as common ground since both of us would require to recruit new legions there. Cisalpine Gaul should be incorporated into Italy, as Caesar had long before intended. This was a concession on my part, since I was that province's legitimate proconsul. I retained command of Gallia Comata and Gallia Narbonensis; otherwise the West was to be Octavian's.

"What about Lepidus?" he said, having forgotten him.

"Let him have Africa."

The East was to be my responsibility, and Octavian undertook to furnish me with all the men I required for the war against Parthia (which, however, events were to compel me yet again to postpone).

We recorded our agreement in writing.

Then, since Octavian protested that his stomach was still so delicate that he must abstain from wine, we went to take our ease in a brothel. Though the boy had formally wed Fulvia's daughter – my stepdaughter Claudia – to seal our pact some months before Philippi, I was amused to see that he selected a boy for his pleasure: a curly-headed ephebe with an engaging grin, whom I might have fancied myself if my eye hadn't already fallen on a luscious negress with oiled thighs that shone like a centurion's armour. She had a thirst to match a centurion's and an appetite for her business that did credit to the establishment. Even today, it gives me a stand to think of her. I bought her indeed from her whoremaster and was sorry when she died of a fever a few months later.

It was a letter from Fulvia that disturbed my complacency a couple of weeks after Octavian had returned to Italy.

Sometimes I think I shouldn't let you out of my sight. You simply can't be trusted. When I feel kindly towards you, which I try to do because we are bound together, husband and wife, one flesh, and as the daughter of a great family that can boast more than a dozen consuls, I respect and value matrimony, well, then, in this mood, I think it is because you are too trusting yourself; you have a noble nature which blinds you to the wickedness of others.

But then, I remember some of the things you have done and the way you have treated me – without the respect due to one of my ancestry and, though I say so myself, character; and then I think it is simply because you are a fool.

You must have been a fool to make the agreement I am told you have made with that little bitch Octavian. You know incidentally that he has never yet boarded our daughter. That tells you what sort of a man he is, or rather not a man at all, not as a man should be. Nasty little pervert, but cunning.

So cunning that my great big stupid Antony fell straight headlong into the pit he dug for him.

I wager that he tried to bag the Eastern provinces and the Parthian war for himself, and that you thought you were clever in dissuading him.

Isn't that so?

It's unbelievable.

How could anyone believe that a cowardly little nancy-boy – we've all heard how he behaved during the first battle, and you should hear what the girls in my sewing circle have to say – would dare to undertake a Parthian war?

Don't you understand? He wanted Italy all the time, and he wanted it because he who controls Italy controls the Republic.

And you gave it to him on a plate.

Well, it's fortunate that your brother Lucius is this year's consul – I'm amazed you had the nous to think of putting him in the job – fortunate because I can use him to make things more than a little awkward for that creature who prefers scented boys who waggle their bottoms to my daughter. Not that Lucius himself is up to much. I've always thought him a milksop, as you know, but I can put some iron in him where it's needed.

I don't know what you would do without me, or where you would be. But I'll make you master of the Republic despite yourself . . .

I wrote to Lucius of course telling him that he must co-operate with Octavian, and to pay no heed to Fulvia's ravings. You might as well tell a drowning man to pay no heed to the water that has engulfed him.

My excuse is that I was fully occupied. Historians never acknowledge the weight of business. Governing an empire is not merely a matter of determining the broad sweep of policy. There are urgent decisions to be taken every day, and each decision requires the consideration of other considerations. If I grant this to that city, what will be the effect on this one . . . and so on. Moreover, the Eastern provinces were in a condition of near anarchy. Brutus and Cassius had plundered them as if they were brigands rather than governors. No doubt they would have pleaded necessity. But the work of restoring order and harmony was exigent and exhausting. I had simply no time to attend to affairs in Italy also. Moreover, I had taken it on myself to raise the money that was needed to pay off some legions, and support those we kept. That was part of my bargain with Octavian and I was determined to keep it.

But was I wilfully blind also? I simply do not know. Perhaps I was; in my new mood of self-doubt I fear I was.

Yet I was constantly on the move. Certain letters sent to me did not arrive. Otherwise, who knows what I might not have done to avert . . .

Critias, I am weary, tell them to bring wine . . .

Night falls fast here, in my Timonium, where I look out on dark waters, swirling waters, of bitter memories and vain regrets. It is very silent at night. Even the sea birds sleep, and the noise of the distant city is stilled.

I have had a life, haven't I, Critias? And now the earth rolls heavily. It is as if it bids me tread no more, ashamed to bear me.

Where was I?

The war of Perusia, my lord. You were about to embark on it.

What should I recount? I wasn't there, but working, raising armies, judging cities, whoring and feasting in the East.

Perusia? Well, if am to leave a record of my life, then I must force myself to it.

Octavian got himself into trouble in his allocation of land. It would have been a hard task even if he had handled it better. The mood of Italy was sour. Those with land feared to lose it, those who had none hoped to win some. There were murderous street-battles in towns throughout the peninsula, fought between citizens and soldiers. Reports came that disbanded legionaries were driven by showers of stones from the lands they had been allocated.

But Octavian made things worse than was necessary. He favoured his veterans at the expense of mine. He held back confiscated estates and sold them for high prices on the open market. He alienated whole districts. There were revolts in Umbria, Etruria and the old Sabine lands.

It is said Fulvia fomented them. To my shame I have to accept that she did. But she was not the cause. That lay deeper, in long-simmering resentment provoked into action by Octavian's brusque measures.

But Fulvia's real offence was against me. She knew my character She knew that having made an agreement with Octavian I was bound to keep it. So she set herself to discredit, and then destroy, Octavian. Even I can scarcely blame him for responding in like manner. Most of all, I cannot forgive her for leading poor Lucius on. When the ass dug his heels in, she stirred him into movement with a goad.

In the autumn it came to open war. To mark this, Octavian dispensed with his unwelcome wife, Claudia, whom he had insulted by his indifference. He summoned Salvidienus Rufus with six legions from Spain. Lucius, belatedly realising that he had overreached himself attempted to break through to the north. Too late; Salvidienus and Agrippa cut him off. He retired into Perusia, and prepared to withstand a siege, hoping to be relieved by commanders loyal to me. Yet I was not myself involved, and knew nothing of what was happening.

It is said that in Perusia Lucius' soldiers inscribed my name on the missiles they shot from their slings: to persuade the besiegers they were making war on the "Hero of Philippi". The siege dragged on throughout the terrible mountain winter. Attempts to break out failed; starvation set in. Fulvia, rather than Lucius, inspired the garrison to heroic efforts. Those who talked of peace were whipped or put to death. An easy release, said some. It was said later that when two magistrates of the city spoke up for surrender, Fulvia had them hanged, and their bodies thrown over the walls.

I would like to think this is not true.

Lucius, at last, acted as a man should, and faced reality. Ignoring my wife, my brother negotiated the surrender of the city. He was promised clemency. Trusting the promise, he submitted, only to learn to his horror that the clemency was restricted to himself alone. Having humiliated him by holding him for two weeks in a cell dug out of the rock, Octavian contemptuously made him governor of Further Spain.

"I know it is what my brother and yours would wish," he said.

Emerging from the interview, eyes bloodshot and flesh stinking after his ordeal, Lucius was marched past the bodies of his comrades as they swung in chains.

He never recovered from this humiliation. The letters he wrote me from Spain were disjointed, incoherent, full of self-recrimination – and hatred of both Fulvia and Octavian. It was with difficulty that I could make sense of what had happened, or what he thought had happened. But I could not doubt that my brother had been broken by these terrible months and their still more awful conclusion. Officers who escaped the slaughter, slipping from the city in disguise, and who made their way to me in Greece, spoke of these things with horror . . .

Months later, when the surviving citizens erected a memorial to those who had died fighting for Republican liberty, Octavian ordered it to be demolished and imposed a ruinous fine.

Fulvia too was spared. She was carried to Rome under escort, and held in custody among the Vestal Virgins.

"This punishment, if you chose to make it for life, will suit her," Octavian wrote. "She is not the sort of woman of whom the Vestals approve, and they will make her feel their disapprobation. But frankly, brother, I should divorce her if I were in your position. By her conduct she has proved herself unworthy of you, and it is evident that she is an obstacle to our common labours, an insurmountable obstacle indeed."

He was right, but of course I could not accept his suggestion. Despite his restrained language it read too much like a command. I arranged, heavy-hearted, for Fulvia to join me in Greece.

When she arrived in Athens I found that her ordeal had not improved her temper. She charged me with deserting both her and my own interest. She also intrigued with agents sent by Sextus Pompey, to whom my mother had fled for refuge, fearing Octavian's wrath. But I would have nothing to do with Pompey. I had given my word to Octavian.

I withstood Fulvia's reproaches with a stoicism foreign to my nature. Perhaps I did feel some guilt. I certainly felt pity for one so enraged against the world.

I left her in Athens. I was not sorry to do so, for her reproaches were intolerable. But I grieved when she died a few months later. For all her faults of temper, she was the only one of my wives who allied herself wholeheartedly to my cause; and if she harmed it, as she did, it was not through malice.

X

He's trying to tell the truth, I'm sure of that, but he always draws back . . . One reason is that the years immediately after Philippi were the years of his glory, years of opportunity too, as I saw even then. He had attained the greatest position in the Roman world, and in the eyes of all he was, when compared to Octavian, as the Sun is to the Moon. And through carelessness and a lordly negligence, he allowed his mastery to slip from him. It is too painful for him to dwell on that.

Then again, he is using me now, or should I say, using these memoirs, in order to establish his place in History – not, in my view, somewhere that anyone should look to find the truth. So again he skates over awkwardness and anything of which he might feel ashamed.

I know of course that for many the very idea of my lord entertaining shame is absurd. But that isn't just. Octavian, whose penetration of others' characters I would never deny, is said to have remarked that Antony, even in his most magnificent hours – perhaps especially then? – was a superb schoolboy. The observation was unkind, what you might indeed yourself expect from a clever – smart-arsed, if you like – little bitch like Octavian. All the same there's something undeniable in it. And don't tell me that schoolboys, even superb ones, can't experience shame. If you want my opinion, they feel that more keenly than adults, because it is so important to them to be well-thought-of.

Moreover, though no husband could, I should say, feel any guilt for being unfaithful to that virago Fulvia, nevertheless Antony did. He

73

knew perfectly well that she was a horror, but she was his horror and he felt responsible to her and for her. It made things worse too that he was having such a splendid time while she was enduring the frightful siege of Perusia. First of all, in Cappodocia, he had a little fling with a really gorgeous girl called Glaphyra, who was (most of the time, but not exclusively) the mistress of the Dynast of Comana, whose name escapes me. Glaphyra was a lady of ample charms (and figure), the sort with whom Antony could feel really comfortable. As a matter of fact, she looked rather like his mother, and she fussed and petted him, and made him easy. He adored short doses of domesticity and jokes, and, though her Greek was terrible, she had a coarse humour, for she had begun life on the streets and worked in a brothel before becoming the Dynast's paramour. You couldn't have found a greater contrast to Fulvia, and it was no wonder that he enjoyed her.

And then there was Cleopatra. My lord always denied that he had made love to her while Caesar was alive, though it pleased him immensely when she hinted that she would have dropped Caesar for him if he had only made a move. So this winter was really the first time that they were lovers. She came to him first in the city of Tarsus, in Cilicia, where he had summoned her to explain her conduct during the war of Philippi.

Well, I suppose everyone by now knows the story of the entrance she made, but in case you don't – and in case future generations do after all have the chance to read this narrative (which I write now, I may say, trembling with fear, agitation and foreboding, if that's not too pompous a word), I suppose I may as well give my version of it.

She had taken her time in responding to his invitation, even though it was really a command. No wonder, I thought, when she did arrive. It must have taken the most imaginative theatrical producer weeks to calculate such an effect as she made.

She approached by way of the River Cydnus in the most mag-nificent galley I have ever seen. The stern was covered with gold – gold-leaf anyway – the sails were purple and the oars silver. The rowers kept time to the music of flutes, pipes, and harps. The Queen, dressed and bedecked to represent Aphrodite, whom the Romans call Venus, lay under a canopy embroidered with dull gold, of the most exquisite and expensive workmanship. Eight beautiful boys, painted cupids, fanned her, and were ranged on either side of the couch where she lay, her fingers delicately dancing on her half-exposed breasts. Her maids were dressed like nereids. The fragrance of burning incense wafted from the galley, and intoxicated the crowds that lined the shore.

Aphrodite, it was said, had come to dine with Dionysos, the god whom Antony so honoured that many thought him his incarnation.

Well, of course it was vulgar, but you couldn't deny that it was also magnificent. And quite amazingly sexy. My lord boarded the galley like a bull in rut, and I confess I was quite carried away myself. (Fortunately I was able later in the evening, when the principals were engaged with each other, to carry off one of the painted cupids, whose apparent and obvious charms proved to be in no way deceptive.) Antony found Cleopatra's equally satisfying, and it is no wonder that he was ready to follow her to Alexandria.

Nevertheless, he wasn't, whatever they thought in Rome, lost in love.

Or was he?

Nobody has known his moods, whims, and emotions better than I, and yet I can't give a certain answer to the question. It still perplexes me.

One thing however I can say, and you can decide for yourselves what it proves.

I can think of at least two dozen women whose favours Antony enjoyed over the years (or the other way round if you like), and if I was asked to rank them in beauty, there's no doubt that Cleopatra would be placed in the lower half of the league table. In a certain light she could even appear ugly, and no one could deny that her chin was out of proportion. You could see that in old age (if she attained that condition) it would hook round and approach the tip of her nose. Then, being small and neat-limbed in youth, but as fond of eating and drinking as my lord himself, she was already inclined to be fat. Moreover, in the mornings, when she had a hangover, she looked more than her age, even then; it can't have been a pretty sight to wake up next to her.

In short, as far as beauty went, she couldn't begin to compare with my darling Cytheris, and I have to admit that even Fulvia was a far more lovely woman.

None of this mattered. Cleopatra had a beautiful voice – she spoke, incidentally, at least eight languages, none of them, I have been assured, correctly – and that was certainly the case with her Greek.

But she played her voice like a musical instrument, and her wit was undeniable. Of course it is easy for a queen, or a general, to win a reputation for wit, since those around are always eager to recognise it, but there is no doubt that Cleopatra was genuinely witty, and so I am only sorry now that I can't actually recall any clever or memorable thing that she said.

Then she was ready to share everything in my lord's life, and that is something so rare in a woman that those who delight in women find it intoxicating. She was happy to gamble, drink, feast, hunt, and review the troops; and seemed to take as much pleasure in all these activities as she did (reputedly) in fucking. She would accompany my lord on rambles through the city at night, and what they got up to on these occasions is perhaps better not written down.

There is no doubt either that she encouraged my lord to drink more than was good for him; and must bear responsibility for his present condition. She encouraged him in the vices that made him less than he should have been. On the other hand, who can love a man without such vices, or one incapable of such magnificent self-indulgence?

But yet, at that time, he did not love Cleopatra with all his being. His interest in her was, he often told me, primarily political. He knew the importance of Egypt and its wealth, and he was, like Caesar, determined to hold the Queen as an ally. If that meant going to bed with her, so be it.

The proof that he was not bound to her is that when it was necessary to go to Italy, he did so, and didn't see the Queen again for more than four years. That gives the lie to his detractors who put it about that Cleopatra had besotted him.

There was another reason why he has been unable to speak truthfully of these years, and that is that it wasn't Cleopatra who had besotted him and held him in thrall: it was Octavian.

He can't now admit this, and he couldn't, in so many words, even then.

When I say he was besotted with Octavian, I don't mean that he wanted to take him to his bed; whether he had done so previously, as some assert and as he boasted more then once when drunk, or not. If he had, that was all past.

But he was obsessed with the boy, and he believed that the agreement he had made with him was the most important thing in his life. It was necessary to maintain the stability of the Roman world, and all his policy from Philippi onwards was directed to this end.

That made sense, even when Antony disowned, as in effect he did, the actions of his brother Lucius and his wife Fulvia.

But just as he may have deceived himself in thinking that his connection with the Queen was primarily political, so he also deceived himself about his relations with Octavian.

The truth was that he craved Octavian's good opinion. He longed for perfect concord between them. He flew, admittedly, into a passion if he thought Octavian had betrayed his trust and served him an ill turn – something that happened every time they made a new agreement. But he always went back.

I can't explain it. Perhaps the rest of this tragic narrative, if we are spared to complete it, will demonstrate what I mean in action.

Meanwhile, take it from me, Octavian mattered more to my lord than anyone else, and to that extent it may fairly be said that Octavian, not Cleopatra, was the love of his life and his evil genius.

If you don't believe me, read on.

XI

Nevertheless there remained a real danger that war would break out again between my lord and Octavian. There were plenty of people ready, with an eye to their own interests, to try to set them against each other, though, as I have said, Antony had no wish for anything but friendship with Octavian, and he for his part was not yet ready to break with my lord. But of course Octavian couldn't fail to be irked by the greater esteem in which Antony was held by both legions and senators.

News came to us in Athens that Octavian had grasped the opportunity given by the sudden death of Rufius Calenus, my lord's legate in Gaul, to seize that rich province, and, more importantly its huge army, of which he made his friend Salvidienus Rufus commander. Then, agents of Sextus Pompey came to Athens to suggest that their master should combine with my lord against Octavian. It sounds confusing, I'm afraid, to read about all this manoeuvring. Let me assure you it was even more confusing, and frightening, to live through it.

My lord was also confronted by a fleet commanded by Gn. Domitius Ahenobarbus. Ahenobarbus had sympathised with Caesar's murderers, though he had been only on the fringe of the conspiracy. He had been outlawed at the time of the proscriptions and was lucky to escape with his life. But, being a man of considerable resource, he had established a position for himself, and now commanded a fleet of at least fifty galleys, which barred our way to Italy.

My lord was ever at his best in the face of immediate danger. He wished to avoid a battle, which could have only an uncertain outcome. So he sailed against Ahenobarbus with only a handful of galleys, making it clear that he had come to parley and not to fight. To prove his good faith he entrusted himself even to Ahenobarbus on his own ship. There is no question but that he put his life in his hands, and I have since heard Ahenobarbus admit that he was tempted to seize this opportunity and slay the triumvir. Perhaps it was virtue that restrained him; perhaps it was admiration for Antony's valour; perhaps he feared to trust his own ability. Who knows? The hearts of men at the moment of crisis are like a deep pool, obscure as a night of mist. I have never had patience with historians who pretend that they can account for why certain things are done or left undone. Even the gods, I suspect, are often baffled by the mysteries of men's actions. That being so, who can claim to read minds?

Antony and Ahenobarbus embraced. Watching, I feared a dagger. But instead there were smiles and loud talk and laughter. This is something which has always puzzled me as a Greek. Though I have lived all my life in Antony's household, and have therefore had the opportunity to observe all the great men of Rome, I am still puzzled by the way in which they can cast enmity aside, and talk as if they were lifelong friends. I suppose the reason is that in a sense even those Romans who appear to be mortal enemies are yet also just that: lifelong friends. They share so much. By that I mean that they have not only friends and relations in common, but that they have the same memories, went to the same schools, and were reared in the same code. So, whenever they speak to each other, even after a long period of estrangement or animosity, they speak the same language; and I don't mean by that simply that they converse in Latin. It goes deeper. They belong to what – if I may coin a phrase – I recognise as the "Establishment" of the world; and this means that, brutal and bloody as their conflicts are, their conversation makes a single and singular music. Of course, this ability immediately to get on easy terms doesn't prevent one man from betraying another to whom a moment previously he has seemed perfectly attuned. The truth is that they are a caste apart from the common run of humanity, and this is why both their achievements and their crimes loom so large.

So now, before the end of the first bottle, you would have thought Antony and Ahenobarbus bosom chums. In their case they found, I must admit, that they chimed perfectly. They sang the same song. And from that day on the deck of his galley under a burning sun, Ahenobarbus protested his utmost loyalty to my lord. He was to serve him for years with absolute devotion, and there was nobody Antony came to trust more completely, few for whom he felt a greater and more true affection. And this was testimony to his own charm and his own greatness, for I swear that on the day when Antony boarded that galley, Ahenobarbus intended to kill him.

Their fleets united, they sailed to Brundisium. This provoked a momentary embarrassment, for it happened that, the previous year, Ahenobarbus, in his role as one of Pompey's pirates, had attacked the city, looting its stores and setting fire to the ships in the harbour. Now he appeared in alliance with Antony who had outlawed him. You can't blame the civic authorities for being perplexed.

They placed a boom over the harbour, and locked the city gates against us. Naturally there were many quick to assure my lord that this was done by Octavian's orders. It later transpired that this wasn't the case; or so at least Octavian protested, finding my lord as usual only too ready to believe him. But till they met there was a real danger that civil war would break out again.

What prevented it was the attitude of the legions. Without approaching mutiny – always a fear which acts as a brake on rash generals – they made it clear that they saw no occasion for battle. They could not be trusted to fight against those whom they regarded as colleagues, and to do so in a cause they did not understand.

This came as a relief to both my lord and Octavian. Negotiations were soon under way, and the pair of them met, alone, in a pavilion pitched a half-mile out of the city.

Their accompanying suites watched anxiously, but soon after the sun had passed its zenith fraternisation between them was under way. Men discovered old friends and colleagues. Wine was drunk. Conversations continued throughout the afternoon, and by the time the sun began to sink it was inconceivable that there had ever been a danger of battle. It looked like a garden party.

I was approached myself, I remember, by Octavian's bosom friend Maecenas. I have to say that although my lord never had a good word to say for him, yet for my part I have always found Maecenas to be perfectly charming. He had such an easy way with him that I very soon forgot the difference in our rank and station; and, though I say it myself, I have no doubt that he made the same discovery with regard to me. Maecenas adored Greece and Greek culture and had an intelligent appreciation of the theatre. We found we had much in common, and I amused him with my stories about Cleopatra and her court.

"A delightful change, I imagine," he said, "from Roman virtue. I'm not at all surprised that Antony should have found charms in the Queen which he never discovered in poor Fulvia."

"Well, as to that," I said, and gave him an enormous wink.

I mention this not to boast, but because unkind people later tried to make trouble for me with my lord by putting it about that Maecenas had recruited me to spy upon him. Nothing could be further from the truth. If I may have spoken a little uncautiously, I am quite certain I told Maecenas nothing that was to my lord's discredit, and certainly nothing that he couldn't just as easily have learned from other sources. You can hardly be surprised that he was interested to hear everything I could tell about Cleopatra. She had that effect on everyone. As for Maecenas, he was simply charming.

"When you come to Rome," he said, "as I am sure you must, my dear, when all this little brouhaha is settled, I do hope you will come to visit me. I've been telling Octavian, you know, that this coldness between him and Mark Antony is quite unnecessary, and I believe he realises this now. The trouble is – between us, you understand, please don't breathe a word to anyone else – that the dear boy is a little jealous of your master. He knows he hasn't equalled his feats of arms, and feels this diminishes him in the eyes of the world. I've told him of course that he has other virtues, other remarkable qualities, but there it is. At bottom you understand he admires Antony enormously, and longs to be certain he has his confidence."

I report this speech in full, just as he made it, because there are many who have said that Maecenas tried to turn Octavian against my lord; and I believe this disproves such evil rumours.

Then my lord and Octavian emerged from the tent. Maecenas clasped my hand, touched me on the cheek, and hurried to join them. I was sorry to see my lord a little unsteady on his feet, because in that condition he sometimes gave vent to careless and undiplomatic language which he had subsequently cause to regret. It was also not unknown for wine to have an effect on him when he was displeased or disturbed. But it seemed that my fears were unfounded. He smiled in his sunniest and most irresistible manner, hugged Octavian to him (I thought the young man stiffened before he realised that this was the wrong reaction), and then called out to the soldiers that they could put their swords up and "all get plastered".

"There ain't gonna be no war," he shouted in the accent of the lowest quarter across the Tiber.

They cheered lustily, and then broke ranks (for when word that the generals were about to emerge had been given, they had been called into formation). The men who that morning had feared they might be at each other's throats, again mingled happily, finding old friends and making new ones. Though I have never myself had a taste for the boozy camaraderie in which soldiers delight, having, as you may have realised, more refined tastes, I confess that I was so relieved at this happy outcome that I suddenly felt enormously randy. It was only then that I realised how frightened I had been.

What was later to be called the Pact of Brundisium promised alas, like most such pacts, more than it eventually delivered. Essentially it was a new carve-up of responsibilities and power within the Empire. Men said that in the long run Octavian gained by what was decided then, and I am afraid this is true. He was to be able to consolidate his hold on the West and even on Italy, though it was still stipulated that both generals should be able to recruit there. As for poor Lepidus, who was by now almost completely ignored, if not actually forgotten, he was still permitted command of Africa – though that wouldn't do him much good, and everyone except the man himself could see that his days of power were numbered.

The truth is that my lord had three reasons for not pressing his own case more strongly.

First, he was secretly a little ashamed of the manner in which his brother Lucius and that bitch Fulvia had made trouble for Octavian. Of course he knew that they thought they were acting in his interests. But this didn't make him feel more kindly towards them. In fact it exasperated him.

Second, he was already preoccupied with planning the war which he knew must be waged against Parthia, for the Parthians' incursions on the Eastern frontiers of the Empire were becoming intolerable. Octavian understood this preoccupation and delighted my lord by offering – "quite spontaneously", as Antony said again and again – to give him five of his best legions for this campaign. Of course he never kept that promise, but Antony wasn't to know that then.

Third, and in my opinion, most important, Antony was so happy to have the chance of being on good terms with Octavian again that he would probably have agreed to anything the little beast suggested. That's what I mean when I say he was besotted with him. Despite all his experience of the iniquity and treachery of men – and some experience of Octavian's sly-booted double-dealing – he still trusted him. He thought that because he felt as he did towards him, that feeling was reciprocated.

To him this was confirmed when Octavian proposed that to seal their new pact, and to demonstrate his own friendship and the pact's permanent nature, Antony should wed his sister Octavia. She had recently been conveniently widowed and was therefore available. I believe that in recent years Octavian has talked of "sacrificing his sister". That's nonsense. She was delighted to have the chance to marry my lord.

XII

Of course by the time I met Octavian at Brundisium all the essentials had been settled by our envoys, Asinius Pollio and that scented fop Maecenas. So when Octavian and I came together I knew everything was hunky-dory. That was a relief.

We embraced. He smelt of young sweat and almond oil.

I said: "You know, when we are together we always agree. It's only when we are distant that disagreements arise, and they are never your fault or mine. People provoke us by telling lies about the other."

"I've always thought so."

"Perhaps we should live together and then everything would be peaches and sweet wine."

"Well," he said, "circumstances prevent that, but I am going to make a suggestion which you may consider the next best thing. It is that you should marry my sister Octavia. As you know, her husband, dear Marcellus, has recently died.

"Marry your sister? Well, that is coming full circle."

I was pleased to see he could still blush.

"There's just one thing," he said. "This marriage is expedient, that's obvious, for it cements our political alliance, but I must tell you, I love my sister."

"I would think the worse of you if you didn't. I'm told she is as virtuous as she is beautiful. Just like yourself in fact."

He giggled at that, and I saw the boy I had known before Caesar's death slip out from behind the mask he had schooled himself to wear.

"So what's this one thing then?"

"Cleopatra."

"The Queen? What of her?"

"Rumour has it that you and she are lovers."

"Oh, rumour," I said, "dear old rumour. All right, I admit we had a tumble in the hay. I'll bet you couldn't resist her yourself if she showed herself eager to be boarded. But she's strong meat, the Queen is, and I'll be glad to have a good Roman wife to protect me from her."

"That's the one condition my sister has made: that you won't see the Queen of Egypt alone."

"Accepted," I said.

I meant that, Critias. The truth is I was elated by Octavian's offer of his sister. There had been moments when – oh to hell with it! I'll tell you what: this made me feel altogether a Roman again. I told Octavian that.

"You know," I said, "there are moments in the East when anyone feels the temptation to go native. Caesar himself succumbed. But you must understand that our relationship is primarily political. I need Egypt. Rome needs Egypt."

"Rome needs Egypt," he said. "Does Rome need Cleopatra? Does Egypt?"

"Well," I said, "I have wondered about that myself."

So we cracked a bottle, though Octavian, murmuring something about his stomach, restricted himself to a single glass.

It was only then, if I remember, that we remembered Lepidus.

We did discuss Pompey, who still held Sicily. But again we agreed that Pompey could wait.

"He's not such a bad chap, you know," I said, "and it would be wise to conciliate him."

"It would at least be wise to appear to do so," he said.

We travelled to Rome together in a golden autumn. As we made our way north, through prosperous fields and vineyards heavy with purple grapes, the mood of the people told us the depths and intensity of their fear in the past weeks. I learned of many prophecies of doom and disaster that had circulated that summer. Was there to be no end, it was asked, of the strife between citizens? No foreign foe, no other Italian city, had been able to destroy Rome; only civil war had brought grief and horror to civil society. I felt as never before the awful weight of responsibility for the health and prosperity of Rome that rested on our shoulders; and I resolved that no act or word of mine should put at risk the concord that we had re-established.

I say this, now, solemnly.

Write it clearly, Critias.

On the terrible field of Pharsalus, when Caesar gazed on the slaughtered Pompeians, his face set and grey with the chill of death, he said: "They wanted it, they sought it."

Death stares me now in the harsh light of day, hovers round my sleepless bed. But I can affirm: this war was not of my making.

Let me say now also. Had I chosen otherwise at Brundisium, it was in my power to destroy Octavian. Even his close friend and confidant Salvidienus Rufus, proconsul of Gaul, had intimated that he was ready to desert him and bind himself to me. I regret that in a moment of carelessness I apprised my colleague of his friend's disloyalty, and that, months after I had departed from Italy, he had Salvidienus arraigned for treason and executed. He was a man of talent whom Rome could ill spare.

In Rome my marriage to Octavia was celebrated, to the disapproval of her mother. I have never had much fortune, or found favour, with the mothers of my wives.

Octavia herself was beautiful as the dawn. The resemblance to her brother was both striking and disturbing. She approached me doubtfully, and with a modest reluctance. But it was not long before I overcame that, and she confessed that she had never known true satisfaction in her marriage with Marcellus. For my part, her eager response exceeded my expectations. Like many chaste and virtuous women, once awakened, Octavia made love with more ardour than any professional.

She was devoted to her brother, and I respected that. She desired nothing more than our continued friendship, and I was able to prove to her that that was my wish also. Yet she confessed herself perplexed by his character.

"It is so hard for him," she said, "to act spontaneously."

Her skin was smooth as pearl, and her limbs were firm as alabaster till they yielded in passion.

Rome burst out in an exhilarated ferment of joy and relief. We jointly celebrated a triumph, and, if there was no victory on the field of battle to justify it, nevertheless we had achieved a greater victory: reason had mastered passion and the reward was peace. Statues were erected to Concord, and we issued coins stamped with the rod of Hermes, messenger of the gods, and with clasped hands denoting our friendship, while the obverse showed two cornucopiae resting on a globe. I myself was inaugurated as priest of the divine Julius, and Octavian allowed himself to be titled "the son of a god". In private he deprecated this, and I riposted by reminding him of my own descent from Herakles.

We gave banquets for the nobility and held street parties for the people; and a young poet (of whom I had never heard) by name Vergil, apparently a protégé of Maecenas, whose taste in literature was superior to his taste in dress, read us a poem hailing the birth of a Golden Age to be fulfilled, if not inaugurated, by a child soon to be born. It was clear that this was a reference to the hopes aroused by my marriage to Octavia, a very pleasant compliment. I seem to remember that I rewarded the young bard, appropriately, with a gift of a golden chain.

Others said that the comet which had appeared after Caesar's murder was the sign and herald of this new age, and indeed the Pythagorean philosophers and numerous astrologers were convinced that one world-epoch was passing and another, more glorious, coming into being.

As a soldier I have never had as much time as perhaps I should have had for such speculations. They seem rather grim to me now.

XIII

Octavia didn't know whether to be amused or shocked when she discovered that I was hailed as a god in Asia.

"Do they really think you are Dionysos incarnate?" she asked, eyes wide as innocence.

"Can't tell," I would reply. "Sometimes I think yes, then no. Actually it's a bit of both, I fancy. Orientals are different from us Romans, you know. Even the Greeks are different. Well, they're half-Oriental. What I mean is" – and you can take that sneer off your face, Critias, I'm not insulting you – "what I mean is, that they have a different understanding of reality."

"Surely what's real is clear enough," she said.

"Think of Plato," I replied – foolishly because of course she had never read a line. In my experience not many women have a taste for philosophy, and I wouldn't trust one that did. So I wondered whether to go on, especially since when she looked at me like that, with her smooth brow wrinkled and her cherry lips held open, I could think of better things to do with her. But she pleaded with me. So I explained to her Plato's Theory of Forms, and his notion of how reality is something beyond our direct experience of which we know only a shadowy representation. I could see she was interested, so I sent for a slave to fetch a copy of *The Republic*, and had him read to her the myth of the cave. For some reason it held her attention. Her lovely breasts seemed to swell. Then she said:

"It's very beautiful, and it makes sense of a sort, but not real sense. But I see what you mean. They don't think you're actually the god, but you appear to them rather as the god might appear if he walked the earth. So he sort of inhabits you. They know quite well that you're really Mark Antony, a Roman general, but they see no reason why the god shouldn't choose to reveal himself to them in your person. Have I got that right?"

"Something like that," I said, and kissed her. "On the other hand it also pleases them to flatter me. Orientals get a kick out of grovelling."

I had to give quite a lot of thought and time to the effort to understand them. That was something that few Romans had ever troubled themselves to do, though I believe that Sulla had some sense of how the Eastern mind works. Pompey of course won his great reputation in the East, attracted to himself a long list of client kings, made grants of Roman citizenship and extended favours and fiscal privileges to many cities. The East honoured him, but, from what I have heard, never took him seriously as a man, though they were compelled of course to respect his power.

And I have to confess also that the century or more of Roman rule had brought little benefit to the subject peoples, or to those client-kingdoms whose rulers acknowledged our suzerainty. Roman armies had laid waste their lands, Roman tax-collectors had stripped them of their wealth. Brutus and Cassius had demanded for example half the produce of Asia as an annual tribute. I was determined to govern in different fashion.

An empire cannot be long held by brute force alone. That is the lesson I wished to teach Rome. We had to persuade Greeks and Asiatics that we were not mere and rapacious conquerors, but had their interests at heart. It was not enough to display a tolerant superiority. I extended active goodwill. I believed that to show regard for Hellenic customs, sentiments and opinion was a sign of strength not weakness (as Cato for example had thought – if Cato's mental processes can be dignified with that verb). Such regard would do more than anything else to reinforce peace and concord. I made it my business to show my respect and regard for native men of property and influence, and to assure them that I stood before them as a shepherd, not a wolf. The day would come, I often told them, when the ruling class in the cities of Asia would enter the Roman Senate, as equals, not suppliants, taking rank with their peers among the Roman nobility. We would create, I said, a new imperial aristocracy.

ANTONY

Many thrilled to hear my words.

Of course, it was to please the common people that I emphasised my own family's descent from Herakles, and the favour I enjoyed from Dionysos. If they took this further and identified me with the god, I was not displeased. Indeed, I confess that when I appeared before them, in great ceremonies, in the garb of the god, and was greeted with hymns of joyful praise, I felt more than human. I was aware of the divinity in myself, even if, an hour later as I sank into a bath and relaxed my limbs, there was everything to remind me of my virile humanity.

It was reported to me that Octavian mocked my public speeches, even imitating the florid and ornate language I permitted myself. Well, I could understand such mockery. I have ever mocked myself too. But when I allowed inscriptions to be raised to "Antony the great and inimitable" I was in no wise succumbing to a crazy vanity. It was policy. The dazzling East will obey only a ruler who dazzles it in return. I did so, proclaiming the great truth that of all the gods Dionysos is he who brings gladness and succour to mere humanity.

Of course not all I placed or secured in positions of power were themselves admirable. Octavia detested Herod, whom I made first Tetrarch and then King of Judaea. Judaea, which Egypt claimed and which I denied Cleopatra, was a most troublesome province. There is no doubt in my mind that the Jews are among the most talented of people. But they are also the most difficult. This is perhaps on account of their religion. Every people of course thinks their own gods the most powerful and beneficent, and that they view them with special favour. This is only natural and proper. Though history shows that gods are often indifferent to states and cities to which they owe protection, yet the conviction of the superiority of the gods whom they have chosen to protect them is universal.

But no other people takes the absurd position which the Jews adopt. They insist that theirs is the only true God and that all other gods are false. And they do this, even more ridiculously, although their god is a mere idea, nowhere visibly represented. Indeed they may not speak his name, while they account it sin to do as all other peoples do, and raise statues in honour of the divinity. It is no wonder therefore that other nations despise them, and they do so all the more vehemently because the Jews declare that they alone are "the Chosen People" of this anonymous divinity. Their certainty of this privileged position is such that they are truculent and rebellious in their dealings with whomever is for the time being their master. For it is another element in their condition, that despite their vast conceit, they have not for many centuries been able to maintain themselves as an independent nation, but have always been subject to others.

Yet though they are in general, and in all political dealings, sly, treacherous and unruly, they have a certain obstinate virtue which I could not but admire. Quite early, I realised that the Jews would never submit contentedly to direct rule from Rome. For some time they had been accustomed to be governed by their High Priests, but – I think the office is hereditary – these men were animated by a fierce and intractable sense of nationalism. Pompey had entrusted the management of the province to a High Priest named Hyrcanus, whose conduct showed yet again that Pompey was no judge of men. I recalled Hyrcanus from the years I had served as a cavalry officer in Gabinius' army, and knew that he could never be a friend of the Roman people. Caesar had therefore had the good sense to put over him a soldier, of no pride of birth, named Herod Antipater, whose family came from Idumaea, in the south of the country near the frontier of the Parthian empire. Antipater indeed sent troops to Caesar during his Egyptian campaign, and could claim that they had saved Caesar's life in Alexandria. When I arrived in the East I therefore decided to trust Antipater's sons – the old man himself was now dead, poisoned by the priestly party – and especially the younger of them, Herod. It was true that Antipater had for a time allied himself to Cassius; but, as young Herod told me, with a rascally smile, which I found agreeable, Philippi had proved the old man's judgement was not what it should have been.

Events in Judaea were immensely complicated, and would continue to be so.

I was soon distracted from the East. The accommodation made with Sextus Pompey at Brundisium proved evanescent, chimerical. I had intended that tranquillity in the West should leave me a free hand to wage the necessary war against Parthia. But, as soon as I had departed Italy, or at least very soon afterwards, Pompey, believing, men said, that in my absence lay his opportunity, drove Octavian's forces from Sardinia, and resumed his blockade of Italy. There were riots in Rome itself, the people clamouring now for bread, now for peace. The two demands were in reality one. Octavian's life was threatened. He wrote to me from the city in unaccustomed agitation.

Octavia begged me to hasten to her brother's rescue. I needed no such bidding.

Messengers, ambassadors, were dispatched. Pompey, gratified to be treated as an equal, consented to a meeting: at Puteoli. To show my confidence in him, I persuaded Octavian to agree to the demand that we should meet on Pompey's galley.

We summoned Lepidus from Africa. Though it was unlikely that he could contribute much of value to the negotiations, I thought it wiser to involve him, lest Pompey should attempt to detach him from us, and form a separate alliance with him, in the event of this meeting failing to lead to a satisfactory resolution. I knew Lepidus to be susceptible to flattery, and, though he was inconsiderable in himself, the legions he commanded remained a force to be reckoned with. So, though Octavian would have been content to ignore him, I judged this unwise; and my view prevailed.

"It is foolish," he protested. "How can we trust him?"

I said: "Trust becomes us."

"Antony," he said, "save your rhetoric for the theatre."

"All right, dear boy. Let me tell you something about Pompey, two things. One, I'm under an obligation to him, because he extended his protection to my mother when you and I were unfortunately at odds. That makes him feel good. It also means that since he believes I'm obliged to him, he expects me to trust him. We'll never come to an agreement if I don't seem to do so. Second, and more important, for years he's been living as an outlaw, an enemy of the Republic. That, you may say, is what he is. Fair enough. But it's not what he wants to be. Deep down, he's a conventional Roman nobleman, and he can't forget that in the civil war with Caesar all those whom that old bastard Cicero called the Optimates – the best-born and those who thought most highly of themselves – were on his father's side. What Pompey wants most of all is to be respectable, and if we treat him as one worthy of respect, he'll act properly towards us."

"Very well," Octavian said, "but I'll make sure he's never out of reach of my bodyguard's dagger."

He greeted us with a flourish. He had grown fat, like his father. Octavian eyed him with incalculable reserve. I embraced him.

"The sea-faring life suits you," I said.

"I take it kindly that you have come here, Antony," he said, "abandoning the soft beds of Egypt."

"Oh," I said, "I have known no soft Egyptian bed in months. I'm a reformed character, you know, a happily married man. We hope to reform you too, Sextus."

"A new age of morality?" he laughed. "Well, we'll see."

Then we drank wine, and he said:

"Let me explain my position, which is that of my noble father. Let me ask you why he opposed the ambition of Caesar? Why noble Brutus and sage Cassius drew their swords against the Dictator?"

"This is old stuff," Octavian said. "Not what we've come to hear or discuss."

Pompey persisted, however.

"It was," he said, "simply because they believed that a man is only a man, not a king or a god. And it is for the same reason that, in the name of the Republic which you, as Caesar's heirs, have reduced to subjection, even to servitude, that I have scoured the sea with my navy: to defend the old ways of Rome and avenge my noble father, victim of Rome's ingratitude."

He struck a pose, noble in intention . . .

"Come off it," Octavian said. "The Republic, as it was, is dead. We all know that though we all give it mouth-honour. We have to. It's the way things are done. But your father, whose nobility I am not going to question, was the first of the dynasts whose greatness showed that the old ways were no longer a practical means of governing the Empire. Let's drop pretence, and talk business."

Pompey looked at me as if he did not care for this manner of plain speech, as if he would prefer we continued to act as senators of old, debating matters into the night, rather than as the men we had been compelled by circumstance to become.

I gave him no encouragement.

Instead, I said: "You have had time to consider the proposals our ambassadors sent you."

"Yes," he said, looking sulky, as one cheated of a scene.

"We grant you the government of Sicily and Sardinia," Octavian said. "In return, you will clear the sea of pirates, a filial duty since that was your august father's greatest work in his time; and you undertake, with whatever solemn vows we demand of you, that you will release the corn-fleet that Rome may be fed, and guarantee its free passage in the future."

"Yes," said Lepidus, speaking for the first time. Normally loquacious, he was abashed by the indifference we had shown him.

Pompey seemed to hesitate. For a moment he looked at the sky, then to the open sea, as if he meditated treachery. He looked at Octavian, and dropped his gaze before the boy's steady stare.

Pompey turned to me and said, "I came here determined to accept your offer. Then when we met, I felt a resurgence of old resentments, the righteous anger I have nursed for so long. And then your colleague here regarded me with such disdain that I felt tempted to tell you what you could do with your offer. Can I trust you?"

"We have trusted you," I said. "Here we are on your ship, at your mercy. So surely you can trust us."

"Very well," he said.

That's the official version, and in truth it was much like that, though I have always thought that this colloquy was by way of being a charade. Yet my lord believed in it, though I'm certain Octavian never did. For him, trust, or the appearance of trust, was no more than a piece of theatre. He cast loose the rope with which he intended Pompey should hang himself. I have to admit that his understanding of Pompey was more acute than my lord's. Octavian, in my opinion, was, and is, a thorough-going cynic. Because he has never kept a bargain in his life, he didn't even then expect Pompey to keep his side of this one. But he achieved what he wanted: corn immediately, for Rome.

That evening, as everyone knows, or knew, as I must say – for who can guess the ignorance of anyone who ever comes to read this narrative? – Pompey gave a banquet on the deck of his flagship. It was at first a merry occasion, which I watched from my privileged position as one of my lord's suite. You would have thought, to hear them talk, that the Triumvirate that ruled Rome was composed of my lord, Octavian and Pompey, and that Lepidus, their butt, was the outsider. Of course he brought it on himself. He quizzed my lord about Egypt, which was scarcely tactful in Octavian's presence, since everyone knew that when he talked of Egypt, he was thinking of Cleopatra. Perhaps he hoped to provoke a quarrel between my lord and Octavian from which he might extract some benefit, poor thing. But my lord was in far too sunny a mood to be provoked. In any case, it was not long before the wine muddied whatever intellect Lepidus possessed. This confirmed what I had heard: that he was now habitually sunk in wine, and made stupid by it – stupider even than the gods had already formed him.

"What sort of beast is the crocodile?" he asked.

"Well," said my lord, "if you must know, it is shaped like itself. It's as wide as it is broad, and as high as its own height. It lives on food, and moves of its own volition."

"Is that so? Remarkable. What colour is it?"

"Crocodile-coloured."

"Crocodile-coloured? Very strange."

"Just so. And when it weeps, its tears are wet."

"Prodigious."

"Does that description satisfy you?" Octavian said. "Can you now picture the beast?"

"Prodigiously so." Lepidus shook his head and drank again.

During this exchange Pompey was drawn aside by his admiral Menas, who talked to him in a manner that seemed urgent, and gestured towards the side of the ship. I drew near, so that I might catch the import of their conversation, fearing treachery.

"No," I heard Pompey say. "Why did you tell me? Had you acted of your own accord as you advise, you would have done me a service. But I cannot."

"You could be master of the world," Menas said.

"You could have made me so."

I have often pondered these words. I suspected then what was later confirmed by Ahenobarbus, in whom Menas subsequently confided, that the admiral had urged Pompey to cut the cable that held the ship to the shore, put out to the open sea, and murder my lord with Octavian and Lepidus.

Why didn't he do so?

He talked, it was reported, of honour. He had given his word, assured his guests of their safety. There are some who do not know how to be made great. Even then I knew that had their situation been reversed, Octavian would have cut the painter with his own hand rather than let such an opportunity escape him.

The drinking continued. Lepidus turned pale, then green, spewed, swigged down another goblet, gabbled nonsense, rose to embrace Pompey, staggered, fell, was carried off by a soldier.

"That's a strong fellow," someone muttered. "He's carrying the third part of the world."

"The third part of the world's drunk."

"So are the other two."

"Not Octavian, not our Caesar, he's too canny. Haven't you noticed, every glass that's poured, he takes a sip, then, when he thinks no one's looking, tips it over the deck."

A full straw-coloured moon rode high in the summer night. A soft breeze blew warm from the south. Someone came forward and hung wreaths of flowers around the generals' necks. Men began to remember old battles, feats of arms, adventures; war, which even that morning had cast its dark and fearful shadow over all, now was made occasion for sentimental memories. Others laughed and cracked jokes, coarse and ribald as soldiers' always are. Even Octavian's bodyguard let his hand fall from his dagger's hilt. A cabin boy, curly-headed ephebe, made saucy eyes at me, promising future pleasure.

My lord rose, swaying, to his feet, took Pompey by one hand, Octavian by the other, and led them to the open part of the deck. He called on the musicians for a rousing tune, and then the three, arms linked, began to dance. My lord kicked his heels in the air, Pompey followed suit and loosed great exultant cries. I thought, as I have often done, that there is something immature, something of the perpetual adolescent, in these Roman noblemen; something which, though we Greeks may view it with disdain, is nevertheless one of the reasons why they, not we, are masters of the world. They have a wealth of animal high spirits, a gross vitality that enables them to enter wholeheartedly into the mood of the moment, even to forget in exuberance the dignity which in sober daylight they so highly prize. To see my lord and Pompey dance, twirling each other round and round in a reeling circle, faster and ever faster, gave one an inkling of the splendid carelessness of self which is the secret, I have often thought, of their success. They retain into middle life the capacity to seize the moment and enjoy it. Because they believe themselves to be beyond criticism, they can play the fool like schoolboys who know the world is made for their pleasure.

But Octavian could never quite forget himself, as the others did. Part of him, I could see, watched the cantrips in which he engaged less wholeheartedly than my lord and Pompey. His eye never lost its look of calculation. Of course he shared, close and reserved as he was, in the momentary release from tension which provoked and animated the dance. But he was the first to stand aside, by which time my lord and Pompey, filled with Dionysiac frenzy, had so abandoned themselves to the intoxication of their wild leaps that they did not remark that he no longer danced with them.

He saw me watching him, and smiled. Then the moon slipped behind a cloud and it was dark. Very soon, it began to rain.

XIV

Octavia hoped to keep my lord by her side in Athens. She loved the city, and the way he behaved there: decorous, domestic, happy to follow intellectual pursuits. They would go together to the theatre and to listen to debates in the Lyceum – debates in which my lord was indeed on occasions ready to engage. Though few in Rome believed this, he had a taste for arguing abstract questions – like the nature of justice.

Moreover, living at ease with Octavia, his health improved; and with that, his temper. I do not wish to give the impression that my lord was overbearing at other times. But he was unquestionably temperamental, now up, now down, now bubbling with life, now sunk in despondency. It is, I have observed, usually thus with men who are accustomed to drink heavily. Drunkenness disturbs the balance of the walk; and the habit of drunkenness works in like manner on the mind. Living with Octavia my lord rarely drank heavily, and never above two pints of wine at a sitting – a measure which, thanks to the magnificence of his frame, he could carry without discomfort. It was only in the camp, in Rome, or, alas, later when in the company of the Queen, that he exceeded this ration, with lamentable effects.

Some Greek scholar, I forget which, has written a treatise on the influence of wine on the intellect and soul which should be read, in my opinion, to every well-born boy at his coming-of-age. The charms of wine are like those of dancing-girls, powerful and corrupting. The drunkard can fix on nothing but the need for another glass; reality slips away from him; he sees things in false proportions; that equanimity which alone ensures happiness and which is a potent aid to success escapes him. Such was to be the sad experience of my lord; but in those happy days in Athens, he seemed to rest in a golden afternoon. No one could doubt that he was not only the most magnificent of men, but the favourite of the gods, his achievement far surpassing any other mortal's.

I used to attend him to the gymnasium, where he exercised with a zeal that was Greek rather than Roman. Stripped and oiled for wrestling or weight-lifting, only a roll of flesh around the belly offered evidence that he was a man of more than forty. His manly beauty belonged to one half his age. I say that with confidence as a judge of these things, even though my own tastes have always run to the ephebe, preferring an unformed, even girlish, beauty to the fully mature and virile. That, you may say, is my misfortune; and indeed it is. But I could recognise that my lord, in those days in Athens, still offered the supreme example I have encountered of manly beauty.

There is no question to my mind but that Octavia adored him. She may have done so at first unwillingly. She had married him because her brother told her to do so, and I believe she had done so without expectation of joy, dutifully, for political reason which she well understood. Though she had an infant son by her first husband Caius Marcellus, consul the year before Caesar unleashed civil war by marching his troops across the Rubicon, she had few warm memories of that timid and devious nobleman.

Seeing my devotion to my lord, she was happy to make me her confidant. That spoke well for both her intelligence and her generosity. She may have believed – there were certainly many ready to tell her – that I had been his catamite; it didn't affect her attitude towards me, or the kindly manner in which she treated me. The truth is that she recognised the absolute nature of my devotion to him. She also had the wit to realise that I knew him better than she did, and could advise her how to please him.

"Keep him amused," I would say, "my lord is easily bored, he needs laughter and gaiety."

"Is that how Cleopatra delighted him?"

"Oh, the Queen," I would say, "she's in the past. Whatever there may have been between them needn't worry you now."

"But isn't it true that she bore him twins?"

"She gave birth to twins certainly."

"And he acknowledged them?"

"You know how kind he is. He wouldn't want to give the lie to a woman, especially one like the Queen whom he needed politically. They may be his children. I'm not saying it's not possible. In the same way her older son may be Caesar's child. You know of course that she named him Caesarion. But who can tell? Anyway, it's all in the past, I assure you."

I wasn't lying when I gave her that assurance. I really believed that my lord had escaped the Queen's web.

"What sort of woman is she? Is she really beautiful?"

"No, I wouldn't call her beautiful, not really. You should see her chin, it's far too big, and a bit hooked. Then she's running to fat, because she's very greedy and dislikes exercise, except when she is trying to please a lover."

"She takes plenty of bed-exercise, I've heard."

"Indeed, yes, but it's news to me that that sort of activity keeps you slim."

I did all that I could, you see, to try to divert Octavia from an interest in the Queen, which could easily turn to an obsession. My lord liked to be easy. He couldn't stand jealousy in women. It was one of the things which had turned him so completely against Fulvia, who was jealous of everyone on whom he bestowed a smile.

Octavia said: "Of course I adore him, you know that, Critias, and I adore my brother too. We have always been unusually close. Our childhood would have been very unhappy if we hadn't had each other. There's nothing I want more than preserving the friendship between the two of them."

"There are, if I may presume to say so, my lady, those about your brother who would wish to break it."

"And those about my lord who have the same intention," she smiled. "Ventidius for instance. I rely on you, Critias, to tell me if you learn of anyone saying evil things about my brother to your master. I know he trusts you with many secrets, and I'm sure he's quite right to do so. But you know in your turn that secrecy between husband and wife is destructive. I'm sure you agree with me that the peace of the world depends on the continuing ability of my brother and your master to work in harmony. That's a lovely word – harmony – isn't it? So you'll help me, won't you?"

What could I do but promise that I would? I did so the more easily because Octavia was so sweet that if I had not been what I am, and in the position which I occupy, I could very easily have fallen in love with her myself. As it was, I certainly felt tenderly towards her.

I have said nothing, I think, of Ventidius whom Octavia mentioned as one she did not trust. This was partly because his blunt manners and rough speech belonged to the camp rather than the boudoir. I confess I had no reason to like him myself. I was even a little frightened of him, and he never treated me with anything but contempt.

Publius Ventidius – or Ventidius Bassus, as some called him, though perhaps with no reason – was a man who had risen to prominence in war, and knew no life but the army. His origins were obscure. Some said he was born in Auximum, an Italian city of no note. Certainly there was a family there of that name, municipal magistrates, who incurred the wrath of Pompey and were expelled from their home town. Some even asserted that the young Ventidius was enslaved as a child, and carried in triumph as a captive by Pompeius Strabo. The truth is that his childhood and youth are utterly obscure. He never spoke of them himself, evidence that there was nothing honourable in his origins. In early manhood it would seem that he served as a common soldier; Cicero even claimed that he was for a time a muleteer, but, as you already know, anything Cicero said about political enemies is suspect; there never was such a liar, not even Octavian is his equal in this respect. At any rate the first authentic record we have of Ventidius is as an army contractor, supplying mules and other necessaries for Caesar. His efficiency was remarked. He was promoted, fought in Caesar's armies throughout the civil war, and, after the Dictator's murder, attached himself to my lord. He was instrumental in the defeat of Decimus Brutus, but later failed to raise the siege of Perusia. That he was not at fault here is shown by my lord's continued trust in him. For instance he appointed him commander of the army dispatched to Syria to check the invasion of the Parthian prince Pacorus; and he did this so successfully that he was rewarded with a triumph – no mean achievement for a mule-driver, men said.

Ventidius was actually the sort of Roman whom Greeks and Orientals detest. He was a bully who had no patience with anything he didn't understand, and who was completely convinced that in every way Romans are superior to others. (Of course he wasn't a Roman himself really, but only an Italian.)

Yet he was a great fighting general and his devotion to my lord was absolute. Recognising this, my lord trusted him in equal measure. This was unfortunate, if only because Ventidius' intelligence, except in military matters, was not equal to his loyalty. He really didn't understand that friendship between my lord and Octavian was in everyone's interest. Actually, though he had never been anything but a Caesarian, he detested Octavian. "The boy is so crooked," he said, "that he shits twisted nails." What he really loathed was Octavian's early effeminacy. He was one of the few who absolutely believed that Octavian had been Caesar's catamite – he may have been right there. Then he knew, as everyone did, that Octavian was for a time the lover of Decimus Brutus, whom my lord called "Mouse", and whom Ventidius loathed as, in his words, "a simpering degenerate". Finally, the sight of Maecenas in Octavian's entourage made him spew; or so, again, he often said. What makes all this odd, and in my view disgraceful, is that the story went about that after his triumph, Ventidius raped one of the Parthian princelings he had taken captive, before the boy was strangled in the Mamertine prison. So you can see why I regarded him as a sort of monster. If all Romans were like him, they would be the vile brutes which many Greeks think they are.

Moreover, Octavia had reason to fear his influence. There was indeed no doubt that he warned my lord against Octavian, and urged him that he wasn't to be trusted. Of course he was quite right, as things have turned out. Curiously, my lord, who allowed no one else to speak against Octavian – his "dearest brother"! – permitted this licence to Ventidius.

There was another thing which commended him to my lord, and this was that Ventidius, perhaps from his days with the mule-train, had an endless repertory of really filthy jokes. Indeed his whole conversation was obscene and scatalogical, to a degree which suggested that he suffered from some disease of the spirit. My lord often said that he liked to talk bawdy after supper because it was the only conversation in which everyone could join, and of course it is true that most men relish a dirty joke. But Ventidius really went too far. I couldn't bear to bring myself to repeat some of his choicer efforts. Cleopatra, who herself has a mind which I have more than once compared to the Cloaca Maxima, that is the Great Sewer, in

Rome, particularly relished a really disgusting one about the priestess of Diana at Ephesus, two candles and a donkey. Frankly, I can't repeat it even to illustrate his debased nature.

So it was not surprising that Octavia, so fastidious, graceful and truly elegant, recoiled from the brute in disgust. Often I urged her at least to make pretence of tolerating him, since his military virtue – the only one he possessed – so commended him to my lord. But she couldn't do so, and it cost her dear in the end. Even though my lord knew that Ventidius had been heard to boast that Antony's armies won greater glory when the imperator was absent, and he, Ventidius, in command, yet this merely appeared to him another example of what he liked to call "the old boy's blunt honesty"; so he was all too ready to believe Ventidius when he dropped poison in his ear regarding Octavia. Even the noblest man will believe lies when they are told him often enough. My lord's reason protested against the insinuation that his wife was more devoted to her brother's interests than to his; yet, when even he began to see that their interests might diverge one from the other, then he too easily yielded to the suspicion which Ventidius, chief among others, had so sedulously fostered.

Alas, it was soon evident that the agreement patched up with Sextus Pompey was fragile. The responsibility for its breach is uncertain. Octavian blamed Pompey, Pompey Octavian. I have preserved letters from each written to my lord, protesting the iniquity of the other's actions. Frankly they make sorry reading being a tissue of lies, which left even then my lord in perplexity. The truth is that both Pompey and Octavian wanted war, and when men are in that condition, they resemble a stag in rut or a bitch on heat.

Octavian, without consulting my lord, but even so sending to him to demand ships and legions, invaded Sicily. More by luck than good management, for in the field there never was a less competent commander, he was victorious, rescued from a predicament of his own making by Agrippa. Pompey fled the island, with only three legions, and for some months waged a desultory war, mere brigandage, in Asia. There it became the duty of my lord's generals to hunt him down, which they did, successfully, if in the end shamefully. That was it: Pompey, taken prisoner, was dispatched. "Cruel necessity", my lord said when the news was brought him. I believe Caesar had uttered the same words when shown the murdered head of the Great Pompey.

Meanwhile far more disturbing news came from Sicily. It was carried in a letter from one of my lord's agents, whom, since he is still alive and in favour with Octavian now, I shall not name. I don't suppose he would himself wish to recall the way he wrote to my lord about the man he serves now.

It runs:

You ask for an account of what has transpired here. My difficulty is to know what was theatre and what reality.

You must know that when Sextus fled the island, his lieutenant, Plinius Rufus, still held Messina with eight legions. Being, as you know, a sensible man, he saw no reason to continue the war on behalf of a general who had deserted him. So he offered to surrender.

Your colleague Lepidus, whose aid in reducing Pompey your other colleague had required, and been glad of, for without it his own military incapacity might have led to defeat, now chose this moment to assert himself. Believing rightly that he had contributed to the victory, he declared that he should be the man to accept this surrender. Octavian was absent, in Syracuse, where he was currying favour with the citizens by sacrificing to the local gods – as you know, they have a thousand of them, so this all took some time.

Lepidus was therefore able to override Agrippa, on account of his superior rank, and so took command of Plinius' eight legions. Consequently he found himself at the head of twenty-two legions – a formidable army if he could secure their loyalty. There was no reason, it seemed, why he should not do so. Lepidus is no great general, we all know that, but his military reputation is somewhat higher than Octavian's.

But almost at once he overreached himself. Before he had merged his own legions with those that had recently served Pompey, and established order and discipline in his new army, he commanded – yes, actually commanded – Octavian to leave Sicily to him.

Now, as to what happened next, it won't surprise you to learn that there is more than one version of events.

Some say that Octavian was all for packing his bags and scuttling off.

I don't know. It wouldn't have been the first time, would it?

But, even if he was, he soon changed his mind. Reports were brought to him that Lepidus' camp was full of disaffection. Some men were deserting, others drunk.

At any rate, Octavian seized his chance. I have no doubt it was all well arranged in advance, but he made what followed appear spontaneous.

He presented himself early in the morning in Lepidus' camp, before the general was out of bed, and, with Agrippa by his side, ordered the men to fall into line.

Then he addressed them, calling them "fellow-Romans" and announcing that he was Caesar.

Well, the name still carries its old magic, and when he saw that that was so, he tore off his breastplate and invited anyone who chose to strike him. (Agrippa's hand would never have left his sword-hilt, you can bet on that.) Nobody did of course. So the little man made a joke about them being more trustworthy than senators.

Then he said, and I got this from one who was present:

"I've had a letter from your general. He tells me to get out of Sicily. It's not a friendly letter, though Lepidus has no cause for complaint against me. So I've come here to ask your advice. Should I obey your general?"

Well, you know how soldiers relish irony, which is their own favourite mode of speech. So the little man piled it on. He said he'd been really alarmed when he got the letter, "knowing Lepidus as I do" – which of course raised a laugh. "Agrippa here," he said, "was all for skedaddling back to Rome. But then," he said, "I had two thoughts: what if Lepidus follows us to Rome and tells us to get out of the city also? We'd have to run again, we'd never stop. That was the first thought. The second was: I wonder if Lepidus' soldiers, men who have won glorious victories even under his command, agree with their general. I wonder if they want to see the back of me. So I came here to ask you."

Well, you have to hand it to him. The little sod had done the trick. They clustered round him. He promised them farms, cash bounties, what you will, even assuring them that if the Treasury clerks wouldn't produce the readies, he'd get it from his own bankers. So they cheered and huzza'd, and that, effectively was the end of your other noble colleague. Lepidus is finished. It's just you and Octavian now. By the way, he's allowing Lepidus to remain Pontifex Maximus. Decent of him, isn't it? He says it's on account of his respect for religious formalities. Tell me another, pull the other leg, sez you, and any other expression of incredulity you care for.

XV

Historians will say I was destroyed – if I am to be destroyed – by my neglect of Rome and Italy, my absorption in the affairs of the East. Well, they will be historians who understand neither the meaning nor the demands of Empire. Occupied with the narrow politics of the city and Senate, they neglect the rock on which Rome's supremacy is based. I have often asked – haven't I, Critias? – what do they know of Rome who know only Rome?

We gained our Empire almost by accident, certainly not by the policy of the Senate. Every man of power I have encountered in my life – and some before me – recognised this. Sulla and the Great Pompey were the architects of Empire, attaching to Rome client-states stretching to the wide desert beyond Syria, and to themselves the allegiance of the native kings and princes. But beyond the Empire lies Rome's only rival in power Parthia, successor state to the empire of Persia and extending even beyond the limits of Alexander's conquests, to fabulous India.

From my youth, it was understood by any who had studied what Greek professors call "geopolitics" that the security of the Empire required the submission of Parthia; not its subjection, for that is beyond us, but its submission to Roman will.

Marcus Licinius Crassus, the fat millionaire who formed the first Triumvirate with Caesar and Pompey, may have sought principally to equal his colleagues in glory and renown when he chose to make war on Parthia; but behind that not ignoble ambition lurked the knowledge that Parthia, like Carthage of old, could not be permitted to survive unchecked, since it was our competitor, vying with Rome for influence over our client-kingdoms that served as buffer-states between the two empires. Chief among these is Armenia.

Crassus, as everyone knows, led his army on the shortest direct route, aiming to strike at the heart of the Parthian empire. But this required him to cross the desert where the Parthian cavalry enjoyed every advantage, and so brought him to the disaster at Carrhae, the name uncannily resembling that of the battle in which Hannibal destroyed two Roman armies. Crassus was killed, his army butchered or carried into captivity, Rome's interests bruised, our prestige trampled in the dust.

Then, in the civil war between Caesar and Pompey, those kings who were Pompey's creatures looked to Parthia for support; they continued to do so after Caesar's murder. The Parthians sent aid to Brutus and Cassius before Philippi; that resolute Pompeian Quintus Labienus even took service with their army and adopted a Parthian name.

Caesar had planned a campaign against the rival empire. Some, like Mouse Brutus, said he had done so only because he was bored, as a distraction from the task of re-ordering the Republic, which he found beyond him. I knew better. Mouse took only the myopic view commonly held by those who have not troubled themselves with the demands, and nature, of our Empire, those who think the politics of our noble class the central and essential matter. Caesar was wiser: he lifted his eyes to the horizon and understood the ground that lay between.

Caesar's murder, and all that followed, made the necessary war impossible. Then, while I was still engaged in coping with the legacy of civil war, in the year of the Pact of Brundisium, the Parthians invaded Syria. Ventidius, my lieutenant, faithfully obeying my instructions, and following the strategy I advised, expelled them in a campaign that brought new honour to our armies.

That gave us a breathing-space.

Octavian in letters tried to deter me. Octavia supported him. Their arguments were different.

He urged that war was premature, that Parthia, checked by Ventidius, presented no immediate danger.

Reading his letter, Ahenobarbus said:

"He's afraid. He knows that when you return in triumph from such a war, your reputation will outshine his, as the sun does the moon."

Ventidius was also scornful of my colleague. He assured me that victory over Parthia would make me sole master of the Roman world.

"That is not what I seek," I said.

"If you are not master," he replied, "then Octavian will be. Rome cannot tolerate two lords any more than a woman can have two husbands."

Octavia's opposition to the war was tender, but not flattering. She was afraid I would be defeated.

"Nobody," she said, "except Alexander has ever succeeded in so vast an enterprise. And from what I have read, for as you know I am a student of history, the Persian empire in his time was as decadent as that of Parthia is now vigorous. In any case, you yourself have admitted that in order to wage war successfully against that empire you will need the support of all the princely states attached to our Empire, and that there is not one of those kings and princes whom you would trust with a dagger in your presence. Oh, I know you make an exception for Herod, mistakenly in my opinion, for he would slit his mother's throat if he thought he could get some advantage from doing so, and anyway he is king only of a piddling little state. Besides," she went on, putting her arms round my neck, and kissing me, "I'm afraid. I don't want to lose you."

I laughed that off of course, made love to her, kissed her tears away, all that. Then, when we lay together, at rest, flesh against flesh, her hair tickling my cheek, I said, "Your brother agrees with you. Why do you suppose that is?"

"Oh," she said, "he loves you too, doesn't he? We all do."

"That's no answer."

"I suppose not. Well, let me think. He was never quite convinced by Caesar himself, you know. I remember talking with him when our uncle was planning his war against Parthia, and he said he didn't think it was a good idea to try to expand our Empire further. 'We've bitten off as much as we can swallow and digest.' Those were his exact words. Strange that I remember them now."

"But I am not planning to expand our Empire, merely to secure its frontiers. Will you write and explain that to him?"

"If he won't believe you when you say so, why should be believe me?"

"He trusts you."

"But he trusts you too, surely?"

"I believe he does when he's left to his own judgement. But there are people around him who have an interest in poisoning his mind against me."

"He's not easily influenced, you know."

"Perhaps not, but he listens to people, everyone does . . ."

"Your friend Ventidius tries to turn you against my brother, I know that, but I know also that you don't pay any heed to him."

"No, but Ventidius isn't close to me as Maecenas and Agrippa are to Octavian."

"Well, I grant you Maecenas is capable of anything, I've never liked him, though he can be charming, but Agrippa's absolutely straight, I'm sure of that."

"I don't know what I would do without you," I said.

I meant that. She was a very nice woman and she did love me, then anyway.

"The person you do have to worry about," she said, "may be Livia. I don't know her well myself, because I'd never met her before she married Octavian. She's a difficult woman."

So she was. For one thing she was – is, I should say – a Claudian. That family, one way or another, has always spelled trouble. For another, she was like hard rock-ice. What went on under her frozen demeanour was impossible to guess. Octavian has never squeezed a child out of her, that's remarkable in itself, since both have proved their fertility in earlier marriages. There are stories about their sexual relations of course; some say he likes to be dominated by her. You know the sort of thing: whips and boots. It could be. Like many timid people he takes pleasure in cruelty. I can't forget the way his eyes shone when we drew up the proscription lists. Just naming men to be killed gave him an orgasm.

Be that as it may, as old Cicero used to say when he was asked a question he couldn't answer, there was no doubt in my mind that Octavian was in some way subservient to her. All the reports I had agreed that he was terrified of offending her.

"Look," I said to Octavia, "difficult as she is, it's essential you establish good relations with her. If she can be brought to see things as I would wish them seen, then there's no question but that Octavian will give me the support I need to wage war against Parthia."

"So," she said, "you want me to support you in an enterprise I fear."

"That's right," I said, and kissed her again to prove it . . .

"Oh," she said, opening herself to me again, "how can I deny you?"

That was why I sent Octavia back to Rome. No other reason, whatever rumour may assert. I needed the legions that her brother had agreed to send me, but which never came. And I hoped that she could persuade him to fulfil his bargain, or persuade his wife to persuade him.

But the legions were denied me. I was cheated of what I had the right to expect.

And so I had to turn elsewhere.

For money, to hire auxiliaries from Artavasdes, King of Armenia.

There was only one person who could supply what I needed.

Cleopatra.

XVI

So it was politics that drove my lord back to the Queen, politics and the failure of Octavian to send him the twenty thousand men he had promised.

That's what I wrote, as you will have read, at his command, and I am bound to say that he was telling the truth as he believed it to be. But I confess I have never been certain.

You will remember that Plato in one of his sublime dialogues (but I do not have the text to hand) compares the soul to a winged chariot with two horses and a charioteer. One horse is mischievous, wild and unruly, the other gentle and biddable. The charioteer represents reason; the unruly steed sexual desire; the tractable one the spiritual element in man. When my lord sent me with his legate Fonteius Capito to summon the Queen to meet him in Damascus, I am certain he believed that the charioteeer was in command of the unruly steed. Alas, alas: how weak and deceptive is the apparent mastery which reason can exert!

The Queen greeted us coldly. She said that she had thought our master had forgotten her.

Though Fonteius, as a Roman noble, was naturally the leader of our delegation, he was thrown into silence by this accusation, which he had the appearance of not having expected, though as a matter of fact I had gone to the trouble of briefing him thoroughly, and had warned him that the Queen would not be immediately agreeable.

Antony's apparent rejection of her after their affair four years previously had wounded her vanity, if it had not touched her heart, which was in my opinion her least vulnerable organ.

"Great Queen," I said, taking over from the silent booby Fonteius, "my lord would, nay could, as soon forget that the sun is hot as let your beauty, grace, and tenderness escape his memory. For him, these years of separation have been like an endless winter."

"I am told," she said, "he has found happiness in the arms of another, who has the incalculable advantage over me of being both a Roman and the sister of Caesar's heir."

"Great Queen," I bowed low so that my forehead touched the marble floor, for I was already, as is proper, or thought proper, in addressing such as she, down on my knees, "who can know better than one of your radiance and eminence that the Great Ones of the Earth are often constrained by duty to eschew happiness; in short, I assure you, that my lord's marriage to the lady Octavia was prompted only by political necessity."

"She is very young, I have heard."

"Too young to please any but a boy."

"And beautiful."

"If your taste runs to the insipid milkmaid style, why then, yes, she is beautiful. But good judges find in her an absence of that intelligence which alone brings beauty to life . . ."

We went on in this vein for some time. Later Fonteius had the good manners to express admiration for the skill with which I had conducted the dialogue.

"I must say you Greeks have a way with you that a plain Roman like myself lacks," he said, "you played her like the most slippery of trouts, and landed her nicely."

Well, I was proud of the skill with words which had enabled me to do so, and rightly proud, for a man should rejoice in those gifts and talents which the gods have bestowed on him, while realising that these are of little account if they are not nurtured and exercised; and to do that is his own work, not a gift of the gods.

At the same time I felt a certain shame. Octavia had been kind to me. I respected her. I felt, possibly to an extent which may be thought unsuitable in one of my condition, affection for her. And I had no doubt that Antony was more blessed in that marriage than in his relations with Cleopatra.

Yet what could I do but his bidding? I was his servant. It is true that I felt more for him than servants are accustomed to feel, and that he regarded me with a certain tenderness which he did not accord to others. It was true also that on occasions he was ready to listen to my advice, and even to follow it. But this was not such a moment. For me to have protested at the instructions I had been given were as futile as to try to arrest the course of the Nile with a word, or order the clouds not to discharge rain on earth. So I reflected that I acted merely as an advocate, and that no one has ever expected lawyers to speak with honesty or anything more than the appearance of sincerity.

I do not suppose that Cleopatra, who, for all her faults, did not lack intelligence, was convinced by my speech. It was enough that she should be given sufficient clear reason to relent. It was in her interest to do so. If, at this moment in his fortunes, my dear lord had persuaded himself that he not only wanted her person, but had need of her assistance, equally it was evident to her that her future was bound up with his. Her position in Egypt even was precarious, where there were those who had not forgiven the murder of her brother Ptolemy, with whom she had first shared the throne. His supporters, now excluded from office, influence, and wealth, still sought revenge. She knew also that Octavian was no friend of hers, and never could be. The fact that she was mother of the boy Caesarion, and swore he was Caesar's son, made her an object of suspicion to Octavian, whose chief claim to the loyalty of the legions was that he was Caesar's heir, Julius his adoptive father. This reflected glory on him which not even his ineptitude in war and battle could altogether dim.

The atmosphere in the Egyptian court was disagreeable. Court life must always be that to a Greek like myself. We delight in the free play of intellect which is smothered in the presence, and the entourage, of Oriental monarchy. We find it difficult to take the pompous ceremonies which were enforced in Cleopatra's court as anything but matter for comedy. And yet – this is our humiliating realisation – we dare not refuse to play our part in the great farce of monarchy.

To be fair to the Queen – Greek by blood herself – she knew it was a farce, though one in which she adored her starring role. Nobody ever, I feel sure, played her part with greater relish. And she could assume in public, when she chose, an awful dignity that was truly impressive, and quite different from her private face. She wore a mask in public, and the abject and servile Egyptians treated it as reality. One consequence was that she never received good advice, for no one dared tell her anything which they thought she would not like to hear.

When my lord and Cleopatra had last been together I had made a special friend of a Greek youth who waited on her, served on her staff, was kept close to her person. His name was Alexas, a gentle boy of the old Dorian type: blond, blue-eyed, straight-limbed. Even if it had not seemed advisable to form a close acquaintance, even friendship, with one who might be privy to the Queen's secrets, I should have found him desirable. As it was . . . well, I need not elaborate.

So, when the Queen released us, and Fonteius had made his way to the Baths – and I pitied anyone whom he picked up there! – I sent a slave to let Alexas know where I was to be found.

He came within the hour, eager and loving as before. Afterwards? I smoothed the hair from off his square and creamy brow and let my finger play a moment on his curving lips

"Tell," I said.

"Tell?"

"Yes."

He giggled.

"I think you convinced her."

"She wanted to be convinced?"

"Up to a point. You know her temper. I've never seen anything like it when she was told that Antony was married to Octavia. At first, when the messenger came to her and she saw that he was trembling, she believed that Antony was dead, and screamed that the news would kill her."

"Fat chance of that."

"Well, yes. But love, you know, naughty old love, is there."

"In a way. Perhaps."

"But then, he said, no, Antony wasn't dead, but there was still something to relate. He and Caesar – whom you call Octavian – were closer friends than ever. 'Good,' she said, a little doubtfully, nibbling her lower lip – you know the way she does when she's calculating. 'But,' said the messenger. 'I don't like that "but",' she shrieked. 'But what can "but" lead to? He's well, he's friends with Caesar, he's free, not captive.' 'Captive of sorts,' the messenger blurts out, 'captive of sorts, he's married to Octavia.' Then, my dear, she positively flew at him, would have scratched the man's eyes out, tore his cheeks with her nails, howling obscenities like a drunken whore, you never saw anything like it, even pulled a knife on him. 'I'll have you whipped with wire, stewed in vinegar, fed to the crocodiles . . .' – though I've never heard they relish pickled flesh! I tell you, Charmian and I had to pull her off the wretch, or he would have been killed. And even that wasn't the end of it. When she had cooled down, which took several hours you may well believe, she had me go question the messenger again and get from him an exact description of Octavia: whether she was beautiful, whether she was taller than herself, what her voice sounded like, and then bring him back to tell her since she wasn't satisfied with my report. Naturally I coached him carefully, telling him to assure the Queen that her rival was quite lacking in physical charms – dwarfish, muttering, inelegant in movement, and, I said, make sure you tell her Octavia's a widow. Nobody can be jealous of widows surely?"

"Well," I said, "you slandered her, but you were wise to do so. My poor Alexas, how can you tolerate that dreadful woman?"

He turned over on to his back, and gazed at the ceiling. For a long time he did not speak. The silence of the afternoon was broken only by the buzz of flies. I waited, letting my eyes feast on his profile.

"You don't understand," he said. "Perhaps you can't. Because you dislike her and fear her too, I think. I can see she's terrible, there are moments when I absolutely detest her. And yet I adore her too. Charmian's the same, and Iras, and everyone around her. We have sessions when we curse her to the moon, weep because she has humiliated us, shake with terror if we have angered her. And yet none of us could leave her even if it was possible. There's probably not one of us wouldn't lay down our life for her. Be honest, Critias, isn't that just how you feel about Antony too?"

"No," I said, "it isn't. There's nobody I would do that for. I intend to survive him. Of course I'm loyal to him and so on. But lay down my life? Certainly not. I wouldn't even do that for you."

"I wouldn't expect you to. This sort of thing isn't very important after all. Just like us. Insignificant people."

"Not important?" I said, and put my hand between his legs and felt him respond.

"Not important," he repeated, not pushing my hand away. "I'll tell you something else though. The Queen will kill your master rather than let him escape her again."

Naturally I was not frank with Alexas. Whatever pleasure I took in his company, I couldn't forget that he was the Queen's servant, as I was my lord's. So it seemed useful to suggest to him that my loyalty was less absolute than it was, for I knew that he would so report to the Queen. Therefore I wasn't surprised that when she summoned me to a meeting the next day, I found her alone, all attendants dismissed, and seemingly eager for an informal and confidential talk.

She questioned me again about Octavia, and this time I spoke more severely than I had done in our public audience, taking my cue (as no doubt he had intended) from the dear boy's account of what he had instructed that unfortunate messenger to say. Of course I didn't go as far in disparagement as the words he had supplied the messenger. It wasn't only that to speak of Octavia in this manner would have offended my conscience; it was rather that the Queen, in this relaxed mood, wouldn't have believed me. She knew Antony well enough after all to know that he was no actor. Since she had doubtless received many reports of how he lived with Octavia, she would know that he was incapable of disguising boredom or simulating contentment where he did not feel it.

"I daresay he found little Miss Octavia restful," she said, sipping wine from a golden goblet.

"Compared to Fulvia," I said.

"But compared to me?"

"There could be no such comparison."

"I'm not restful. I know that." She smiled and purred and to demonstrate her perfect good humour invited me to take wine.

"I'm not restful," she said again. "I wouldn't wish to be restful. She must bore Antony, I'm certain of that. Everything I've heard about her suggests that she is virtuous. I can read that message below your careful words also. And virtue of that sort's a bore. Charming at first for Antony, but it couldn't hold him. He has too great a soul."

Then she questioned me about the war my lord planned against Parthia. I protested I was no soldier, had no understanding of strategy. She brushed my objections aside.

"Octavian has denied him the troops he needs?" she said. "And so he turns back to his old Cleopatra. Why should I help him who abandoned me?"

"Great Queen," I said, "you are of too noble and generous a nature to imperil a great enterprise because you feel you were slighted or aggrieved. Besides . . ."

"Besides?"

Her fingers clawed at the soft fur of the black cat that lay purring across her thighs. Her eyes glinted like the cat's. I was aware that without warning she could spring like the cat.

"It's not for the likes of me to speak high politics to you, Great Queen. But I say this. My lord will march against Parthia. He will do so whether you aid him or not. If you do not, and he is victorious, then he will remember who were his friends when he needed them, and who were not. If he makes war and is defeated, then he will blame those who declined to send him help, blame Octavian and blame Cleopatra. And you must consider: without the men and money he asks you for, his enterprise is perilous, defeat more probable, and worse than defeat . . ."

Her hand leapt from the cat to her lips. She held it there, fingers pressed against ruby lips, eyes dark and questioning . . .

"Octavian," I said, "has no cause to love you, or your son Caesarion. My lord stands between you and the resentment of his partner in Empire."

She jumped up, sending the cat flying from her lap. It stood arching its back and swishing its tail.

"When I demanded Judaea from him, he denied me, though it is an old possession of Egypt's, and gave it to Herod, whom I detest."

"The Jews," I said, "are awkward. Herod is a sort of Jew himself. He understands them. Or so I have heard my lord say. I believe he thinks that you would find Judaea more trouble than it is worth. But there are other territories. I don't know which, but I believe my noble colleague, if, when he is absent, I may so dare to term him, has a list of those my lord will offer to you."

"Your noble colleague," she said, "territories."

She spat, directing her spittle, neatly, into a tall onyx jar.

"By what route will he advance against Parthia?"

"That I cannot tell you. I have heard him speak of the folly of Marcus Crassus."

"The key to Parthia lies in Armenia. Its king, Artavasdes, is not to be trusted."

"No doubt you will tell my lord so yourself, but I shall warn him as you direct. I am honoured by the confidence you show me."

"Confidence? If I chose, I could have you whipped the length of Alexandria's sea front."

Then she smiled. That was the worst moment, for I couldn't be sure whether she was smiling at the picture (decidedly unpleasant to me) which this thought presented to her, or whether indeed she had spoken the words so lightly that she had forgotten them the moment they floated from her mouth into the hot air of her boudoir scented with hyacinths. As if she had caught this thought of mine, which she may well have done, for her ability to seize on what those with her had not expressed in words was one of her most disconcerting qualities, she now leaned over a bowl of pink hyacinths and pressed her nose, against the flowers.

"I'm telling you a war against Parthia is a rotten idea," she said, and smiled again, this time as if inviting me to share a joke. "If you asked me the first rule of war, I'd say it was 'don't invade Parthia'. Can't we stop him?"

"You may be able to do so, Great Queen, but only if . . ."

"Only if?"

The smile was replaced by a frown.

"Who am I to give you advice?"

She paid no attention. I remembered that Alexas had told me she had a habit of throwing out questions which required no reply, or observations, which had no real significance, but were uttered merely to allow her time to elaborate her thoughts in her own mind.

"Very well," she said. "I'll send your lord a formal reply by way of that idiot Fonteius. He must know he's an idiot, so I assume that he wants my personal answer, not Egypt's, to come by way of you. I don't know why he trusts you. I wouldn't, any more than I trust Alexas. He's very sweet of course and devoted to me as I suppose you are to Antony, but I wouldn't trust him with a secret. Pansies always babble, that's my experience. And they're frightened of pain. I was watching you when I made that joke about having you whipped. Still, if Antony trusts you, well, I'll have to make use of you. So, here are the two conditions I'm adding to the formal acceptance of an alliance Fonteius will carry back. First, he's got to get rid of Octavia, publicly, decisively, irrevocably. Second, he must agree to marry me. That's all, I think. Tell him if he jibs at either condition, he can whistle tunes from his arse before I'll send him any help."

XVII

Ahenobarbus advised me against committing myself to the Queen. He had the Roman distaste for what he called Eastern intrigue.

"I don't say little Octavian's not a shit," he told me repeatedly, "but what I do say is that he's a Roman shit. So we know where we are with him."

He urged me to fetch Octavia back, resume my marriage, employ her to mend my fences with her brother.

"We don't need to crush Parthia," he said, "all we need is to give them a bloody nose."

Should I have listened to him? I have no doubt historians will say I should. In the long hours, as darkness gives way to dawn, and sleep is denied me, unless I have gone to bed drunk – and even then, nowadays I often find myself awake before it is light, and have to send for a slave to come to read to me in order to banish the evil thoughts of that hour – then I regret that I tossed his advice aside.

But what else could I do?

The message you had brought me from the Queen promised glory beyond compare. It seemed a small thing to risk losing respect in Rome when I felt assured that I would bring the city and the Roman People a victory and riches on a scale which neither Caesar himself nor Pompey had won.

Apart from the Queen's promises, I had two good reasons for believing that my star was in the ascendant.

First, Artavasdes, King of Armenia, engaged himself my ally by solemn treaty, and undertook to provide me with a force of some fifteen thousand light cavalry. It was the lack of such troops capable of matching the Parthians for mobility which had doomed Crassus, and, by his own account, rendered even Ventidius' glorious victory less complete than we would have wished.

Second, while I waited for Cleopatra at Damascus, there came to me a Parthian noble, by name Moneses, exiled by Phraates, the cowardly master of the empire. Moneses, a man of rare dignity and former power, a nobleman whose estates extended further than a horseman could travel in a day's hard riding, assured me that bitter dissension was tearing the fabric of Parthia in shreds, and that my invasion would be the signal for a general uprising of the disaffected against Phraates. Moneses, in his ill-fortune and apparent sagacity, resembled the Athenian hero Themistocles, and impressed me by his frank and open manner. For he also warned me that I should not accept his report without confirmation: "I am," he said, "a victim of Phraates' tyranny. I seek revenge. My views are partial. Therefore seek evidence elsewhere that what I tell you is truth and not the mere dreams of a revengeful exile." I rewarded him with the governorship of three cities: Larissa, Arethusa, and Hierampolis.

Cleopatra arrived and our reunion was cordial, even though in the privacy of our chamber, she reproved me for what she termed my infidelity. As I had promised, I conferred on her certain provinces of old Phoenicia, also Cyprus, and that part of Arabia Nabathea which lies upon the ocean to the south.

We also went through a ceremony of marriage. This was to provoke argument and hostility in Rome, fomented there by friends of Octavian who wished me ill. They wilfully misunderstood the nature of this union. I was of course well aware that it did not conform to Roman Law, and that my wife according to that code remained Octavia, whom I had no desire to insult by exercising my right to divorce, as Octavian had disposed of his own first and second wives.

But they order matters differently in the East, and there it seems natural that a great man should have more than one wife, or wives of different orders. Besides, as I then declared, the greatness of Rome appears more in giving than in receiving kingdoms; and it is proper for persons of high birth and station to extend and secure their nobility by leaving princes and successors born of different queens. My ancestor Herakles, as is well known, did not trust to the fertility of one woman, or to the fortune that would spare a single line of descent, but scattered his favours widely. Why should I not do likewise?

I expected my fellow Romans to understand that these sentiments were, so to speak, a rhetorical flourish, even to be amused by them.

Criticism was aroused too by my decision to honour the little twins Cleopatra had given me four years previously with the names of the sun and moon. The objection was absurd. It should have been obvious that I did this only to please and flatter the Queen.

In any case I was too busy to pay heed to the ridiculous susceptibilities of those of my compatriots whose vision did not extend beyond the Alban Hills which fringe the eastern horizon of the city. I was fully engaged with business, and experiencing one of the greatest pleasures a man may know. I mean of course the ordering and assembling of a mighty army.

Though I lacked the twenty thousand legionaries Octavian had promised, I nevertheless commanded sixteen legions, of whom at least half were veterans. Six were brought from the Caucausus where my marshal P. Canidius Crassus, most trusted of friends, had been establishing the northern frontier of Empire. I had ten thousand heavy cavalry from Spain and Gaul, while the forces of our auxiliaries amounted to some thirty thousand troops, the most valuable being the Armenian cavalry.

"Never," said Ahenobarbus, "never in the history of the Empire has so magnificent an army been arrayed."

"And we march against the wrong enemy," said Canidius.

"What do you mean?"

"The general knows."

Of course I knew, and said nothing. Ironical now. For months Canidius had argued, in fierce letters, that Parthia could wait, that my true enemy was Octavian, that I stood against him as Pompey against Caesar – "or, if you prefer, Caesar against Pompey"; that, like Sulla, I should employ the might and wealth of Asia in securing my sole pre-eminence in Rome; that only then, with the full resources of Empire behind me and "no enemy in your rear", would it be safe to turn against Parthia.

I would have none of it.

Canidius was not alone. My stepson Scribonius Curio, a youth who more resembled in character his father, friend of my childhood and adolescence, than his mother, fierce Fulvia, pressed the same advice on me.

"You forget," he said, "I have known Octavian all my life, and in a peculiarly intimate manner. We were at school together and that gives me an insight into his character. I quite see why you are fond of him. He has great charm and great intelligence. But I assure you that he is not to be trusted. Frankly, I would not trust him round the next corner myself. I remember once, there was a teacher who criticised Octavian's Greek style – we would have been about twelve at the time. Well, even then Octavian was as conceited as he was vain, and quite unable to accept such criticism. So what did he do? Why, he sneaked on the teacher, and said he had made a pass at him, felt him up, even buggered him, I can't remember the details. So of course the teacher was dismissed, brought before the courts, sentenced to be whipped – so many lashes that the poor man nearly died of it – and driven out of Rome. I don't know what happened to him in the end. And he was a really good teacher, and quite right about Octavian's Greek style. What's more, there wasn't a word of truth in the accusation the little beast brought. Of course like most teachers, the man was inclined to fall in love with some of his pupils or fancy them at least. You know that's often the case with the best teachers. But he was far too timid to put his desires into practice. I know that, because it was me he doted on, not Octavian, and I assure you he never went further than to stroke the back of my leg when he was correcting my work. But nobody would listen to me because little Octavian was so charming and persuasive. The most I could do was give the little beast a nasty fright next time we wrestled. How he howled! So you can see why I think you're wrong to trust him. People don't change, they merely pretend to."

"They have been known to," I replied, as chillingly as I could. Curio was a dear boy, is one indeed, but I found this irritating. It occurred to me that he had always been jealous of Octavian. No wonder, you may say . . .

Well, actually, if I can take this moment while he goes off into dreams of Parthia, let me say that, no, I wouldn't say any such thing. But then I've always found Curio madly attractive. He on the other hand is crazy about girls. What my lord has forgotten is that when on some subsequent occasion Curio told the same story – forgetting or simply not caring that I was there to overhear it – and my lord again suggested that people had been known to change, Curio shook his head and said, "No, they grow more like themselves." As he spoke these words and looked at my lord, who was red-eyed and shaking, for it was morning and he had not recovered from the previous night's excesses, so that he had, as I've seen so often, to employ two hands to grip the first cup of wine of the day and guide it to his lips, a look of the most profound and touching pity softened Curio's face, which had been set in anger as he spoke of Octavian; and he approached my lord, laid his arm around his shoulders, and hugged him, holding him for a long moment like a little child in a loving father's arms.

What a good thing it is that my lord never asks to read over with his own eyes what I have written. He would hate my understanding that he was the object of his stepson's tender sympathy.

I get distracted. I have no time to be distracted. Critias, stop me if my thoughts wander again.

Where was I? Parthia? That's right . . .

At Zeugma on the Euphrates I parted from Cleopatra who at my command returned to Egypt. It was later, I believe, put about that I delayed the start of the campaign on account of the delight I enjoyed with the Queen. This was nonsense. There was no delay. Those who spread the story were either malicious or ignorant of the organisation required to set a mighty army on the march. On the banks of the Euphrates I addressed my troops.

"Soldiers: we are joined together in the greatest enterprise ever undertaken by a Roman army. Never in the long history of Rome have we marched against an empire so powerful as that which faces us today. Some generals would try to hide the magnitude of the task from their troops. I am not such a general and you are not such soldiers as to be unable to face reality. There are great dangers before us. We shall suffer hardships. There will be fierce battles. Some of us, many of us indeed, will not return, never see Italy again.

"Why should I hide such things from you?

"We are brave men able to look truth in the face.

"Many of you are veterans. You have fought beside me in great battles. We conquered then; we shall conquer again.

"Some of you are young, untested recruits. You are about to encounter what you have only imagined before. I trust you. I am confident you will behave in a manner worthy of your glorious fathers and remoter ancestors.

"And there will be great rewards: rich plunder and the deeper reward of knowing that you are men worthy of respect. Generations to come will point at our deeds and wonder what manner of men were capable of such courage and endurance."

Then I reviewed the troops. To grizzled veterans I recalled the battles we had fought side by side: this man had served in Gaul, that at Philippi, the next at Pharsalus; all were eager to share their memories with me. To the young recruits I spoke in a different manner asking if their centurions took proper care of them, if they were being paid promptly, if they were in need of anything. I even asked to see their knapsacks.

Then I halted at the centre of each legion, and enquired of the legates who most deserved promotion. Those who were named I summoned before me and advanced in rank on the spot and in the sight of their colleagues. I did this so that all might realise that in the midst of my concerns for the well-being and security of the Empire, even while my mind was full of the problems of Grand Strategy, I could still trouble myself about the details of my soldiers' lives. I showed them that they were my first, my eldest, my true family. In this manner I instilled in them the love of war, of glory and of myself.

We advanced to the river. Cavalry had already forded it, and were drawn up on the further bank to guard against any sudden attack by the enemy, though scouts had reported that only a few light cavalry skirmishers were to hand. Then engineers set to work to construct and launch bridges of boats by which the legions could cross over into Mesopotamia. It was not till dawn that the crossing could begin.

The chill of night made sleep difficult. The dark was never silent. I myself moved through the camp encouraging the sentries and young soldiers too excited to rest. We were all aware of the dangers of the morrow. A feeling of solemnity mingled with expectation of a day of glory. Officers reported to me that men were repeating in whispers the most memorable passages of my speech, and that the spirit of conquest fired the imaginations of all. At first light the advance began.

For three weeks we marched across the northern fringe of desert, then into the foothills of Armenia. The roads were poorer than we had been promised. In particular, to my distress, the mule-trains that dragged the siege machinery found it impossible to keep pace with the body of the army. I was compelled to detach two legions under the command of Oppius Statianus to protect the baggage train that was forced to take a longer road further north. There were disquieting reports that Artavasdes was slow in bringing up the supplies he had promised.

Nevertheless by midsummer we had advanced five hundred miles and arrived before our first objective, Phraaspa, capital city of Media Atropatene, a vassal state of Parthia. I had been assured by Artavasdes and Moneses that this city was barely fortified, and would have no choice but to surrender. It proved otherwise. Phraaspa was built on a hill and surrounded by strong walls. Had we had the battering rams with us, we should no doubt have made short work of them. But the siege train was still delayed. Ahenobarbus, ever more prudent than adventurous, counselled retreat: Canidius assented. But it would have been ridiculous to turn away from the first check. I therefore gave orders for earthworks and mounds to be thrown up and we prepared for a long siege. There was little timber in the surrounding district, which made the construction of new battering rams impossible.

Our situation soon resembled that which Caesar had encountered at Alesia in his Gallic war against Vercingetorix: we, the besiegers, were besieged in our turn, for Phraates or his marshals brought up a huge Parthian army and invested our camp. Then word was brought that the Parthian cavalry had cut off Statianus and the baggage-train, and destroyed his legions. This was the first intimation we had of the treachery of Artavasdes, who had collaborated with the Parthians. Had he remained loyal, their attack would have been beaten off, and in time the reinforcements would have reached us.

Danger has always inspired me, and I was happy to find that the men's confidence in me was such that they were in no way dismayed by what a lesser army would have regarded as a calamity. They continued to prosecute the siege with vigour and determination. But it was clear to me that our position had become perilous. Not only was it impossible that we should receive the aid I had expected; there was also a real prospect that we would soon suffer famine: for the supplies we had carried with us were almost exhausted.

I therefore determined to bring the enemy to battle, in the expectation that if we drove off the investing army, the city would yield, or, even if it did not, we should be able to forage safely.

So, at the head of ten legions, three heavily armed praetorian cohorts and ten troops of Spanish cavalry, I broke camp and headed for the fertile plains where the harvest was already stored in granaries. For a day and a half the Parthian army tracked our movements, but gave no sign of being ready for battle. It seemed that they were looking for an opportunity to fall on us in line of march.

In order to lure them on, I gave orders that our tents should be struck so that they might think we were planning to withdraw. They approached closer, and their commander drew up their army in crescent formation. For an hour we marched past them, each army in full sight of the other. The coming-and-going of their skirmishers suggested their uncertainty. Then I gave the order to our cavalry to wheel and engage the enemy. The charge took them by surprise, so that they were unable to use their bows except just before the impact. At once the legionaries swung round also, taking the enemy on either wing. For a moment I had hopes of the decisive victory we required. Indeed, we would have had such a victory if the enemy had been Roman or even Gallic troops accustomed to stand their ground and fight. But that is not the Parthian way of war.

We Romans are accustomed to the war of battle. We seek to engage the enemy in open field, in order of line or phalanx, and fight hand to hand till one army gives way. This is the warfare of civilised men, as the history of the Greek states and the wars of Alexander as well as our own have demonstrated. But the Parthians do not fight like that. They shrink from the decisive battle. Throughout that campaign we discovered that whenever we faced up to them boldly, they never offered resistance, even when they outnumbered us by three or four to one. Their style of fighting is to advance within sight of the enemy and then try to provoke him to action by taunts and insults, and by tormenting his troops with flurries of arrows. But when the enemy offers to engage, the Parthian runs away. They have no feeling for true war; no feeling for those Roman virtues of absolute obedience, manly courage, self-sacrifice, honour; in short, everything that we understand by the word virtue. Instead they see nothing dishonourable in cowardice, flight, and the self-interest that permits a man to prize his own life more highly than victory.

So at our first determined onslaught, the whole Parthian army wheeled round, and took to flight. We pursued them for a dozen miles at least, and though we slew some and took a number of prisoners we were quite unable to obtain the decisive victory which I had sought and knew to be necessary. I confess I was baffled.

We were a true army, imbued with the true military spirit, capable of maintaining our cohesion while enduring the fiercest attack, impervious to vain fears, obedient to command, steeled by training in privation and effort. The army that I led against Parthia was as staunch and gallant, as formidable a force as that which I had known when with Caesar I took my share in the conquest of Gaul; it was as fine as that with which I conquered at Philippi. No civilised force could have been its equal. And yet, there we were, several weeks' march beyond the frontiers of Empire, impotent, because the enemy would not stand and fight, but melted away before our bravest and most terrible attacks. It is absurd that brave men, composing a fearsome and disciplined army, should be thwarted by cowards, but that was our unhappy position. That was the reality I am brave enough to confront. The question whether Rome can ever subdue Parthia remains unanswered; but I fear what the true answer may be.

With winter approaching, our danger increased. Fear of famine is the strongest fear an army knows. I therefore sent messengers to the Parthian Emperor offering to withdraw if he would return to us the standards and captives taken at Carrhae; in this way I would be able to show that the war had not been in vain, and that Roman honour had been restored. But no answer was forthcoming. It seemed to me that I had little choice but to try once again to bring the Parthian army to battle. In this my zeal overmastered my judgement of what was possible. But both Ahenobarbus and Canidius, the generals on whom I most relied, argued against what they regarded as a desperate proposal.

Ahenobarbus said: "Too many things are against us: the season of the year, the shortage of food, the nature of the country, barren and deserted as so much of it is, the nature of the enemy who are certain to retreat still further, drawing us still further from our base . . ."

"And eventually to disaster," Canidius added.

I argued that the threat of battle might yet so alarm the Parthian

Emperor that he would at least yield to the modest demands I had made, but Ahenobarbus said:

"As long as Parthian territory is occupied, I do not believe that Phraates will listen to any proposals. At this time of the year he is fully aware of the advantages he possesses."

My stepson Scribonius then spoke up:

"You may be right. I fear you are. Nevertheless the imperator's suggested course is still worth attempting. At the very least it will salvage our honour. Consider: if we are compelled to retreat without recovering those standards and those poor unfortunate Romans who have been held captive for so many years, then Octavian, who is jealous of Antony's renown, will be able to present this campaign as a great disaster, even though we know that we have done things never before attempted or achieved by a Roman army, marching further to the East than any Romans have ever done before, and rivalling Alexander in the audacity of our enterprise. Therefore I am prepared to volunteer to lead an embassy to Phraates. At the very most these negotiations will cost us a few days; they may result in a happy conclusion."

So it was agreed.

XVIII

Scribonius set off to attempt negotiations with the Parthian Emperor. Nobody but my lord thought he had any chance of success. The army was nervous and impatient. The prospect of the retreat was frightening, but they would all rather have been on the move than held waiting before Phraaspa, in a place they had come to loathe.

It was still hot at midday. Flocks of ravens circled in the sky over our camp. The men were alarmed, regarding them as birds of ill omen, which indeed they are generally supposed to be.

Often I heard my lord mutter: "I want peace! I need peace! But I must preserve my honour!"

During the day he made the round of the camp urging the men not to despair, speaking to them of glory and victory. Because he was Antony, he still found them ready to believe – while they were in his company. But when he turned away, the murmuring began. They talked of the sweethearts they would never see again.

The desert stretched pitiless around us, like a waste of silence. Men said they would die there, and the tramp of the guard wandering through this immense tomb that seemed to enfold the camp could scarcely wake my lord from the reverie into which he sank as soon as dusk fell, chill and oppressive. What cruel memories he pondered as he sat alone, sinking cups of wine that could not now, it seemed, intoxicate him, I even then shuddered to think. I found myself moving silently and unobtrusively too, lest he engage me in conversation. But most evenings he preferred silence.

Now it appears to me that the thought which he turned over in his tormented mind was this: aware of the power which he had won for himself by his mighty deeds that had given him an aura of invincibility, he dreaded the wound which news of his defeat would deal him. In the past, in every encounter with Octavian, he had opposed his military renown to the boy's cool insolent self-assurance. Did he then fear that, robbed of that prestige which victory wears, he would find himself Octavian's inferior?

Sometimes he spoke, and the words were such as I could not repeat to his generals. Perhaps they were a sort of soliloquy, he being so accustomed to my presence that he was often unaware of it.

"The first step of retreat," he said, "will open the way to weeks of daily battle, as the enemy hang on the heels of the army like a wolf-pack. That is why I remain inactive, which decision if it is a decision you are wrong to fault in me. Of course from a military point of view, our being here is now worthless. Don't think" – and here he would look at me as if seeing me, and I would find myself no longer able to evade his weary bloodshot gaze – "don't think, my dear Critias, that I don't understand that. Yet, from a political point of view, our establishment here still has some value. I am not only commander of the army, I am also imperator, and for a Roman imperator to be based deep within the empire of our enemies is not nothing. No, indeed. In affairs of state retreat is nearly always fatal. I learned that lesson from Pompey's blunders. One must never admit to a mistake, for then the whole world takes you at your word, and the consequences are terrible. To admit an error is to be open to contempt. Reputation is not all, but reputation is worth six legions. I have heard Caesar say so. When one makes a mistake, one must hold one's course; that then makes it right."

So he clung on, catching at wisps of hope, all the more eagerly because he knew then that Artavasdes had played him false, and that in the retreat through Armenia (which in sober moments he knew he must embark on), would be the more dangerous since, far from being able to look for help from the king, he would find the Armenians hampering his progress and even joining the Parthians in sniping at the flanks of the army.

Yet every day, as Scribonius still did not return and he began to fear for his safety too, I could see that his distress grew more acute. It was clear that Phraates was playing a cruel game with him by delaying his response. Yet he felt he could not move till he knew the worst, and his hopes now rose, now sank – not precisely in time with the level of the bottle, but according to the wavering of mind and spirit.

"Why," Ahenobarbus asked, "does our general adopt the most dangerous of all courses – waiting for a reply? I am amazed to find him so lacking in his old ability to make swift decisions. It is playing hell with the nerves and morale of the men."

Yet here Ahenobarbus was perhaps wrong. Simply because they had been accustomed to look to my lord for victory, because they knew his courage and resilience, and trusted in his genius, there were still many ready to believe that he was nurturing a plan. This was especially the case among the junior officers, who saw him only in the morning when he forced himself to look cheerful.

Old soldiers too muttered: "He's a deep one . . . he's a crafty bugger . . ." And indeed no one could fail to admire the brave face that he wore when he spoke to the troops, and his ability still to joke and appear radiant and confident. Few besides myself knew the effort this cost him, or saw how deep shadows darkened his face when he had retired from the public eye.

I saw how he was prolonging his meals, as if by indulging in the pleasures of the table – even though it was ill-furnished – he could, forget his cares. Then, dull and heavy, with only wine to comfort him, he would sit for hours as if his faculties had suffered a numbing blow, while he waited for the end of this terrible adventure. It came to me as I watched this stubborn hero wrestle in his troubled mind with the impossible demands which our situation imposed on him, that here, a few months after he had placed himself on the pinnacle of glory, he suffered a presentiment that the first backward step would mark the beginning of his ruin; and for this reason he clung still to the summit and to the illusion that he still retained the ability to choose. He was caught in the charm of self-deception; and I loved him too deeply to be the one to dispel delusion and compel him to confront reality . . .

XIX

Scribonius Curio returned to announce failure. Phraates was obdurate. At the same time he extended a promise which was to prove mere deception: that he would permit me and my army to withdraw from his territory unmolested. I could not believe him sincere. Yet, this word running round the camp raised the spirits of the soldiers who believed that their return march would be easy and without danger. Many therefore relaxed their vigilance; others burdened themselves with spoil; and for a little it seemed that I commanded a caravan rather than an army. However measures were soon taken to restore discipline, and we withdrew from Phraaspa. As we reached the summit of the hill behind which the city would soon be hidden, I drew up my horse and looked back. Our abandoned camp was in flames and the city beyond shimmered rose-pink in the blaze of noon. Birds of prey hovered over the ground we had occupied and then with heavy beating of wings wheeled away and directed their course towards our line of march.

For two days we travelled without incident, centurions efficient in forcing stragglers to keep in touch with the main body of the army. The elation of our advance was no more; men kept their heads lowered, and the songs they sang were no longer the rude ballads of happier days, but laments for the girls they had left behind them and the homes they might never see again.

On the third day, breasting another hill below which a river valley extended itself, I observed that the banks of the river had been broken, and though there had been no heavy rain, the waters had flooded the road by which we must travel. This was the first evidence we had

137

that the Parthians had no intention of keeping their emperor's word and permitting us to withdraw in safety. I therefore ordered the officers commanding the flanks and rear to make ready for battle, and henceforth the army marched in the form of a square. While this retarded our progress, and thus put more pressure on our supplies, it provided an effective guard against the possibility of a sudden attack. For four days we were engaged in frequent skirmishing with the Parthian cavalry, inflicting losses on them, and still continuing our movement towards the west. The spirits of the men were raised both by the action and by the precautions I had taken.

Then, one of my officers, Flavius Gallus, possessed of greater courage than judgement, exceeded his orders. These were of course to repel all attacks but not to break ranks in pursuit of the enemy. But Gallus, being, I suppose, convinced that he had given such a check to the enemy that there was advantage to be gained from forcing home his attack, became detached from the main body of the army. Word was brought that he was surrounded. Canidius, commanding the rearguard, either because he was not alerted to the full extent of the danger, or because he underestimated the gravity of the task, sent only a small detachment to his aid; and this too was surrounded. He then repeated his mistake. When I learned of what was happening I spurred my horse to the rear, and took command myself. At the head of the third legion I engaged the enemy who were between us and the encircled Roman troops, and the impetus of our charge was such that we were able to break through and relieve our friends. The Parthians in their usual manner scattered, understanding that they had altogether lost their earlier advantage. Never in the whole campaign did they prove able to resist the organised assault of my veteran legions.

Yet this day was our first disaster. No fewer than three thousand of our men fell, and twice that number stumbled wounded back to the camp. Gallus himself was brought in on the shields of his loyal legionaries. His eyes were closed and a trickle of blood ran from his mouth. An arrow had pierced his neck and the surgeons were unable to remove it safely. I held his hand as he died spitting blood.

That evening I went round the camp visiting as many of the wounded as I could. It was touching to know their loyalty, and to see how many were more concerned with my safety and the well-being of the army than with the wounds they had themselves suffered and the pain they were experiencing. One man, a veteran of Philippi, pressed my hand. "I don't matter," he said, "as long as you are safe, for then the army will escape." I wept tears at these words and they fell from my eyes on to his dying face. In a little while it was over for him.

The next morning the first frost of autumn struck before dawn. The mist cleared and I saw on the other side of the valley a great host of the enemy arrayed as if for battle. Scouts reported that Phraates was so confident of complete victory that he had sent his own bodyguard to lead the attack; but he himself was absent, for he never risked his person in, or indeed near, battle. This we learned from captives taken by our outposts.

I saw that it was necessary that we should give a severe check to the enemy if we were not to be constantly harassed on the line of march. So I spent the early hours of the morning going round the camp addressing the troops whom the centurions had summoned on parade. I thanked them for their efforts of the previous day, praised their courage, and assured them that they had fought in a manner of which their ancestors would have been proud.

"Courage and greatness of soul," I said, "are displayed in adversity rather than in times of prosperity. I can offer you no ease in the days to come: only stiff and bloody battles, hard work, long marches and a supreme test of courage. If you were not Roman soldiers I could not speak this truth to you. I would have to tell lies to instil courage in your souls. But you are Roman soldiers and so I can speak truth to you. If you were not Roman soldiers I might myself yield to despair and fall on my sword. But, since you are Roman soldiers, I can smile at misfortune and meet danger with an easy mind."

Then I raised my arms aloft and prayed to the gods that if my former fortune was to be followed by some future evil, it should fall only on me, but that my army should emerge from the dark valley of trial safe and victorious.

So the men turned to the business of battle with resolution and a grim smile on their lips.

Seeing us ready for battle, the Parthians with much flourish of banners, blowing of trumpets and yells of mingled fury and dismay, yielded ground. Their army again melted, dissolving faster than the morning mist before our eyes, and we were able to resume the retreat.

But then we were faced with a new danger, for we had entered the hill country, and found ourselves harassed by the enemy from the higher ground. I therefore devised a novel means of defence. The light-armed troops were covered by the legionaries who would place one knee upon the ground, and receive the arrows on their shields. The rank behind covered those before with their shields in turn. This unusual fortification protected all from the enemy as the sloping roof of a house guards against the rain.

Moreover, whenever the Parthians, assuming perhaps that our men had sunk to their knees in exhaustion, or finding that they could make no impression with their arrows, came to spear-point, defence was at once turned to attack; and, as ever at close quarters, the enemy were driven off, though such was their readiness to take to their heels, their losses were always smaller than would have been the case with more disciplined and courageous forces.

Yet, though these tactics were invariably successful, they had one unfortunate consequence: our march covered less ground every day, and the shortage of supplies became acute. Even had the country which we were traversing provided grain for the men or fodder for the horses, it would have been impossible to send out foraging parties. And so though we won each daily battle, we grew daily more enfeebled. There was such a shortage of grain that many were reduced to scratching the earth for roots and herbs. One of these proved dangerous, for, when eaten raw, it deprived men of both memory and sense. They could be seen turning over stones as if in desperate search for an antidote, though none could explain what he was looking for. Then they succumbed to bile and vomiting, which unless they were provided with the stomach's sovereign remedy, wine, so weakened them that they died. I mention this oddity to show the hardships that befell this most noble and courageous army; and to highlight the courage and endurance of those who persisted in their duty.

The hills gave way to mountains and with their approach came renewed hope that the Parthians would abandon the pursuit. Once again, captives seized by our outposts seemed to confirm us in this expectation. It was possible, they said, that a few Medes might continue to harry us, but they would do so merely to protect outlying villages. The main body of the army had had enough, for they knew then that they could never defeat us in battle. More was said to this effect, and accordingly our spirits rose.

A debate ensued as to whether, in those circumstances, it was necessary to subject our men to the hardships of the mountain route, where moreover we could not look for water, and must endure thirst as well as hunger. Might it not be wiser to turn back into the plains again and take the easier passage? My staff were evenly divided.

But the matter was settled by the arrival of a Parthian deserter by name Mithradates, a cousin of Moneses. At first we were suspicious of him, for experience had given none of us any reason to believe anything a Parthian said unless we found evidence to confirm it. Yet, in our perplexity, I resolved at least to hear what he had to say myself, and to judge its credibility by his manner of speech. This appeared to me manly, and since he also spoke warmly of his gratitude for my kindness to his cousin, I listened to the warning he delivered.

He indicated a ridge to the south-west.

"Under that hill," he said, "the main body of the Parthian army waits in ambush. At the foot of the mountain is a wide plain, and they hope that you have been sufficiently deceived by the information you have garnered from captives, who were, I must tell you, planted on you for that purpose, to think it safe to exchange the rigours of the mountain for the delights of the plain. If you take the mountain route you will suffer thirst and exhaustion, but if, deceived by these captives, you choose the plain, then the fate of Crassus awaits you."

I rewarded him with gold, and summoned a council where I informed them of what Mithridates had said. Some were ill-disposed to trust him, but others argued that we had no reason to trust the information which the captives had given either. Ahenobarbus suggested that we torture some of them to see if they spoke differently; that way, he said, we should be certain which course was wise. But I had already determined that I should follow Mithridates' advice. As I explained to the council, it was impossible that a Parthian army should be lying in wait on the mountain route; all too possible that they would be lying in wait on the plain. "If all Parthians are liars," I said, "they are not all fools."

I was soon proved right, for when we took the mountain route, our rearguard was immediately pursued and engaged by the enemy, angered that we had not been deceived by their lies and chosen the way of the plain. The rearguard, commanded by Canidius, repelled the attack, but our progress was further delayed, and the men's sufferings from thirst increased. Still more disasters were to follow. The first stream we came upon proved to be salt and bitter, and it was with great difficult that the centurions drove the soldiers from its banks. Night fell while we were still in the mountains, for, though our guides assured me that a river of fresh water was but a few miles further on, it would have been imprudent to press forward in the dark.

But I gave orders that the rest should be brief, and that all should be ready to march at first light. I hoped in this way, not only to steal a march on the Parthian light cavalry who were still nibbling at our rear, but to alleviate the men's thirst as soon as possible.

Unfortunately it was a night of thick mist, which still clung about the mountains when I gave the order to strike camp. This occasioned some confusion. Word ran round first that we were lost, second that the Parthians were among us, and third that I myself had been killed. For the only time on this epic campaign, the men gave way to panic. Soldiers lost contact with their fellows and many were running wildly and alarmed about the disordered camp, shouting that we were betrayed, that all was lost, and that every man should seek his own safety. At this moment the Parthians did indeed begin to harass the rear, and if it had not been for the courage and good sense of a centurion of the Third, who seized the eagle and bore it towards the enemy crying out that he cared not if he perished since his comrades had abandoned their duty, all might have been lost. But others, shamed or inspired by his example, rallied to the ranks, beat off the enemy who fled as soon as they encountered stern and characteristically Roman resistance, and so saved the day. At this moment, made aware of the rumours concerning my own safety, I showed myself to the troops riding up and down the line, encouraging the men both by my presence and with words. In this way, order was restored, and we advanced to the river where sustenance was found.

Six days, ninety miles later – for being still in mountainous country where the roads were poor, we could not maintain the regular marching pace, we came to the River Araxes which serves as the boundary between Media and Armenia. When we set foot on the further shore, the men knelt down and kissed the ground; then they embraced each other in gratitude for their deliverance from the greatest dangers and most arduous march that any Roman army has ever undertaken.

Our withdrawal from before Phraaspa had taken twenty-seven days of bitter journeying. In that time we had fought eighteen battles and defeated the Parthians in all of them. Our losses were twenty thousand foot and four thousand horse, more than half of whom had died not in battle but from sickness, disease or the harsh cold of the mountain nights. We had endured extremes of temperature, and at the highest point of the march, the men had tramped through knee-deep snow. We had experienced frosts so severe that men's hands were frozen to their sword-hilts. The wounded lay in wet uniforms which the night rendered icy shrouds; and yet, save for that one occasion the army maintained its discipline, its composure, its confidence. No army of Rome has ever achieved so much, so magnificently.

XX

You have probably realised that in his account of this in reality disastrous campaign my lord is playing a part. He is pretending to be Caesar. The tone is just that, or so it seems to me, of Julius' account of his Gallic wars. There is the same combination of an assumed detachment with an intense egotism. My lord, like Caesar, never made a mistake. If anything went wrong, it was as a result of chance, rather than any misjudgement on his part. And of course nothing really went wrong; disaster rewritten becomes triumph. He proceeded, as you probably know, to celebrate a triumph; and to make matters worse, held it in Alexandria, an innovation which could certainly be defended as expressing his sense of what a universal empire such as Rome's had become must show itself to be, but nevertheless an innovation that was regarded as an insult by the Roman nobility. It was to supply Octavian with incendiary material for the propaganda war which he soon launched against my lord.

So this account of the Parthian campaign is certainly dishonest. Curiously, though, there is one respect in which his account does himself an injustice – such as Caesar would certainly never have been guilty of. It understates my lord's personal heroism, even though it was that, and his almost unfailing cheerfulness and affability, which kept his army from either disintegration or mutiny. There were so many occasions during that terrible retreat in which he seized a sword or a spear from one of the legionaries and put himself at the head of a counter-attack. He was wounded six times in the twenty-seven-day retreat from Phraaspa.

Of course he himself regarded what had happened only as a

check. Convinced that Parthia must be subjected, he was quite ready to resume the campaign the following year. Once again he asked Octavian for the twenty thousand men he had promised him. Once again, his colleague found excuses. To make matters worse, he dispatched Octavia to her husband with merely a tenth of that number. This was doubly provocative.

Would my lord go to Athens to meet Octavia? The matter was fiercely debated. He himself declared it impossible. In his camp on the fontiers of Armenia, he was fully occupied preparing his new army. How could he tear himself away? My own opinion is that, knowing he had treated Octavia badly, and made uncomfortable by guilt, he could not bring himself to see her. Perversely, he was resolved to insult her further, as if by piling indignity on indignity, he could justify his earlier cruelty. It was behaviour unworthy of his generous nature; knowing this, he yet continued in the same vein. It made little sense, but then of how much in our lives may that be said!

Others, who did not understand him as I did, plagued him with advice, urging him to follow the path of duty, rather than inclination – though this was not of course how they put it. Ahenobarbus, for instance, certain that my lord's position in Rome required to be consolidated, pressed him to come to a reconciliation with Octavia and receive her into his household again.

"It's being put about," Ahenobarbus said, "that you're turning into some sort of Levantine. Our friends in Rome are disturbed. They notice that you haven't been there for six years now, not in Italy for three. They're beginning to fear that you are forgetting what you really are. Well, you can satisfy them by setting up with your wife. If you send her back to Rome, you not only declare yourself an enemy of her brother, because he'll take it as an insult . . ."

"It's an insult he's going out of his way to invite," said Scribonius Curio.

"Precisely. Nothing he'd like better than to be publicly insulted by you."

"Which he'll present as an insult to Rome itself."

"But what," said my lord, "is his sending me a tenth of the troops he's committed to send me, but an equally open insult?"

So the argument went round and round.

And what part did Cleopatra play in this?

On the face of it, she kept out of the argument. Indeed she wrote to my lord to say that he must decide his future course without reference to her, or to her needs, or even to their children. She would always be his loyal friend, but she made no demands on him. She realised that he must place the security of the Empire and his own position at its head before any obligations he might suppose he had towards her.

Unfortunately this letter has disappeared. It really was a master-piece. My lord broke out in cries of admiration for her selflessness and understanding. He was, he said, quite overwhelmed by it.

My dear Alexas, who had been entrusted with the delivery of the letter, then asked what reply he was to carry back to the Queen.

"Tell her, tell her . . ." said my lord, and then burst into tears, unable to tell Alexas what he was to tell the Queen. A letter, it was later agreed, was to be drafted; and I was to be charged with preparing the first draft . . .

"What does she want to hear?" I asked Alexas.

"My dear, how should I know?" he said, opening his blue eyes very wide.

"It's all flannel, isn't it?" I said.

"My dear . . ."

"But of the very highest quality, I grant you."

"In confidence," he said, "the Queen is on edge. She can't believe that Antony will abandon her. She can't believe he won't. It's playing hell with her temper. I must say I'm glad to be away from her for a little."

From the orangery beyond wafted in the scent of blossom. Alexas stretched out on the couch, his tunic rucked up. He was a little drunk, his speech thickening. From over the rooftops came the wailing of women. Then there was only the soft wind in the trees.

"I've heard her say she would like to thrash Antony, the next moment . . ." – he made a vague passing movement with his hand. "She doesn't know her own mind, never has." He let his long thin-fingered hand rest on his naked thigh. "It doesn't matter to us, does it, what they do?" he said. His lips were invitingly open.

Later he said: "I may be effeminate, but I thank the gods I'm not a woman. Women are hell, aren't they?"

Even so, Cleopatra had to be answered. I drew up the draft of a letter, committing my lord to nothing – in the most flowery language you can imagine, naturally. Alexas had helped me, whether he intended to or not. He had shown me the Queen's uncertainty and therefore the nature of her dependence on my lord.

I explained this to Ahenobarbus who trusted my judgement when it concurred with his, all the more because he disliked and despised me. He often said he couldn't understand Antony's willingness to have a creature like myself about him. He called me, in my own presence, a painted child of dirt. Of course when I heard him say this I allowed myself only a little smile, as if in acknowledgement. Well, I thought, I am what the Romans have made me. But, distrusting me as he did, Ahenobarbus nevertheless knew that I was intelligent. He couldn't believe I loved Antony, because he couldn't believe a creature such as I capable of love; but he recognised that I had his best interests at heart, precisely because I was, and would be, in his view, nothing without him; not, you understand, that he acknowledged me as anything anyway.

Having heard me out, he said: "Granted you're right" – at which words he treated himself to an enormous disdainful sniff – "and the Queen is uncertain of him, I don't see that it gets us forward."

I explained, with many professions of my own unworthiness, too flowery and insincere to be repeated here, and in any case too boring (but in my experience Roman noblemen like Ahenobarbus will swallow any self-abasement on the part of their inferiors and judge it merely proper), that it strengthened his hand in the debate about what my lord should do. It meant that he was still able to keep the Queen at arm's length, whereas if she had, as we feared, already established a complete ascendancy over him, there would be no such hope.

"If however," I said, "it could be arranged that he should agree to receive the Lady Octavia, then such is her virtue and charm, if I may be permitted to say so, that I do believe he would happily be re-established in marriage. I have been in my lord's service since childhood," – He glowered and harrumphed at that – "and I know him well enough, if again I may presume to say so, to know that he will always be governed by some woman. It is better for all of us and especially for himself if that woman should now be Octavia."

Now I confess that here I made a mistake, and from it all our subsequent catastrophe followed. I addressed my words to the wrong man. Ahenobarbus had many virtues, or so they say; but delicacy in argument was not one of them. Had I spoken thus to Scribonius Curio, who was a man of great and sympathetic understanding, all might have been well. But Ahenobarbus was one of those proud, in that absurd saying of which Romans are so fond in their self-congratulatory fashion, of taking the bull by the horns. Accordingly he launched on his argument to my lord with all the subtlety of one galley ramming another. He told him it was his duty to receive Octavia. He told him he would be a fool to send her back to Rome. He even said that if a degenerate pansy like Critias had the intelligence to understand this, he couldn't comprehend how my lord could be blind. In short, if he had been paid by Cleopatra to win Antony to her side, he couldn't have made a better job of it. But of course he wasn't in her pay. He really did detest her. He was just a stupid blundering Roman nobleman with as much tact and sensibility as the dull ox he resembled.

How I came to make such a mistake myself I can't think. The consequences were most unhappy. My lord dispatched a sharp letter to Octavia – I drew it up with tears in my eyes – commanding her to return to Rome, since she had failed to bring him the troops he required, and appeared to be more conscious of her duty to her brother than of the greater duty she owed her husband, a duty which indeed extinguished that owed Octavian. In short it was a letter so stupid and brutal that I was quite ashamed to have inscribed it.

Curiously, Alexas quite misconceived my role in the affair. He was overwhelmed by relief and joy, and gave me keen evidence of his gratitude, which sentiment, he assured me, Cleopatra would also entertain towards me. It would have been unkind to set him right, and in any case I saw no reason to deny myself the pleasures he offered me.

XXI

When my lord and Octavian were on apparently easy terms, they had been able to treat my lord's affair with Cleopatra light-heartedly. Once, Octavian wrote, reproving my lord, but in comradely tones, so that my lord was able to reply in like manner, saying for instance:

"What about you? You're not entirely faithful to Livia, are you now? I bet you're not. Just remember, dear boy, that I know a good deal about your tastes, personally and by repute. You don't suppose Mouse Brutus didn't boast that he'd had you? Now of course you're grown up and differently orientated no doubt. But my congratulations – or commiserations as may be – if between the time I write this and you receive it you haven't bedded Tertullia or Terentia or Rufilla or Salvia Titisenia, or a selection of other lovelies. By my ancestor Herakles, does it matter a damn who or what or where or when or how often you do it to or with? Sex, dear boy, is mere animal activity, and, as far as I'm concerned, the Queen is just a piece of female flesh . . ."

Would that it had been so!

Of course now any letter written in this vein, and my lord tried to recapture it more than once, but the copies have vanished, was more likely to infuriate Octavian than charm him. Though he was given to lechery himself, as everyone knows, he had, under the influence of Livia, become a prude. His friends would have called him fastidious, but in my opinion he was really a hypocrite; and I believe he was always jealous of my lord's ease of manner and careless superiority.

As for Octavia, for whom as you know I had great respect and admiration, I do not know if she ever realised how badly she had been used by her brother. If he had kept his word to my lord, then my lord would never have rejected her. Of that I am certain. I believe that Octavia knew this, though she could never bring herself to confess it openly. My evidence is admittedly mere hearsay, but I have been told that, returned to Rome, she met her brother only on formal occasions when her absence would have occasioned talk; but had no private or intimate dealings with him. And it is surely noteworthy too that she continued to care for Antony's children by his marriage to Fulvia, bringing them up in her own household and treating them just as she treated her own daughters.

For a while our affairs improved. Though my lord did not feel strong enough to launch a second expedition against Parthia, he did march into Armenia, arrest the traitor Artavasdes, and turn that unruly kingdom into a province of the Empire; Canidius was established as proconsul. As for Artavasdes, he was carried to Alexandria, where he would be paraded in my lord's triumph, subsequently suffering the well-merited penalty of execution.

That triumph was indeed magnificent, what ever lies were later disseminated in Rome. My lord was dressed in a golden robe and held the sacred wand of Dionysos. The captives were marched through the city which had never seen anything like this before. Alexas later told me that the citizens of Alexandria were so struck by the splendour presented to them that they abandoned their habitual cynicism and scepticism – for the Greeks of Alexandria believe they have seen everything and that nothing can surprise or impress them – and that they really did believe that my lord was a god incarnate; but the dear boy may have been trying to please me, or he may have been too credulous himself.

The captives were then presented to Cleopatra seated on a golden throne which was mounted on a silver platform. Her children were placed on little stools or thronelets on the lower part of the dais; and the vast crowd huzza'd and scattered rose-petals over them. It was reported in Rome that the captives declined to offer the customary obeisance to the Queen, but this is not true. They did as they were required. Then, amidst general enthusiasm, my lord took young Caesarion by the hand and proclaimed Caesar's son joint-ruler of Egypt with his mother. This was something which Cleopatra had been seeking for many years, for it was long customary for Egypt to be governed by the heir to the throne in association with the reigning monarch. Moreover Cleopatra hoped by this means to demonstrate that her son, and not Octavian, whom she feared and resented, was the true heir of Caesar.

Even so, it was remarkably generous of my lord to make this gesture, for in truth the legions by their enthusiasm displayed on so many occasions in the previous ten years had shown that they accepted him as the true inheritor of Caesar's glory.

Then, further to please the Queen and to display his own magnificence, he declared their little son Alexander Helios, a boy of astonishing beauty, King of Armenia and Media, and his younger brother Ptolemy King of Phoenicia, Syria and Cilicia. Of course these were mere honorific titles, which nobody could take seriously, though Octavian later made great play of them in his propaganda; but the children looked quite charming, Alexander in Median dress with turban and tiara, and Ptolemy garbed like the successors of Alexander in long cloak and slippers with a bonnet encircled with a diadem. Cleopatra herself wore the sacred robe of Isis, many-coloured to signify that that goddess enjoys a universal power.

We knew this was all play-acting, to please the people and the Queen. It was unfortunate that no thought had been taken as to how this quite harmless and gorgeous spectacle would be represented in Rome. It is true that Ahenobarbus had warned against it, but he was so old-fashioned in his opinions that little note was taken of his words. For myself, I rather blame Scribonius Curio, admirable though he was in almost every respect, for not realising how Octavian would use this affair to poison the mind of Rome. My lord would have listened to Curio, whom he had every reason to trust, and whom he loved, partly on account of the love he had borne his father, whom the young Curio in so many respects resembled.

It has often been said since that from this moment my lord was seized with a folly which amounted to madness, and that he had lost all sense of proportion.

This is a libel as I now intend to prove.

First, far from neglecting politics or his relations with Octavian, he immediately turned his powerful mind to a statement of his legitimate grievances. I know this for sure, and can swear to the dating, because I was instrumental in drawing up his letter of accusation.

He made five principal points.

First: that Octavian had broken his word by failing to send him the troops he had promised.

Second: that, when Octavian had seized Sicily from Sextus Pompey, he had, contrary to their agreement, taken the whole island and its revenues for himself, rather than sharing them with him.

Third: that he had never returned the ships which he had borrowed from my lord.

Fourth: that after reducing their colleague Lepidus, without consultation, to the status of a private citizen, Octavian had taken to himself Lepidus' legions, province, treasure, and tributes which again should have been shared.

Fifth: that Octavian had allotted all the public and confiscated lands in Italy to his own time-expired veterans, leaving none for my lord's men; which was again in breach of their agreement.

I quote this in detail in order to show that my lord was still in full possession of his intellectual faculties, and attentive to business. Moreover, he was justified in every one of these charges.

This was proved in turn by the feebleness of Octavian's response.

First he declared that Lepidus had proved incompetent and so resigned his power and authority to him, Octavian. Then, with honeyed words, he said he was ready to share with his colleague Antony all that he had acquired by war . . .

"And that's damn all," said Ahenobarbus.

"In any case," Curio said, "when has Octavian ever kept his word to share anything. Remember, I was at school with him, and I know. He's greedy as a stoat."

Finally, Octavian, having declared that by the same token he expected Antony to share Armenia with him, had the insolence to claim that my lord's veterans had no need of lands in Italy "because my lord could comfortably settle them in Armenia and Media".

As though that was the same thing.

All the same, insolent and feeble though the letter was, it didn't betoken what was to follow. Within a few weeks word was brought that Octavian had launched an astonishing attack in the Senate on my lord. He accused him of every sort of immorality, of betraying Rome's Empire in the East in exchange for the foetid embraces of an Eastern harlot queen, of adopting Oriental religion and dress, and of giving territory won by the heroic exertions of the legions to the harlot's bastards.

Then, acting swiftly, he created such fear in the city that several hundred of the nobility and equestrian order, fearing their lives were in danger, fled, and made their way to my lord's camp. Rome was again on the brink of civil war, brought to that point by the malice and ambition of Octavian.

XXII

This war was not of my making, not of my seeking. It has been forced on me.

I proposed that both Octavian and myself should demit office. The period of the Triumvirate, already itself broken by Octavian's expulsion of our colleague Lepidus, was approaching an end. Let us, I said, restore the old forms of the Republic.

My suggestion was ignored. Instead my colleague of ten years delivered a violent attack on my public conduct and private morals. Was Rome, he asked, to be governed by a habitual drunkard enslaved by the charms of an Eastern harlot? This was intolerable. Octavian also employed pamphleteers, some obscure, others men of birth but ignoble character, to poison the minds of senators, equestrians and people against me. One, Marcus Valerius Messalla Corvinus, once an adherent of Marcus Brutus, who described him as a "noble youth of talent and distinction", prostrated himself before Octavian and obliged him by accusing me of Oriental extravagance and Oriental vices; he would be rewarded with a consulate originally reserved for me. This same Messalla conveniently forgot how I had spared his life when he made his surrender to me, rather than to Octavian whom he then distrusted, after Brutus' defeat.

In response I dispatched to the Senate a dignified statement of my achievements, proving the legality of all my acts, and rehearsing the covenants I had made with Octavian, which he had broken. To ensure its reception I entrusted it to Cn. Domitius Ahenobarbus and Caius Sosius, designated consuls for the coming year. Even my enemies in the Senate, I fondly thought, must acknowledge that my conquest of

Armenia and expansion of the frontier of Empire told in my favour. Sosius performed manfully. He delivered an eloquent speech in my praise. Meanwhile Ahenobarbus, no orator, sought to rally support among the Conscript Fathers. Sosius, thinking that the tide had turned in our favour, made a second speech denouncing Octavian's infringement of our agreements; he proposed a motion of modest censure. Legality, it seemed, might prevail.

The prospect alarmed Octavian. Knowing he was in the wrong, he acted to subdue just criticism. Though he no longer possessed any official position, the Triumvirate having expired, he immediately raised an army in Italy, summoning retired veterans, and the armed bands maintained by his associates. He marched on Rome – a capital offence in the days of Republican legality. He entered the Curia at the head of an armed force. Placing himself between the two consuls, whose legitimate authority he thus defied, he accused me of treason. Overawed and terrified, the Senate behaved like women. Not one man dared raise his voice against the adventurer. Then Octavian dismissed them, no doubt with scorn; he ordered them to reassemble on a day which he would name when he would produce documentary evidence to prove me a traitor.

The situation was grave. Sosius and Ahenobarbus took counsel together, concluded that their lives were at risk, and fled the city. They were followed by more than three hundred senators, some old Republicans, others loyal to me personally.

Then Octavian, acting on no right but only on his personal authority, declared that Sosius and Ahenobarbus were guilty of desertion. It was a rich stroke. If they stayed they were dead men. If they departed they were traitors. Not even Cicero acted with such brazen contempt for legality when he had Catiline's associates executed without trial. Octavian then appointed, without consultation or even show of legality, two consuls of his own creation, one, appropriately perhaps, a cousin of Messalla. In the following year, he declared, he would hold the consulship himself and Messalla would be his colleague.

Such were the acts of the man who accused me of breaking the laws of the Republic. By violence, actual and implicit, he had secured for himself power in Rome, mastery over Italy.

I repeated nevertheless my willingness to resign my powers. I had, I said yet again, no wish for war. I had an army of thirty legions, men tried in battle, and a large fleet. If I had sailed to

Italy, Octavian could not have withstood my might. Let this be remembered when history comes to judge. Moreover, since I had with me the duly elected consuls, my army was the true army of the Republic, Octavian's merely his own faction.

Furthermore, the justice of my cause may be estimated by the roll-call of those who had left Rome to join me. Ahenobarbus himself was formerly an adherent of Cato. Could there be better evidence that I was true to the Republic?

XXIII

The effort of dictating that last chapter has exhausted him. In the middle of it he called for more wine, drank fast, and now sits with his eyes glazed but fixed on the sea which gleams a hundred feet below us. Sea birds shriek, but I doubt if he hears them. His thoughts are distant. Or so I assume.

Now he has begun to snore. When he wakes he will drink again, inviting oblivion. Can I blame him?

So I must resume the narrative myself.

Everything he said in that last passage was true, and everything was less than the truth. Isn't that the way with all historical exercises?

When he arrived at Ephesus with Sosius, Ahenobarbus was both disgusted and alarmed to find Cleopatra with my lord. He urged that she should be sent back to Egypt. Rome, he said, might fight a war against Cleopatra, never against Antony. He may, I fear, have been right. Indeed I thought so even then, though I was also inclined to question his opinion because I knew of his distaste, even hatred, for the Queen.

Others disagreed, chief among them Canidius, whose word carried weight because of his exploits in the field of battle. He argued that Cleopatra could not be safely dismissed. She had furnished us with men and ships. More important, without her help, the army could not be paid.

He had reason on his side. So did Ahenobarbus. Therefore my lord's inclination conquered.

My lord then expressed his resentment of Octavian by divorcing Octavia. This was a blunder. As soon as the intention was mooted, I besought Alexas to urge Cleopatra herself to advise my lord against so precipitate a course.

"Persuade her," I said, "that it is not in her interest that my lord should either provoke Octavian to war or give him such a valuable weapon of propaganda as this divorce will prove."

"My dear," he said, "you have seen the pyramids, I think?"

"Certainly."

"Persuade them then to march across the sands. That were as easy. The Queen hates and fears Octavia; she longs to see her humiliated."

By this action my lord betrayed himself. He was soon to be more terribly betrayed by one he had trusted.

L. Munatius Plancus was an old Caesarian. He had served on the Dictator's staff. At the time of the proscriptions he had proved his zeal for the Republic by willingly sacrificing his own brother, whose property he had inherited by special dispensation. A friend of my lord's brother Lucius, he had stood by him in the siege of Perusia, from which he had escaped while acting as an envoy proposing truce. Later he had been forgiven by my lord, and resumed his service. My lord, in his generosity, made him proconsul of Syria, where he proved efficient, though men talked of his lust for deflowering under-age girls, some as young as nine or ten. Unlike Ahenobarbus, he had engaged in gross flattery of the Queen, and made good use of her favour to enrich himself. He even appeared, successfully, in theatrical performances at court; he had indeed a peculiar talent for low comic parts. But it was a bitter comedy he played now.

Either because he was resentful of my lord's greatness, or because, as some said, my lord had detected him in peculation, or, as I have always believed, because he could not endure long in the same company since men there discovered his vices and displayed open contempt of him accordingly, he now deserted my lord and fled to Octavian. It may be of course that he sniffed the direction of the wind. I do not know. I know however that desertion was not sufficient to satisfy this nobly born rat. He carried the lust for betrayal in his heart.

Arrived in Rome, he at once sought an audience with Octavian. It would be nice to think that he was received with some distaste. Surely not even Octavian could welcome such a man? But if he did not welcome him, he welcomed the news he brought. Antony, Plancus said, had deposited his will in the Temple of Vesta. He, Plancus, knew its contents, for he had been a witness; and they were, he said, scandalous.

This news delighted Octavian, but for a little he did not know how to put it to effective use. Since many who happen on this narrative may know little about Rome, I should say that it is customary for noble Romans to lodge their will in the care of the virgin priestesses who tend the flame of the goddess Vesta. Now such documents are regarded as inviolable. The Vestals have a sacred duty to guard their contents till the death of the testator. Never are they revealed till then. Moreover, any attempt to coerce the Vestals into breaking the seal is regarded as gross sacrilege. So, although Plancus declared himself ready to swear to the contents of the will, Octavian, knowing that the word of such as Plancus was not worth a Spaniard's fart, was in a quandary. He was desperate to see the will in the hope that it would prove as damaging to my lord as Plancus assured him was the case; but he dared not command the Vestals to produce what they were bound to keep inviolate. Moreover, he was, I have been told, afraid of his wife Livia who, for all her faults of manner and her greed for power, was so narrow and rigid in her opinions, that she could not have countenanced an act of sacrilege.

Indeed I have heard that she told him roundly that no man was permitted to enter the shrine which the Vestals tended, nor might force them to surrender what had been entrusted to them. Moreover, it is said that when he then urged her, as a woman, to do what was forbidden to him as a man, she spat in his face. This may not be true, though I should like to think it is. What is certain, because I have this from a special friend of mine in Octavia's household, with whom I have kept in touch despite my lord's rejection of his wife, is that Livia warned Octavian that if he yielded to temptation and committed this sacrilege, their marriage would be barren. I know this because Octavia in great distress revealed Livia's fears to her dresser, who in turn told my friend with whom she was in love. So I have no doubt that this is authentic.

So he organised a robbery. It seems that it was bungled. The gang were discovered, and all but one killed resisting arrest, as was most convenient. The survivor, a Greek youth, having been put to the torture, no doubt, told a ridiculous tale, which nevertheless received credency.

He said he had been recruited in a tavern by an agent of Antony's. The intention, it seemed, was that the burglary should be blamed on Octavian who would be supplied with a false will, very damaging to Antony.

Naturally Octavian would then have this read to the Senate, whereupon Antony would cause the true will to be produced, and thus discredit Octavian. The whole thing was to be presented as a conspiracy aimed against him.

This farrago of nonsense was believed. I suppose the poor boy was disposed of before he could retract it. The Senate then required the Vestals, for the safety of the Republic and the Roman People, to breach convention (that is, break the law), and deliver to their keeping Antony's will, that they might determine whether it contained matter injurious to the State, etc., etc.

As it happened – surprise, surprise – when the Vestals reluctantly bowed to the command of the Senate, the document was handed, not to the August Fathers themselves, but to Octavian. I am told he had it in his possession for fully forty-eight hours before he caused it to be read to the Senate. Well, a lot can happen to a document in that time.

It seemed, or was made to seem, that my lord had declared Caesarion to be Caesar's son – well, one has only to look at the boy's nose to see that he is indeed that – and had left huge legacies to him and to Cleopatra's other children. Nothing in contrast was left to Octavia or to my lord's children by her or Fulvia. Cleopatra was acknowledged as his wife, though by Roman law no Roman citizen may marry any but a Roman citizen – as my lord well knew so that whatever ceremonies he went through with the Queen had no legal standing.

Then there were the arrangements for his funeral. If my lord died at Rome, it seemed, he had directed that his body should be carried in state through the Forum and then transported to Alexandria to lie in the mausoleum of the Ptolemies.

The agitation was considerable. It was fomented further by one Calvisius, who regaled the senators with lurid tales intended to demonstrate my lord's slavish infatuation with the Queen. For instance, he said, Antony had once scurried from a law-court in the middle of a speech by the learned orator Furnius merely because word had come to him that Cleopatra was passing by in her litter. Moreover he had bestowed on the Queen the great library of Pergamum, no less than two hundred thousand volumes. Calvisius himself had once seen Antony press Cleopatra's foot with his own as a signal of some future rendezvous.

This last accusation was particularly absurd in view of what the old fool had already said regarding my lord's relations with the Queen. If they were half of what he asserted, what need of such signals or secret signs of intimacy?

But the truth was that Calvisius had been suborned by Octavian and was a man of no independent judgement. In any case his speech was mere tinder to set the blaze of rumour alight. Soon the most ridiculous and obnoxious stories were current in Rome. Octavian's friend Maecenas, without a blush, declared that Antony was accustomed to deck himself in Egyptian robes and participated in the most abominable rites with which the corrupt and loathsome depraved wretches of the Nile Valley celebrate their vile gods. This from Maecenas – I ask you!

Someone else popped up to assert that when my lord was presiding over public business in the presence of kings, tetrarchs and other dignitaries, he was accustomed to break off abruptly if by chance love letters from Cleopatra were present to him, enclosed, to make matters worse, in onyx and crystal.

All this, and countless other absurdities, were to the excited populace as wine is to the habitual drunkard. Wild rumours swept through the city, and indeed all Italy. It was asserted, and believed, that my lord and Cleopatra intended to descend on Italy at the head of an army more terrible than Hannibal's. Moreover, when they had obtained victory, Antony would surrender Rome itself to Cleopatra and transfer the capital of Empire to Alexandria. His favourite oath was "So may I deliver my edicts on the Capitol".

If any objected that Antony had ever been a faithful servant of the Republic – and few were bold enough to say so – and that no Roman other than a lunatic could have sunk to such treasonable degeneracy, then an explanation was immediately forthcoming from Octavian's spies. Antony, they said, had been bewitched by the Eastern sorceress.

And this seemingly made perfect good sense to the deluded mob, who sallied forth to burn his house on the Aventine to the ground; yes, even that house decorated with the most delicate and gorgeous wall-paintings, for some of which I had myself served as the model. I regret a particularly fine depiction of myself as Paris delivering judgement to the three goddesses. Alas, that such high art should fall victim to blind and witless fury!

No wonder that Octavian so easily persuaded the Senate to strip my lord of his imperium, and deprive him of the consulship he was due. Only one man, C. Coponius, once an adherent of Pompey and a man whose family had entertained long enmity to the house of Plancus, was bold enough to oppose this motion, declaring that in his opinion the will was a forgery, and that anyone who believed a word that a creature like Plancus said had himself taken leave of his senses. For speaking this courageous truth, he was to be the victim of a street assault at the hands of thugs in Agrippa's pay.

Only when Agrippa himself, in collusion with his little master, appeared in the Senate to urge that my lord be named a public enemy, did Octavian draw back. And no doubt this was by design. It was his intention that the war he planned should not seem a renewal of the civil wars which had destroyed so many noble families. His war would be waged against Cleopatra. It was she, he said, who was the true enemy of Rome, and Antony merely her tool.

Yet, even then, all was not lost. Though Octavian spoke of war, he was not yet ready to engage.

When this news came to us, Ahenobarbus, furious on account of the insults he had received, as well as alert to the way in which the crisis was developing, urged that we launch an immediate invasion of Italy.

"We must crush the viper now," he said, "or fall victim to its sting."

But my lord would have none of it. Even now he sought peace.

"Never," he said, "will I consent to invade Italy and bring down the horrors of war once more upon the unfortunate inhabitants of my native country which I dearly love."

Let this be remembered when the balance is weighed!

Yet there can be no doubt that Ahenobarbus' strategy was wise and

I am still at a loss to understand my lord's reluctance to obey military sense.

Ahenobarbus was beside himself.

"If I could ever believe that little toad Octavian," he said, "I could credit his assertion that Antony is indeed bewitched."

"No," said Curio, "he is merely entranced."

"Comes to the same thing. For the greatest general of the age to reject the strategy that alone can save him is a sign of . . . I don't know what. That he's out of his right mind, for sure."

Alexas told me that Cleopatra herself was begging my lord to move against his rival.

"She has the heart of a lion," he said, "but nevertheless she is afraid of what will happen if he does not take the initiative."

This information merely exposed the cause of his indecision. He knew he could not invade Italy in the company of Cleopatra, and yet he was strangely reluctant to order her back to Egypt. It was obvious to the world that he was indeed infatuated. Yet I could not believe it, and few had a better knowledge of him than I. Certainly, much of the time, he delighted in her company. Certainly many nights she shared his bed. So much gave ballast to the common opinion. But at other times I saw a spasm of dislike cloud his face when she spoke. If he was indeed dependent on her, as he had never been on any other woman, even Fulvia, then he resented this inferiority. Yet, offered the opportunity to break free, he would not move.

For the record of history, let me say this: in my opinion my lord was sincere in his refusal to carry war into Italy. He was weary of civil strife. He knew the horrors it had unleashed on Italy so often. He could not believe that even victory would justify their renewal.

Once, late at night, lounging half-drunk on the terrace of his villa, gazing across the dark sea to the distant mountains of Greece, rising like heavy clouds full of foreboding, he murmured:

"In any case civil war settles nothing. Civil war is a hydra. Every victory causes new enemies to sprout heads. I am too weary to imitate my ancestor Herakles, and slaying the monster is beyond me. There must be some other way."

Perhaps in his tormented heart he still could not comprehend the depth of the animosity Octavian felt towards him. He retained tender feelings for the grim young man whom at moments he still saw as a pretty boy. He could not believe that Octavian was determined to destroy him.

As proof, I offer this letter which he dictated to me, and sent to Octavian.

I do not understand the game you are playing. What have you got against me? It can't be my rejection of Octavia, which would never have happened if you had kept your word to me. You can't think the Queen so important. Egypt is important, yes, that's true. Egypt is indeed vital to the well-being of Rome. You can surely agree with me on that. Without the rich harvest of Egypt there will be scarcity, even famine, in Rome. And she governs Egypt. That is why I first befriended her. Since then she has given me aid in terms of men and money. Armenia would never have been added to the Empire but for the help she gave me, when, I am sorry to remind you, you failed or were unable to provide me with the legions you had sworn to send me. How can I fail to feel grateful to her?

This quarrel which has broken out between us is not of my seeking. I can't believe you want it either. People have been telling you lies. The quarrel has been fomented by those who wish neither of us well, for some personal gain that they seek.

Let us meet together, alone, just the two of us, and I am sure all will be resolved between us. I am puzzled and dismayed by what I hear of your behaviour. Nevertheless I still cherish a deep regard for you.

Come on, kid, fix a meeting-place. You know we always agree when we are together. It is only when we are separated that trouble brews up. Always because of lies told by others.

That refrain again! My lord had too noble a nature to understand Octavian's selfish, jealous, and ignoble temper.

XXIV

I do not believe that my lord can ever continue his narrative. Therefore, for his sake and for his reputation, it behoves me to carry it forward.

At first the news from Italy offered hope. Followers of my lord who had fled from Octavian's implacable temper brought word that all was in confusion. Octavian, they said, had been faced with near mutiny, which he had appeased only by promising a lavish donation, which however he could not raise, for even the bankers were doubtful of his success and feared that they would never recover any loan they made him. So he had imposed new and terrible taxation, demanding a quarter of the annual income of every citizen. No wonder riots broke out, and the public buildings, where the taxation records were stored, were burnt to the ground in many municipalities. Octavian's response was immediate and brutal; suspects were arrested and put to death, either by the sword of the legionaries eager to earn the extra pay they had been promised, or by crucifixion. Detachments of the army were lodged on private citizens and small towns, and not withdrawn till a large sum of money had been surrendered.

None of this oppression was legal. Octavian, prompted, it is said, by Maecenas, justified it on grounds of "higher legality".

Then it was reported that he was preparing to compel all Italy to swear an oath of personal allegiance to him; anyone who broke such an oath would be deemed guilty of treason. No one had ever before demanded such an oath from Roman citizens. Yet, terrified, men thronged to the fora of towns all over the country to attest their loyalty – which was in reality their subservience.

Yet all was not yet lost. Italy, men said, secretly, in taverns and chambers, had no quarrel with Antony. How should it have when he had brought unprecedented glory to the Empire and deserved so well of the Republic? As for Cleopatra, many thought, correctly, that the threat of Eastern domination and the establishment of an Oriental monarchy was remote and chimerical. And yet, the immediate terror practised by Octavian stifled such doubts.

One friend of my lord's, by name Geminius, slipped out of Rome and came to warn Antony of the intensity of the agitation being raised against him. But, by an unhappy stroke, Cleopatra determined that this man, though as honest as any, was a spy sent by Octavian. She therefore gave orders to her people that he should be received with insults and treated with contempt.

Geminius, near despair, came to me and asked if I could arrange that he should have a secret interview with my lord. This was difficult, but at last I was able to smuggle him into an ante-chamber and, by some tale, draw my lord from Cleopatra's side to speak to him.

Unfortunately Antony had been drinking deep with the Queen who by this time, or at least on this occasion, had the harder head. Seeing my lord sway as he approached him and hearing that his speech was slurred, Geminius said in a manner that was regrettably petulant:

"One part of what I have to say should be communicated to you at a more sober hour, but the other part is unmistakable whether you are drunk or sober. Italy has no wish to war with you, Antony, but Octavian's propaganda has raised a storm of fear and hatred of Cleopatra. The war being planned is nominally directed against her, and the legions which will not fight Antony will zealously seek to destroy her. Therefore, if you send the Queen back to Egypt, either there will be no war, or, more probably, for Octavian's purpose to destroy you is fixed as the polar star, you will be victorious, since his legions will fight you only half-heartedly."

No one could have given better advice, or in a more decorous manner; it will be observed that he said not a word against the Queen.

Yet Cleopatra who, suspicious, had followed my lord from the room where they had been drinking and concealed herself behind a curtain that she might hear what Geminius had to say, before my lord could make any response, burst forth in angry denunciation of honest Geminius.

"Piece of filth. Spy of the little monster . . . sent to divide and conquer . . . to weaken Antony by depriving him of half his army . . . dung in a silk stocking . . . Octavian's catamite . . ."

That was the purport of her speech, delivered in the tone, and with the terrible temper, of a fishwife from the Piraeus.

Geminius, she said, would be fortunate if he escaped torture and he would do so only because he had proved himself guilty without it. All this while Antony stood silent, his head hanging and his hands alone moving in little convulsive twitches. In his heart he knew Geminius spoke truth, and yet he dared not defy the Queen. At last he gave vent to a deep groan, like a bull sore wounded awaiting the stroke that would dispatch it, and slumped to the marble floor in what was either a swoon or, alas, a drunken stupor. But it may be that he sought refuge from perplexity in a willed oblivion.

Geminius turned away, and with heavy tread departed into the night. In a little I slipped after him, to see if there was anything he required, anything more he wished to say. He looked at me as if he had never seen me before.

"I am surprised she allowed me to leave unmolested," he said.

"My lord has had the same advice," I said, "from Ahenobarbus, Scribonius Curio and others."

"Dragons," he said, "fix those they seek to devour with their unsleeping eye. Antony is a man possessed. There is nothing for me here. I have been deceived in my understanding. I have perhaps wilfully deceived myself."

Soon after he slipped from the camp and was said to have returned to Rome. This report confirmed the common belief among the Queen's entourage that he was indeed a spy. Even Alexas could not be shaken from this delusion.

Others too began to desert, sometimes for trivial reasons. Quintus Dellius, often used by my lord on diplomatic missions, gave out that Cleopatra had planned to murder him, merely because at dinner one night he had complained that they were compelled to drink sour wine, while in Rome the likes of Sarmentus enjoyed the best Falernian. Who could believe such nonsense? This Sarmentus by the way was one of Octavian's lovers, or, as the Romans have it, "pet delights".

Dellius like many others had switched his allegiance often before. He had been a Pompeian who had deserted to Caesar, then a partisan first of Dolabella, subsequently of Cassius, abandoning them too when their cause promised badly. In himself he was no loss; but as a portent his defection was disturbing. I said to myself: the swallows are leaving us, as winter looms harsh.

In Rome Octavian now declared the Triumvirate finally at an end. In return for surrendering this power, the Senate obediently granted him imperium, without limitation. He disdained the old title of dictator; it was associated with Caesar, whom he still claimed as his father, but he feared to style himself so for in the opinion of many it was Caesar's assumption of the dictatorship for life which had provoked his murder. But in reality his powers had grown to those which Caesar had enjoyed and abused. With the impudence that was habitual to him he announced that this imperium had been granted to him not only by the will of the Senate, but spontaneously, as a mark of confidence, by All Italy.

This was absurd, since Italy had no means of granting any office; but no one there dared to remark on this at the time.

The wagon-engine of Mars was set in motion – to employ a fanciful phrase beloved by Roman versifiers.

War was formally declared: on Cleopatra, the foreign foe, and done with all the pomp and ceremony of a traditional rite, though it is quite possible that Octavian invented the form employed. There was no mention of my lord.

Privately, I am told, Octavian let it be understood that while his own friendship with Antony was no more, their disagreements were merely personal and private. Neither Rome nor Italy, he said, had a quarrel with Antony. But if Antony in his degeneracy did not abandon Cleopatra, then as her creature he must share in the destruction that was to be her lot.

I suppose most declarations of war partake of fraud to some degree; few can ever have been made with such effrontery and dishonesty as this – private spite pretended to public virtue.

When Antony learned that war had become open, he could not at first believe it. He had reposed such trust in Octavian that it was bitter for him to root out the last shreds of his confidence and affection, and to understand that Octavian had determined to destroy him.

"But I trusted him," he said again and again, then retired to his chamber and wept. In a little he summoned me and told me to fetch his armour-bearer.

"Antony is Antony still," he said. "The cub will learn what it is to have aroused the lion."

Then he looked out to the sea and the grey clouds scudding low across it.

"At Pharsalus," he said, "when Caesar looked on the bodies of the Pompeians fallen in battle, he said only: 'They wanted this war, not I.' Critias, if I fall, see that the world knows this was Octavian's war, not mine. I have done all that a man of honour could to avoid it."

Then he turned away to put his armour on.

Alexas that night told me that the Queen had received word of war with mingled jubilation and terror, one mood swift on the heels of the other.

XXV

It was not long before dire prodigies of nature were spoken of. All mighty wars are preceded by such things. Pisaurum, a colony which my lord had established on the Adriatic, suffered an earthquake. Word had it that the whole town and all its inhabitants were swallowed up. Then my lord's statue in Alba began to stream with sweat. However often it was wiped dry, the sweat returned. It will be observed that both these occurrences took place in territory controlled by Octavian.

On the other hand it is true that at Patraea, in my lord's presence, the temple of his ancestor Herakles was struck by lightning. I attach less credence to another report that the statue of Dionysos, the god to whom my lord had so often and with good reason been compared, suffered an even more remarkable fate. This statue at Athens was swept up by a whirlwind and transported from the Gigantomachia into the theatre. The same wind cast other statues, familiarly known as the Antonii, to the ground, while those around them remained erect. These tales, however improbable, found many believers.

I have to confess however that Alexas came to me with another tale to the authenticity of which he was ready to swear.

"It's the most alarming thing, my dear," he said. "You know that galley of the Queen's to which she has given the name *Antonias*. Well, just listen. Some swallows built their nests in the stern, and then others came and put them to flight, and – guess what? – began to eat the young birds. The sailors swear they have never seen anything like it, and they're all in a panic. You know how superstitious sailors

175

are. One of them, a rather gorgeous hunk actually, was absolutely shaking with dread. You must admit it's awfully odd."

"What does the Queen have to say about it?"

"Well, you can imagine! She's livid, abolutely livid. She ordered the boatswain to receive forty lashes, nobody knows exactly what for, except to put her in a better temper."

"It's all too silly for words," I said.

"Yes, of course. But it must mean something, mustn't it? I do get the shivers sometimes. All the same, I suppose we're bound to win, aren't we? From what I've heard I can't imagine Octavian being a match for your general. I mean, I know his type only too well, my dear."

"Yes," I said, "I'm sure you're right."

I would have felt more confident if my lord had been his accustomed self. But it was hard to get him to attend to business. From time to time he roused himself and displayed his characteristic energy. But too many nights were spent in drinking late with Cleopatra and some of her courtiers and his junior officers, and too many mornings lying late in bed. When he did rise, he was crapulous, idle, and seemingly indifferent to the unreadiness of his forces for the war that was almost upon him.

For instance, he had almost five hundred well-armed ships furnished with eight or ten banks of oars. That sounds impressive, but the reality was less so. Few of the ships were fully manned, some indeed had less than half the required complement. So his officers, instead of devoting their days to training, were obliged to scour Greece and seize men from the villages to work the galleys. Few were anything but reluctant, and the quality was low. Some were beggars or vagrants, others muleteers, others decayed peasantry, many mere boys. Ahenobarbus remarked that they looked to him like the scum of the earth.

"The few who have enlisted willingly," he said, "are drunkards in search of free wine."

Even so, it was impossible to man all the ships fully.

The deficiencies of our navy lent weight to the argument which Ahenobarbus, Sosius and Scribonius Curio all urged on him: not to chance a naval battle, but to withdraw from his base at Patraea on the Gulf of Corinth into mainland Greece or even Macedonia, and so compel Octavian to march against him over difficult terrain where supplies were scarce. In this way, they said, you will exhaust him before battle is joined. Moreover, since we are already standing on the defensive, let us take all the advantages which a defensive war offers, and fight where we are most sure of victory. I have no doubt that if my lord's judgement had not been clouded, if he had been indeed his own absolute master as in all his wars, he would have adopted this plan, would indeed have formed it himself, even without the advice of so many of his senior commanders.

But he was not by himself, nor was he indeed fully himself. When Cleopatra heard the advice that was mooted, she came at once to Antony and asked if he intended to desert her, and abandon Egypt to its fate.

"You must have it your own way," she said, "fight your war as you think fit. Though I am a descendant of the great Ptolemy, the bravest and most admired of Alexander's marshals, I lay no claim to military genius. I am only a poor weak woman who has risked all for love of you. If you withdraw into Greece, you leave the sea to Octavian. You surrender Egypt to him, for there is then nothing that can save my poor kingdom from his wrath. I shall be a queen in name only, deprived of land, wealth and honour. But you must do as you think best. You are the general, I am only a woman who loves you. However, even I can see that by surrendering the sea you deprive yourself of my Egyptian corn-ships on which, as I have understood it – forgive me if I am wrong – you have been relying to feed your army."

This last argument was potent, but had only half the cogency of her eyes brimming with tears, her trembling lips, her artful pallor. When she threw herself at his feet, and, clutching his ankles, begged him not to desert her, or abandon her to the insults of Octavian – for she could not, she said, follow him to Macedonia, since duty would draw her back to defenceless Egypt – what could the poor man do? What could anyone in his position have done?

I suppose exactly what he did, which was to raise her up tenderly, kiss her tears away, trace a smile from her lips, and tell her not to be a goose . . .

"Could I desert my cat?" he said. "How could you ever imagine me capable of such cruelty?"

Truly, women do not need logic, while they can shed tears.

XXVI

I am not, you understand, deeply versed in the study of war. Though I have perforce lived a great part of my life in and around camps, I have never borne weapons. My temperament is not the warrior's. I delight in art and artefacts; things of beauty seem to me more admirable than feats of slaughter. I am not even one of those queens who lust after the embraces of the rude soldiery. I prefer the delicate, the pretty, the frankly effeminate; and to tell truth am more at ease in the company of giggling girls than boisterous men-of-war. For this reason, though I feared Cleopatra, I yet, unlike so many of my lord's household, relished the atmosphere of her court. Yet now I find myself a chronicler of war. It is rather ridiculous.

I have already rehearsed the arguments for and against an Italian campaign. I might add only that my lord had opposed this for one other reason, apart from his disinclination to carry war again into the peninsula: this was that a landing on the Adriatic coast was fraught with danger, on account of the paucity of natural harbours. But those who favoured the Italian plan believed that this difficulty could be overcome. However it remained a sound strategic reason, as even they were forced to admit.

In any case it was too late to think of that. The opportunity had been let slip. We were compelled to stand our ground in Greece and await Octavian's attack.

In the spring my lord transferred from his winter quarters on the Gulf of Corinth, and established himself at Actium, on the south shore of the Gulf of Ambracia. Even Ahenobarbus, though he still regretted the form the war was taking, admitted that this was a

magnificent and admirably chosen anchorage. Since it was essential
to keep the supply lines to Egypt open, ships and men were stationed
from Corcyra in the north to Methone, the most southerly point of
the Peloponnese, which controlled the sea-routes to Egypt. For greater
security garrisons were also established in Crete. Meanwhile the bulk
of the land army, some nineteen legions, fifteen thousand auxiliaries
from Asia and twelve thousand cavalry, many being veterans of the
Parthian and Armenian wars, had their camp on the southern shore
of the isthmus that opens into the gulf. My lord assured everyone that
our position was impregnable, and, "as we know, the boy Octavian
is no general". This was true, yet, as Ahenobarbus reminded him,
Marcus Agrippa's grasp of strategy and tactics was not to be despised.
Ahenobarbus was worried too by the quality of some of our legions.
He repeatedly drew attention to the consequences he feared from
Antony's inability for several years to recruit in Italy.

My lord laughed at this:

"Don't be so narrow-minded," he said. "The highlands of Illyria
and Asia breed stout hearts and strong bodies. In any case many of
our troops are the children of Caesar's soldiers established in frontier
colonies. They will fight bravely, believe me."

"Good enough to die anyway, I suppose," Ahenobarbus muttered,
unconvinced.

The advice which Cleopatra gave was inconstant, contradictory.
Now she urged my lord to strike against Octavian with all his forces;
now she begged him to stand on the defensive, that, above all, he
might protect Egypt.

"As long as Egypt is inviolate," she said, "we shall win in the end.
The wealth of my kingdom is yours to provide the sinews of war."

Alexas told me that in private she was equally changeable.

"She is brave as a lion," he said, "yet terrified. The truth is that,
for all her talk about her great ancestor, Alexander's marshal, she is
aware of her ignorance of war, and, like all women, expects defeat.
Moreover the contempt which she publicly expresses for Octavian
conceals a secret fear. She really has come to believe that he is indeed
Caesar's heir, and, though she seduced Caesar, as you know, she was
always afraid of his cruel and incalculable nature."

"Does she really love my lord?"

"She loves only Cleopatra," he said.

My lord's moods were likewise shifting, his judgement tossed on every wind that blew. There were days when he seemed his old self, his true self, as he moved among the soldiers with a cheerful word of encouragement or commendation here, a light and ribald jest there. On such mornings he walked with the magnificent assurance of the god men had hailed him as. The sun glinted on his golden head, and he wore his battle-stained armour with his old accustomed swagger. Wherever he passed, the soldiers cheered and were encouraged by the magnificence of his presence. He was often accompanied by his eldest son, Antyllus, now a youth of thirteen; a boy of astonishing beauty and charm of manner, with a remarkable likeness to his father when young, and no resemblance in character, I am glad to say, to his mother Fulvia. The troops delighted to see him, and took confidence from his presence in the camp. Antony, they said, would never have kept the boy whom he adored with him if he had not been certain of victory. When my lord presented the boy to the troops he let it be understood that this was his true heir. Even Cleopatra, though jealous of all that connected Antony to Rome and so seemed to exclude her, could not but confess the merits of the lad and take pleasure in his company; this, although his frank and open demeanour served to emphasise the deficiencies of her son Caesarion who, perhaps on account of his disputed paternity, which weighed heavily on his mind, was both furtive and deceitful in manner, timid in the presence of the troops, and easily cast down by his fears of the future. All this I had from Alexas who knew the boy well and pitied him, though adding that he was "a mean and dismal little bitch".

Our position did not improve. Indeed for it to have done so would have required some gross mistake on the part of the enemy, or some disaster to have overtaken Octavian's fleet. As it was, it could not improve because my lord, trapped in immobility and held in the vice of an indecision foreign to his nature, could not bring himself to take any positive step. This alarmed me. I had never known him incapable of decision, and nor had any of his generals.

In the spring the war began to turn against us. Agrippa seized the port of Methone, in the extreme south of the Peloponnesus, and so lay athwart the supply-line to Egypt. Then Octavian nerved himself to carry his army across the Adriatic and land in Epirus. He marched south with an unaccustomed celerity, perhaps in the hope of catching my lord unprepared. We were indeed unprepared, but, receiving news of the strength of our army, and conscious that Antony himself was in command, Octavian's brief splutter of courage expired, and he declined the battle which he had seemed to invite. Instead he established a camp on the high ground to the north of the Gulf of Ambracia, dominating the road that led to northern Greece.

Worse followed. Agrippa, who possessed the strategic intelligence which controlled the campaign, for he had, as my lord acknowledged, as keen a sense of the business of war as Octavian's was blunt, seized the island of Leucas, and then Corcyra, Patraea, and Corinth, so that he contrived to cut our communications with Egypt. The strategy which the Queen had forced on Antony, either by her reasoned argument or by her charms, was thus stifled. It became necessary to send troops into Boeotia to forage for the supplies which we had imagined were secured by the connection with Egypt.

Ahenobarbus raged at my lord. We were, he said, caught in a trap as a result of the general's lethargy and subjection to that woman. Alas, there was much truth in what he said. An attempt to lure Octavian to battle failed. So did two sallies intended to cut off his water supply. We found ourselves besieged, in an inhospitable spot, as summer brought fever on. The foul water on which we were compelled to rely caused many of the soldiers to suffer from dysentery. Malaria was rife. Every day saw burial parties at work. Cleopatra did not dare to show herself to the Roman troops, who blamed her for their wretched condition.

Still my lord walked boldly among the men and despite his private anxieties displayed a cheerful countenance. This encouraged many to endure their suffering without complaint. But I knew his private distresses. I saw how he winced at the approach of Cleopatra whom he at last recognised as the prime cause of his predicament. Ahenobarbus, who had long refused to speak to the Queen, or even to name her by her title, now besought Antony to abandon her to his enemies and to make the best peace he could.

"For," he said, "there is still no question but that Octavian's legions will refuse to face you in battle. They know what victories you have won. Many of them have served under you. They admire you and distrust their own general. So, since he has proclaimed this war is against that woman, the only way to escape this mess she has landed us in is to hand her over to Octavian, and then negotiate.

In this way you will, I am certain, safeguard your own position and rescue our army from this trap which otherwise looks certain to end in disaster."

"If I did not recognise the courage which alone has made it possible for you to speak to me in this manner," my lord replied, "and if I did not understand that it is your friendship which alone permits you to speak so bluntly and with so little regard for my feelings, I would be angry. You say this war is against the Queen. You are mistaken, my friend. She is the mere pretext. I am the cause. It is bitter for me to accept that the boy Octavian, for whom I have ever entertained warm and even tender feelings, should so treacherously have determined on my destruction, but I can no longer hide from that painful truth. If I followed your advice and surrendered the Queen to our enemy, I should lose my honour but save neither my life nor our army. Octavian who still views me with a fearful respect would conclude that Antony is no longer Antony, and would despise me. No, Ahenobarbus, I have tied myself to the stake, and bear-like must fight my battle to the end. But I will not yield to despair. I have enough experience of the shifting fortunes of war to know that no battle is lost till the field is strewn with the bodies of the slain. Antony is Antony still, and my will remains indomitable."

Ahenobarbus sighed and turned away. From that moment hope withered in his heart. When Antony called on him not to despair but to crack another bottle and talk over old times – "for in our present misfortunes that is one pleasure that is left to us" – he sighed, and, sighing, consented. But I observed that during the drinking that went on late into the night, he grew ever more sombre, his face darkened, and he fell into a melancholy silence.

Soon afterwards we received more bad news. My lord, perhaps because he felt he had dismissed Ahenobarbus' plea for peace too abruptly, dispatched two envoys, M. Junius Silanus and Q. Dellius, to Octavian, to enquire whether a meeting between the two generals might provide grounds for a negotiated settlement. That was the sum of their mission. I say that clearly because there have been rumours since that my lord actually proposed to follow Ahenobarbus' line exactly. Though he might have been wise to do so, for the arguments were good, if shameful, this was not the case. It was rather that this evidence of the sad condition of the morale of so many of his friends

– for he could not doubt that Ahenobarbus spoke for many and not only for himself – prompted him to hope that a means might yet be found to avert more open war. That was all. I can say this with confidence, since I myself drafted the instruction Silanus and Dellius carried with them.

In vain. No sooner had they arrived in Octavian's camp than they deserted. One of their staff who bravely demanded the right to return to Antony reported that Dellius was last seen gobbling a dish of pork and beans and calling out to Octavian that there was no such food to be had where he had come from. And it was no doubt in the expectation that such a report would have a still more lowering effect on the morale of my lord's troops that Octavian acted with such apparent generosity, otherwise quite uncharacteristic of his mean and cruel nature, in allowing this envoy, whose name I unfortunately forget, to return to the camp.

Two days later my lord attempted to break what had now become a blockade. He ordered one of the allies, Amyntas, King of Galatia, a man who owed not only his position but also his life, to my lord's clemency, to force Octavian's lines at the head of two thousand cavalry. This had become urgent, for my lord could not doubt that the traitor Dellius had revealed all he knew of our plans and projects, and, worse, would have exposed the nakedness of our position. But Amyntas in turn played false, and led his men straight into Octavian's camp having negotiated his surrender to the outposts. No doubt he hoped, thus ignobly, to keep his crown. Octavian, he rightly assumed, was not the man to be disgusted by treachery.

It is a rule of politics, that parties are destroyed by internal dissension and desertions. Unity of purpose cannot be maintained where there is uncertainty, rivalry, infirmity of will, disaffection. Then one sees the discontented and faint-hearted slip away. Even the best lose conviction, while the passion and intensity that may yet fill the worst are directed against their fellows more fiercely than against the nominal enemy. And if this is true of a political faction, how much more so is it true of an army. Though I am no soldier, I have seen and read and heard enough of war to know this: victory or defeat is primarily determined by morale. It is hard to ask any man, even an iron-hearted, dim-witted foot-soldier to die for any cause; it is doubly hard when he feels the cause is lost, despaired of by his chiefs, and when he sees treachery spring like noxious weeds on every side.

I was playing *micatio* with young Antyllus. It was not yet dawn. He had woken me from my sleep because, he said, he had been suffering a nightmare.

"There was blood everywhere," he said, "a river of blood and it was flowing towards me. A cock without a head was carried past me, and I felt myself pressed down so that my head was under the flow of blood and the cock's head thrust into my mouth was choking me. Then I woke. Look, I'm covered in sweat still. What does it mean, Critias?"

I could not tell him. The clear implication of his dream was something better disguised from his waking self. So I rose from my couch, and put my arm round him, merely to still his trembling, and sought a means to divert him. The game *micatio* is of course simple, but it serves as an agreeable distraction, and distraction was what the boy needed. So we thrust out our fingers and shouted the total number displayed, and in a little the rose-colour returned to his downy cheeks. In a little he had also won a tiresomely large quantity of my money. Not that that was very important. The coinage we were issuing to pay the troops, with my lord robed as consul and Cleopatra depicted as a goddess, was thoroughly debased, adulterated with mean metal.

"Why is Octavian resolved to destroy my father?" Antyllus asked.

"Because," I said, "he feels his inferiority. My lord your father diminishes him."

"It seems an inadequate reason," he replied.

"Perhaps so. If you live long enough you will come to know the essential meanness of men."

"Is my father mean?"

"No," I said; and did not add, "only weak and foolish in his dotage."

We were interrupted by a banging at the door. A look of anxiety again crossed the boy's face. He smoothed his tunic over quivering thighs and I rose to admit whoever was knocking. It was a centurion whom I recognised; a veteran of the Parthian campaign in which he had been decorated for bravery. He looked at me with dislike, and demanded the general.

"He is still asleep," I said. "It's not yet dawn. Can I take a message?"

"No," he said, "you'd better rouse him. It's urgent."

This was how the word was brought that Ahenobarbus had followed Silanus and Dellius and deserted to the enemy.

It seemed that he had slipped away, in a small boat, under cover of the moonless night, taking with him only two of his personal staff.

My lord rubbed sleep from his eyes, bestowed a rough kiss on Antyllus' gleaming locks, belched, and said, "Sad news. No need to wake me. Would have kept."

The centurion asked if he wished a pursuit to be ordered. "He may not have got far," he said, "it's a very small boat."

"Pursuit? By no means." He gazed out beyond the camp to the sea, still grey but touched with streaks of pink. "Maybe he has a mistress in Octavian's camp, and is fled to join her. Critias, give this centurion money. Antyllus, I am sorry, boy, that you see me as I am, authority melting from me . . ."

(Sweat from his statue, I thought.)

"It's not so long," he said, speaking half to the boy, half or more than half to himself, "since kings leapt to do my bidding, eager as boys called to a rat-hunt. And now? Well, poor Ahenobarbus, I'm not the first he has deserted. But I am Antony still. Critias, arrange for my council to meet at noon."

"Would you have me summon the Queen also, my lord?"

"She'll need no summons."

I suppose historians will call that day's council fateful. For me, acting as its secretary, it was pitiful, cruel, and chaotic; impossible, as I discovered later, to prepare a coherent minute. People spoke at once, interrupting each other, in no sort of order. My lord lounged at the end of the table, his back turned to the camp and the sea, the wine flask at his right hand. His face was already flushed and his voice thickening. In the Queen's face I read a horrid satisfaction: Antony was truly and completely hers now. There was no means left by which he might evade her. Yet at the same time a dark look crossed her face, and she bit her lip in anxiety. In thus taking possession of my lord, she feared that she had also signed her own death warrant. And yet she would not release her grip.

At last Canidius hammered the table and obtained silence. He said:

"The time for waiting is past. Every day we grow weaker. Every day there are more desertions. Every day the net closes more tightly on us. Every day makes defeat more certain. Therefore we must act now. There are only two courses open to us, if we are not to die in this stinking trap. Either we break the blockade with the fleet – a dangerous venture since our ships are under-manned, and Agrippa has proved himself a skilful admiral. But if we succeed in breaking out, then we can retreat to the sanctuary of Egypt. But I warn you Octavian will follow hard on our heels, and press home his advantage. The respite will be short and the prospects of victory poor. Alternatively we withdraw into Thrace or Macedonia. There we have allies. Dicomes, King of Getae, has promised reinforcements. Octavian will be compelled to follow, and in doing so, will find it hard to maintain contact with the fleet on which he depends for supplies. In time we shall bring him to bay on ground of our own choosing. It is no disgrace to abandon the sea to Octavian, whose ships, under Agrippa, have proved their worth in Sicilian waters, but it would be shameful to surrender the advantage which so great a general as yourself, in command of veteran troops, may yet hope to wrest from the enemy. It would be folly to entrust the legions to the dubious waves. Therefore I am for war by land."

Canidius might have carried the day had my lord been sober and in full possession of his mind and resolution. But if he had listened it appeared he did not grasp what was being said. From time to time a low groan escaped him, and twice he muttered Ahenobarbus' name. On each occasion he followed it with a deep draught of wine, and shuddered as he returned the cup to the table.

Seeing this, I passed a note to Scribonius Curio, whom I knew to be still devoted to my lord, and who was indeed observing him with a look of profound pity; I suggested that he should call for an adjournment of the debate to the next day, for whatever reason he could devise. But before he could speak, Cleopatra herself struck up.

"Aye," she said, "follow this advice, this Roman advice. Romans desert you daily, while Egypt holds true. But follow this Roman advice, desert Egypt, hand me over indeed to Caesar's mercy, for I perceive that in your Roman eyes I am sole cause of your misfortunes.

Flee to Macedonia and leave Egypt to . . . to what? The boy Octavian with his adder's eyes? I have risked all for you, shared all I have with you, reposed my trust in you. But now you must do as you think fit."

Saying this, she covered her face with the wide sleeve of her dress, and, with an anguished howl, fled the chamber, leaving all the generals and staff embarrassed. My lord drank wine and closed his eyes.

That evening, or perhaps the next, he called me to him in order to dictate letters. I found him on a couch being massaged by a Nubian. The black fingers worked the oil into his flesh, and as he pressed and kneaded the bloated body old wounds revealed their scars. I waited till at last he gestured to the Nubian and rose from the couch, fleshy but still magnificent, and held out his arms for a slave to slip a dressing-gown over him. Then he dismissed the slaves, poured two mugs of wine, and handed me one.

"There are no letters," he said. "There is no business."

"How can that be, my lord?"

"None anyhow that I care to do. Why are you still here, Critias?"

"Where else should I be, my lord?"

"Where others have run to. Here is gold. Take it, and make your peace with Octavian."

"He has no interest in such as I; nor I in him. You mistake me, my lord. I am Critias, raised in your household, devoted to your service. I am no Roman nobleman."

"Do you say so? Then honour has strange bedfellows."

He drank his wine off at one gulp, and seizing the flask, replenished his cup.

"There are few," he said, "to whom I can speak openly. Curio perhaps. Few others. If I die in the battle that must be fought, take charge of Antyllus. Carry him, if you can, to Octavia. She'll care for him. If that's impossible, then, seek some distant refuge for him. Somewhere in Greece perhaps. You're not a man for the mountain caves, I think, but where you think fit."

"I'll do what I can, my lord; but I have heard you say often that no battle is lost till the field is abandoned, and that strange things can happen in war."

"Strange things have happened," he said; and the weariness in his voice was that of a man who has travelled long miles in waste places. "Six months ago I commanded an army as fine as any I have ever led. Today I walk through the camp and men avert their gaze, muttering ceases when they catch sight of me, and some turn their backs. One soldier this afternoon addressed me boldly: 'Don't fight by sea,' he said, 'don't put your trust in rotten planks. Leave that to the Egyptians and Phoenicians, let them play ducks and drakes if they choose. But this sword of mine has served you in thirty battles, these feet have marched with you from the sands of Media through the icy mountains of Armenia. These wounds,' he said, displaying them, 'I got in your service. Let us fight by land, foot to foot, and we'll still show them what manner of men we are.'"

"That was a brave and noble speech," I said, "a heartening one."

"Heartening? Aye, if his fellows had cheered him. But not one cried out, 'Well spoken, Publius'. Instead they turned their heads, or lowered them, and dared not meet my eye. Canidius is right. We should withdraw to Macedonia and meet Caesar there."

I had never before heard him call Octavian by the name he has usurped. I did not like to hear him use it then.

"But we cannot do so. The army will not march. After today I know it will not fight or stand its ground or anything, but run away, desert, disintegrate. It is no longer an army, you see, merely a collection of men. And so there is no choice. It must be the Queen's way. Men will say I'm being led by her, won't they, Critias?"

"I fear so, my lord."

"It is not so. It is necessity that has me by the nose and drags me on. Six months ago . . . do you ever get drunk, Critias? I've never seen you drunk, careful Critias. Well, I've no choice. I welcome wine's sweet oblivion. You'll care for Antyllus as I asked. How strange that now I find I have only such as you to trust . . ."

A desperate compliment, not untinged with contempt, and yet I treasured it, treasure it still.

Then he said: "One other thing. Find Curio – I can still trust him, I think – and tell him to see that Ahenobarbus' goods and treasures are sent after him to Octavian's camp. If he crossed over in a little boat, he must have left much he values behind."

XXVII

Cleopatra won the day, whether by her arguments in council or by means of other persuasion privately. As Alexas remarked to me, "None of the generals who were for the Macedonian option found themselves in bed with Antony."

So we took to the ships, leaving Canidius in charge of the land army. For three days the seas were too high to permit an engagement. (I was dreadfully sea-sick myself.) Then the wind softened and fell away. For another day however there was no movement. It was as if, on the edge of decision, neither commander dared to loose the hazards of war.

On the fifth morning, before dawn touched the sea with rosy fingers, my lord had himself rowed in a little boat from ship to ship. Boarding each, he encouraged the men, ordering them on account of the weight and strength of their ships, to hold their ground and fight as firmly as if they were on land. Later some would remark that he lacked that cheerfulness which the prospect of battle usually awoke in him. His expression was grim; his sentences short, even abrupt. Yet he was encouraged by the resolution of sailors and soldiers and by the confidence which his visits so obviously inspired.

It was his plan that the pilots should stand as firm as if they were at anchor, and await the attacks of Octavian's lighter ships. And he judged that this was wise because between the two fleets was a narrow strait where the current ran fiercely.

But it so happened that towards noon a breeze blew up, and the sea running fast, our ships were involuntarily drawn towards the enemy. But, because no command had been given, the attack was half-hearted. Soon, in the open sea, our ships were surrounded by Agrippa's lighter vessels, which were more easily manoeuvred. Yet they did not dare come to close quarters on account of the weight of our ships and the ramming-power of their great beaks. Accordingly the contest bore more resemblance, as I thought, to the siege of a town than to what I had expected a battle at sea to be like. The enemy assailed us with light spears or javelins and fire-brands, while our men, having the advantage of a higher station on account of the greater depth of our ships which, in the context of this strange battle, made them resemble the tall towers of a besieged town, replied in like manner, also hurling bolts from catapults upon the foe.

All was confusion, and I confess that my own fear was such that I covered my head with my cloak and could not for some time look on what was happening. But when I discovered that things continued in this manner and I had received no wound, I grew ashamed of myself, and, looking again at the confusion around me, began to feel as if I was the spectator of some strange and gripping drama in the theatre.

Nobody, as I have heard my lord say often, really knows what is happening in a battle, except for what is immediately around him. He cannot see its shape, and it is for this reason that many a battle has been unnecessarily lost, or alternatively won against the odds. For what is immediate may encourage or terrify and so set in motion an insensible process which encourages some to advance, others to flee; and thus in this inconsidered manner changes the developing shape of which however the agents of such a change have been perfectly unaware.

All was certainly uncertain, pell-mell, confused, and no advantage positively gained by either side, when, all of a sudden, a great yell of fury, dismay, or terror broke out from the soldiers on the deck of our ship. Following their gaze, I saw to my amazed horror the Egyptian ships, Cleopatra's flagship in the van, hoist their sails and proceed with such speed as they could muster, which was considerable, for the wind was now with them and full in their sails while their rowers also worked their utmost, away from the battle in headlong flight.

And the reason for this has never been explained. In my opinion, it was not treachery, as some averred even then – for cries of betrayal were loud and furious – but a blind panic which had taken possession of the Queen.

When he saw her flee, my lord, who till that moment had shown all his old vigour in organising the battle which was by no means lost, gave the order to tack about, and followed by some forty ships of the right wing, set off in pursuit of the Queen.

For myself, I was baffled. It had seemed to me, in my ignorance of these matters, that we had been holding our place, and that, if Cleopatra had launched her ships at the enemy instead of heading in the opposite direction, the engagement would have terminated successfully, and the day been ours.

As it was her flight made that impossible, and ours inevitable.

Later it was put about that it had always been the strategical plan to attempt a break-out; and so the battle was not to be deemed a defeat, but even a victory, since it had achieved that end.

But I know from the expression of my lord's face as he sat in the prow of our vessel, and he gazed on Cleopatra's sails flying before him, that this explanation is false.

It is true all might have ended that day if we had held our ground and fought the battle to the end and yet been defeated, while as it was my lord could claim to have saved the Queen and her treasure, a hundred of our ships and more than twenty thousand of our veterans who had fought on board. Yet we had lost at least twenty ships and five thousand men; and had been driven from the position in which we might still hope to win the war.

Towards evening we caught up with the Queen's flagship. A little boat was lowered and my lord and his staff and intimate members of his household were ferried to Cleopatra's vessel.

He went straight to her cabin, and remained there till it was near dark. What transpired between them is not known certainly to anybody. Cleopatra gave her version, which was in time relayed to me by Alexas; but it was so frankly incredible that I see no purpose in repeating it.

What is unquestionable is that when my lord returned to the deck, he sat in the bow of the vessel, having wrapped himself in his cloak, and remained there, silent, refusing to speak to anyone throughout a wakeful night. He refused wine, and his face was as blank as marble. Some say he wept, but I saw no tears, and believe he was beyond them.

Moreover, for three days till we reached the port of Taenarum, on the southernmost tip of the Peloponnesus, he refused to see

Cleopatra, who remained sulking or terrified in her cabin, and also declined all food and drink. For most of the time he sat unmoving, and what his thoughts were during these days and nights I do not care to think. Certainly they were such as none would wish to have.

At Taenarum however he roused himself, perhaps because he could no longer hide himself in the limbo of the sea voyage in the course of which neither action nor decision was possible. Dry land forced him to contemplate reality again. While we waited there for any stragglers from the battle to join us, he abandoned his brooding on the disaster which had engulfed him, and was, for a moment, himself again.

But the news soon brought to him was of fresh catastrophe. Canidius had been left in command of the land army with orders, when the sea battle was determined, to retreat into Macedonia, thence, if it seemed right, to Asia and Syria. But the soldiers, when they saw the sea battle lost, and understood that they had been abandoned, as they saw it, by Antony, refused to obey his commands. They were certain that Octavian would receive their surrender eagerly, for they judged that he had no stomach for a battle, and they guessed that to avoid its dangers, he would reward them with generous donations, and only their officers would be put to death. So they felt no scruple in indicating their intention to surrender; and things fell out, I believe, as they had hoped. Canidius and a few of his senior officers, knowing the temper of their troops, slipped away by night, and made their way south to inform my lord of these events.

Whereupon, with his old accustomed generosity, he released all who wished it from their oath of loyalty, gave them such treasure as might secure their future, and a passage to Corinth where they might either negotiate the terms of their surrender to Octavian or flee, if they preferred, to remote and barbarian lands.

And never, it may be said, has a defeated general behaved with such magnanimity to his followers. In nothing did he more truly prove his greatness of soul.

XXVIII

When we arrived in Egypt my lord refused to accompany Cleopatra to the royal palace, and instead established himself in a house beyond the Pharos. He told the Queen that he must seclude himself in order to be able to devote all his energies to organising the resurrection of their fortunes. "If I am in your company," he said, "I cannot hope that your charms will not distract me from this necessary task."

Of course this was not the true reason for his withdrawal; nor did Cleopatra believe it. Alexas with whom I kept in constant touch – for among other things his own terror and depression were now such that only in my company and bed could he experience any pleasure – told me that the Queen was thrown into agonies of self-pity and fearful suspicion by my lord's conduct. She was certain that he plotted a means of saving himself at her expense, for she could not forget that Octavian had summoned the whole of Italy to war against her, not Antony. Of course I did what I could to allay this distrust. While I had no warm feelings for Cleopatra and recognised her as my lord's evil genius, I yet saw that they must now stand together. Moreover, I feared that in her suspicion of my lord, she would herself make overtures to Octavian, offering to surrender her lover to save her kingdom. And Alexas could not conceal from me that this was indeed the case.

Then I said: "My dear, I know Octavian. I have studied him for years. And I can tell you one thing for certain: he will promise whatever things will serve him, and break that promise as easily as you might snap a twig between your fingers. Tell the Queen, in whatever manner you find possible, that if she betrays my lord thinking thus to save her life and her kingdom, she merely hastens on her own defeat."

"I can tell her nothing," he said. "She will not hear what displeases her."

"That's why we are in the mess we are."

A few days later we were ensconced in the house which my lord began to call his Timonium, naming it after that sceptic and misanthrope, Timon of Athens, for (he said) "experience has taught me that he was wise in his contempt for mankind". Canidius arrived, to report occasion for further grief.

The army, left in our camp when we took to the ships, had at first refused to believe that my lord was in no position to return to lead them. They expressed an intense desire to see him, and refused for several days to listen to the overtures of Octavian's legionaries who insisted that they had been deserted. However, when he did not appear, they began to question their position, and soon fell into despair. Indeed they were so wretched and so bereft of confidence (Canidius said) that when he, in accordance with the plan agreed with Antony, gave orders that they should prepare to retreat into Macedonia, they flatly refused to obey. What started as passive mutiny soon turned violent, and Canidius understood that his own life was in danger. So he fled the camp under cover of night, and with great difficulty made his way to Alexandria.

For my part I could not think that Canidius had behaved well or in a manner fitting his high reputation as a general. But my lord was too great-hearted to reproach him. Instead he drew Canidius to him, and kissed his grizzled cheeks.

When Canidius, who was exhausted, begged leave to retire to rest, and permission was granted, my lord turned to me and said:

"Why do you look so amazed, Critias? What would you have had me do? Upbraid him or punish him for the misfortune of having acted in the same manner as I myself. I think myself happy to have so noble a companion in dishonour."

It was soon after this that he began dictating to me the narrative which I have here presented, and which circumstances compel me to bring myself to its unhappy conclusion.

For much of the day, for several weeks, he found himself incapable of action. He would dictate a little, sometimes this narrative, sometimes urgent and anguished letters to those who might still, he hoped, be of some help to him. But this hope was weak, though the language of the letters was often strong, at least in the form in which I eventually cast them. Yet even as I wrote, I knew the appeals were futile. Authority had fled from Antony, and even men of virtue – or of self-proclaimed virtue, or commonly reported virtue – found no reason to respond to his pleas. And many of those to whom these appeals were directed were men of power incapable of pursuing any course except that which they judged to be in their own interest. My lord was the setting sun, and they turned their gaze to the rising Phoebus that was Octavian. Such news as we received was bad. Our party had disintegrated. One example may stand for many. Herod of Judaea was one who owed everything to my lord's favour, without which he would have been no more significant than a cockroach. If any of the kings and princes of the East was indebted to my lord, it was Herod. Yet no sooner had he heard of the disaster of Actium than he prepared to carry his legions over to Octavian.

My lord merely dismissed the news with a weary sweep of his hand.

"Herod?" he said. "Romans have deserted me, and should a Jew be loyal?"

Cleopatra however, who understood the baseness of Herod's nature better than my lord, believed that he was not yet utterly lost to their cause. She therefore determined to send an embassy to him, bearing treasure, with promise of still greater riches to follow, if he would stand by the man who had made him, and form an alliance with Egypt. When I learned that she had selected my dear Alexas, on account of his charm of person and Herod's notorious depravity, to lead this embassy, I begged him with tears in my eyes to find some means of declining so hopeless and dangerous a task. But of course there was nothing he could do but obey the Queen who would certainly have had him put to death if he had defied her. So he set off, and all turned out as I had feared. Herod received him with kind words, accepted the treasure, gloated over it, then, yielding to his lust, raped Alexas, and had him thrown into chains and carried to Octavian as evidence of Herod's commitment to his cause. I never saw my dear friend again, and believe that he was put cruelly to death.

My lord meanwhile, ignorant of Cleopatra's attempt to draw Herod back to their side – for I saw no reason to lull him with false hopes by reporting what Alexas had imparted to me – sank ever deeper into despair. For days his only solace was to be found in wine. I could not blame him, though I did not share his taste. For years he had had recourse to wine in order to heighten his appreciation of the moment; it was cause for exuberance. Now he drank to dull his awareness, and sought sweet oblivion. Most days he found that by the early evening, but would then wake in the night, compelled to creep open-eyed through the wasteland hours before dawn. Sometimes he would call out to me then, seeking reassurance or whatever words of comfort I could drag from a mind that knew there was no comfort.

Generally, towards noon, when he had sunk no more than a pint of thick red Cyprus stuff, he would gaze out to sea and assemble fleets and armies in his imagination. This was the hour of fevered hope. Legions were summoned from distant provinces, alliances re-formed, urgent letters dispatched to generals who were no longer in posts of command where they might receive them. For a little hope revived, and with it determination. Several times he called for his armour, and allowed himself to be dressed in the manner of the imperator which, briefly, he still believed himself to be. Then he would draft orders summoning a council or make plans to visit Cleopatra and set resistance to Octavian in train. "Egypt," he would say, "is a mighty stronghold, from which we shall not be easily dislodged. When the boy Octavian understands the strength of our defences, he will be ready to negotiate. You know, Critias, how when we meet together Octavian and I always find points of agreement, as the love we bear each other blossoms anew."

I found these spurts of hope, in which there was no reason but only self-deception, painful beyond endurance. Yet what could I do but feed his fantasies? I was certain no action could save him, and yet any action seemed preferable to the lassitude into which he would soon relapse.

But as Phoebus Apollo's chariot fell away from the zenith, defiance departed from him, and he gave way to self-pity. Enough of nobility was left to him to spare Cleopatra in his reproaches. Though in his heart he knew that she had been his destroyer, and that, whatever he felt for her, itself a shifting and uncertain love or lust, was the prime cause of his ruin, he disdained to confess this, or bewail the passion that had made him less than Antony. And indeed, on the rare occasions when he spoke of the Queen, he still clung to the pretence which had informed his conversation and correspondence with Octavian, that his alliance with Cleopatra was founded in his understanding of political realities. Thus he remained able, even in his grief and self-abasement, to pretend that he was a rational being in control, under the gods, of his own destiny. And I suppose this was of some comfort to him; how rare it is for men to be able to acknowledge the vices that have destroyed them!

Much of his talk in twilight hours was devoted to Octavian; and it was what he saw as the young man's treachery that so deeply perplexed him.

"I never gave him cause to fear me," he said again and again. "I never broke my word to him, reneged on any agreement that we made. I ever treated him as my colleague, equal in authority and power, and I believed that together we were working to sustain Rome's Empire without limits. Why then, why then, has he turned against me?"

And then the tears would flow as he compared the glory that had fled with his present state, and his gaze remained fixed on the pitiless waste of ocean till darkness descended.

In these days I spent many hours also with young Antyllus, whom I tried to shield from his father's dereliction. But the boy was too intelligent to be deceived. He understood that his own life was in danger. More than once he expressed regret that he had not been left in Rome, in Octavia's household, for he knew that he could have trusted her to protect him. He also spoke bitterly of his father's desertion of Octavia, for he understood well that it was his rejection of her in favour of the Queen that had precipitated disaster. I tried to persuade him that, no matter what course my lord had followed, Octavian was determined to destroy him. But all he said in reply was that Octavia would never have permitted her brother to move against her husband if he had proved loyal to her. And I could not argue fiercely for I suspected that the boy might be wise in his judgement.

Nevertheless Antyllus loved my lord and was eager to do anything that might be in his power to aid him in his perplexity.

XXIX

At last my lord roused himself.

"If all is lost, he said, "let us yet act as if much may be regained. Antony is himself again."

Indeed the transformation was remarkable. One day there was this quivering hulk, corrupted by self-pity, fat, grey-haired, his face tear-streaked, his eyes bloodshot. The next he went to the baths and returned refreshed, his bearing erect, and decision in his voice and eye.

"Critias," he said, "you have been patient with my moping. Now I shall present you with a glorious finale to the memoirs you have been inditing. Or, if the gods favour us once again, I shall see that you have new and more splendid chapters still to write."

Saying this, he decked himself in purple, and called for his chariot that he might be carried to Cleopatra and the court. For he had resolved, as it seemed to me, that he would in his last days give the world cause to remember him as he had been in his glorious prime rather than as one broken by treachery and defeat. He would, whatever befell, leave a name at which the world should wonder, so that posterity might say "this was indeed a man".

And though this bravado touched me more painfully than his previous gloom, for I well understood the demands it made on his weary spirit, I yet greeted his renewal with a smile and in a manner intended to suggest that I still reposed confidence in his genius, and in the star that guided him.

Nevertheless I trust that none will take it amiss, or think the worse of me, if I confess that from this day on, I made plans which would enable me to escape Egypt when all was done, and to carry with me these records of my lord's career, and such treasure as was rightly mine or as I could with safety lay hands upon.

Word was sent to the Queen to expect my lord, and when he entered the palace he found her sitting on the royal throne in the great gallery that, on one side, opens upon the sea. With that grace of manner which she could assume so royally, she rose to greet him. They embraced in the sight of all, shed a few tears, made pretty speeches and then retired to her chamber.

When they emerged, my lord announced that henceforth their old society of the "Inimitable Livers" should be renamed the "Companions in Glorious Death"; for, he said, "If we are doomed, let us depart in our native magnificence; and if we are not, why then, we shall cheat death by looking him in the eye, without fear or foreboding."

Then he bestowed on the assembled company a smile such as only the gods may offer; and everyone observed that he had returned to them, returned indeed to life, in the garb of Dionysos.

That night they held a great banquet, and the feasting continued for the next seven days.

When, at the end of that time, some were exhausted, all yet knew a release from the fear in which we had been held since Actium, for Antony had sounded a trumpet of indomitable defiance. It was then that word came that Octavian, having marched his army by way of Syria and Judaea, where Herod fawned at his feet and provided him with ample supplies, had captured the easternmost Egyptian port of Pelusium, which surrendered so easily that there were accusations of treachery. Some suggested that Cleopatra had given orders to the commander of the garrison to yield without a fight, for she still hoped that, abandoning my lord, she could negotiate a separate peace with Octavian.

I cannot say whether this was true, for, since the loss of my dear Alexas, I had no longer a means to discover the secret thinking of the Queen or her advisers.

That Cleopatra had such a hope, I am however certain. However she valued, or had valued my lord, she valued her kingdom and her life more highly. And yet she loved him in her way, as far as she was capable of love. But she loved herself more.

Antony himself, I must say, had openly advised her to abandon him and make such terms as she could with Octavian. That was the measure of his love and his nobility. He even wrote to Octavian offering to retire to Athens and live there as a private citizen, if Octavian would promise to safeguard Egypt for Cleopatra and her children. "In this way you will avoid the uncertain perils of battle," he said, "for you know that when that is joined, the gods alone determine the outcome."

This was rhetoric of course, and I never thought that it had any chance of swaying Octavian. In my opinion he knew well that superiority in men and supplies is what decides battle; and he had no intention of throwing his advantage away. Moreover, innately suspicious, he could not, I'm certain, believe that my lord would ever be content to live as a private citizen – or indeed that others would permit him to do so. By now Octavian was a fighting dog with his teeth locked on his rival's throat.

Nevertheless Octavian, with his accustomed prudence, did not immediately reject my lord's proposals. Instead he sent an ambassador to the Queen; and he did this because, however certain he was of victory, and with reason, he yet in his innermost heart was conscious of his inferiority to Antony, and feared that the chance of battle might expose this, and again turn against him. And nothing testifies more surely to my lord's greatness than his enemy's hesitation at a time when all that had supported that greatness had been torn from Antony; and he stood naked but for his courage and his will against the malignancy of Fate.

So, for a little, Octavian flattered Cleopatra and assured her that she could expect every favour from him, provided she banished Antony from her dominions. At first she believed him and was persuaded that her cause was not lost, though Antony's was. So she replied that she was deeply conscious of Octavian's generosity of soul, and now should be permitted to share the throne of Egypt with her son Caesarion; for, she is reported as having said, "I myself am but a weak woman who has been led astray and I require the support of my son if Egypt is to be governed and prove a worthy ally of the Roman People and their imperator Octavian Caesar."

There are some who say that when my lord learned of what had transpired in these negotiations, he was angry and threatened to have Octavian's ambassador whipped; that he turned in fury on the Queen, and assured her that if she abandoned him, he would kill himself and carry her to the Shades with him.

But this is nonsense, as is proved by the fact that he himself had suggested this course of negotiation to the Queen. Yet, though his reason had led him to urge this policy on her, his heart was wounded by the alacrity with which she followed his advice. It could not but pain him to discover that she was ready to abandon him in order to save herself. Yet his hurt was assuaged when she assured him that she had done so only because he had advised her thus and because she believed that this was the only way by which he might himself escape Octavian's revenge.

"If you are allowed to retire to Athens and live there as a private citizen as you requested," she said, "and if Caesarion and myself still govern Egypt, who knows what some further turn of Fortune's wheel may bring us? Defeat is never absolute, so long as we both remain free."

He believed this, or chose to believe it, because he wanted to, and because she followed her words by kissing him on the lips; and he found no taste of treachery in that kiss.

It was however young Caesarion who put a stop to these negotiations. He had never impressed me as a youth of spirit comparable to Antyllus. He was thin, undersized, positively scrawny, timid even furtive in conversation; his lips were thin, his nose crooked and his eyes squinting slightly.

But now he spoke up boldly.

"You have always assured me that I am Caesar's son," he said, "which is the title Octavian claims for himself. That being so, it is impossible that he should keep his word and allow me to live. In my opinion, he is only trying to detach you from Antony, that he may destroy us all the more easily, and utterly. I would rather put my hand in a serpent's nest than trust Octavian's words. Therefore, though our situation is indeed desperate, I believe we have no choice but to try the test of battle."

When my lord heard these words, he was deeply moved. Embracing Caesarion, he exclaimed that it might have been his father Caesar speaking.

All were convinced by the boy's inexorable logic, even Cleopatra, though she did not yet abandon all hope that she might still save something from the wreckage. It was at this time that she ordered all her treasure – precious metals, jewels, ivory, ebony, and spices – to be collected together and transported to the mausoleum which she had built near the tombs of the Ptolemies; for she understood that while she was in possession of such great riches, she retained the power to bargain with the conqueror.

That day too Caesarion was admitted to the ranks of the Ephebia and Antyllus received the *toga virilis*; for Antony said that since both had behaved in a manner worthy of true men, they should be granted the status of adults.

Octavian's advance-guard was by then approaching the outlying suburbs of Alexandria, and he himself was encamped near the Hippodrome or racecourse.

"Now is the moment," cried my lord when this news was brought to him.

And on the last day of Caesar's month he led such troops as he could muster against the enemy. Meanwhile forty ships were drawn up alongside the shore, and he marched at the head of some twenty-three legions, some Roman, others Oriental, against Octavian.

The decision to threaten Octavian's flank from the sea proved mistaken, for the ships, as soon as they were free of the harbour, were treacherously carried over to Octavian and surrendered to him. Then the infantry refused to fight, and some deserted, others fled, while only a small portion of the force retreated in orderly fashion. Therefore, although my lord at the head of the cavalry scattered those immediately opposed to him, nothing substantial was gained by this action, which was to prove indeed the last of Antony's countless victories.

He himself returned to the palace and embraced Cleopatra as if indeed he had come back in triumph. But he did so only because he knew that an appearance of dejection would spell final ruin of their cause. The Queen, to his mingled gratification and sorrow, was deceived by the shreds of magnificence he still retained, and, for a little, truly believed that he had conquered Octavian.

But he knew better, and his next move shows the desperation to which he was now reduced. He ordered me to compose a letter challenging Octavian to decide the issue in single combat. I penned this missive with the utmost reluctance, for I knew that Octavian would receive it with contempt, as a gambler's last throw of the dice. And indeed the reply was brusque: "Antony," Octavian wrote, "might think of many other ways to end his life."

For a while I did not dare to pass this message to my lord, and sought to pretend that no reply had been received. However when he had enquired searchingly of others, and been assured that a response had indeed come from his rival, he chided me kindly, even teasingly, and asked whether I supposed he was no longer man enough to hear evil news.

I do not think he had ever supposed that Octavian would accept the challenge. He knew the boy too well, and could not imagine he had acquired the physical courage he had always lacked. Moreover only a fool would have risked a game that was all but won in such a manner; and Octavian was sharp as he was crooked.

That evening, having resolved to put all to the test of a final battle the following day, my lord ordered a great banquet to be prepared, and said:

"Call my sad captains. Let us have one more gaudy night. Whatever the morrow is fated to bring, and no matter how the gods determine the issue, Antony is Antony still."

When they were gathered together and had feasted on such delicacies as were still to hand – lobster, kid, and salad dishes as I recall – and when all had drunk deep of the finest wine, my lord rose, and spoke as follows:

"Tonight," he said, "we remain masters of our fate. Tomorrow you, my servants, may belong to another master, while I lie stretched on the sand, of no consequence to any but the fowls of the air."

Many wept to hear him speak thus, and observing this, he attempted to strike a more cheerful note, assuring them that he would never yield to despair, and that his expectations of a glorious victory were at least equal to those of an honourable death.

But he dwelled on the words "honourable death" with a sincerity which he could not impart to the prospect of victory; and there can have been none there who did not feel that we were sharing a funeral feast . . .

At last the company dispersed, and Antony took leave of them with gentle words, some tears, many kisses, and the distribution of gifts.

Then I accompanied him to his chamber, where he disrobed and called for more wine and music, for, he said, "I wish my sleep on this which may be the last night of my life, to be harmonious." I sat by him till slumber rescued him from anxiety, and he slept as calm as a little child. I observed that the lines of grief and worry were smoothed from his face, and the grizzled veteran resumed his youthful beauty.

It is said that in the darkest hour of night, when the city had fallen silent, a ghostly music was heard in the streets, and that this was accompanied by the songs of praise which worshippers direct to Dionysos. Then the music and the cries faded away, till only faint echoes were heard from the sands beyond the city. Those who claim to have heard this music say it was the god at last deserting Antony whom so many had worshipped as his incarnation.

But, for my part, I heard no such music and believe that the tale was subsequently put about by Octavian's agents. Furthermore, as a rational Greek, I have always believed the gods to be indifferent to the actions and fate of men. Tales that suggest otherwise are for children, and belong to the youth of the world which is now spent. In any case, even if this were not so, it was clear to me that Antony had long been deserted by Fortune, the one god who certainly counts.

In the morning I did not march with him to battle, but occupied myself with private matters, among which was the elaboration of a plan which might secure young Antyllus from the vengeance of the victor. I am also not ashamed to say that I advanced plans for my own safety.

There was no battle. My lord's forces, some of whom were the wretched scourings of the camp, lost such heart as they had when they surveyed the mighty army which Octavian or his generals had drawn up against them. Most immediately signalled their willingness to surrender, and though my lord led a small force of cavalry against the enemy, they were quickly and ignominiously routed.

It was not yet noon when my lord returned to the palace and his face told me that no words were needed. Someone, in an attempt to stir him to renewed action, brought word that the troops had deserted on the orders of Cleopatra who was still attempting to make a separate peace with Octavian.

For a moment he stood rock-still, as horror-struck as his ancestor Herakles when his enemy Hera set Lyssa, who is also known as Madness, upon him, and drove him to slay his own children. He swayed, like a tall tree before a winter gale, and would have fallen had I not moved to support him. Then he loosed a great cry of rage and agony that echoed round the near-deserted palace. And then, after a long silence, he unleashed a torrent of words, cursing the Queen as the woman who had led him astray and brought him to his doom.

Much of what he said was incoherent, but I could not doubt that he remembered how Ahenobarbus and others had urged him to dismiss the Queen from his camp, so that Octavian should not be able to rally all Italy to his cause against the foreign woman; and how he had resisted them, refusing to believe that the woman whom in a manner of speaking he truly loved could do him any damage. In his agony he knew what others had long known that Octavian could never have made successful war against him alone, that indeed, without Cleopatra, there was no adequate cause of war; that, if he had remained true to Octavia, no breach would have been fully opened between her husband and her brother.

All these thoughts, regrets, recriminations coursed through his anguished mind. No one who loved him could have seen the dereliction of his once splendid presence without sharing his grief and pain.

Then a runner entered bearing word that the Queen, choosing death before dishonour, had stabbed herself. At once Antony, ashamed of the accusations he had that moment levelled at her, turned on himself and cried her virtues.

"What is life," he said, "to me now that the only being for whom I valued it has fled? Why do I hesitate to follow you to the tomb?"

Then he turned to me and holding out his sword, ordered me to kill him.

But I could not do so.

He summoned Eros, his armour-bearer, and gave the same command to him.

Eros took the sword, but when he gazed on Antony, could not meet his eye which still shone with the pride of a wounded lion.

"My lord, I cannot," he said, and turned the sword against himself, falling on it so that it entered deep into his belly, and he lay on the marble, spewing his guts.

Again Antony said to me:

"Critias, can you refuse me?"

And again I could not do as he wished . . .

"If Cleopatra could, why then so can I," he said, and looking at Eros, muttered, "brave Eros, you have shown me the way."

For a moment still I thought to dissuade him, for I could not imagine him dead, or contemplate the image of his lifeless body. But I bit back the words. There was nothing left for him on earth . . .

So, with a smile which recalled his finest hours, he drew a dagger from his belt and plunged it into his bowels. Then he fell upon a couch, and blood ran from his mouth.

I knelt beside him and held his hand, waiting for him to die; for I could not bear that he should die alone. So we stayed like that a long time, but he could not speak. And I confess that I was afraid lest Octavian's soldiers enter the palace and find me there. When I heard footsteps approaching at the run, I pissed myself, but still I held my master's hand.

But the man who entered was Diomedes, a secretary to Cleopatra and he carried from her a request that my lord should join her in the Monument.

To this day I do not know if the word that she was dead was a mere rumour, or whether it was a lie she had let loose, now that she had nothing to hope for from my lord. Her summons now would seem to contradict this, but that is not necessarily so. She was the most changeable of women.

Hearing her name, Antony opened his eyes, and seemed to under-stand what was said. He made a feeble gesture with his hand, which I interpreted as meaning that he wished to be with her. So I called slaves to fetch a litter, and we carried him to the Queen. The streets were deserted for none dared to be abroad since they expected Octavian's troops.

We reached the Monument, but the Queen was too afraid – for no reason I could understand – to allow the door to be opened. So it was necessary that ropes be attached to the litter, that it might be raised to the window from which Cleopatra beckoned. When the ropes were tied, I leaned over and kissed him on the lips, which I had never done before. He stretched out his hands, and they were all bloody, for he had been pressing them against his wound so that he would not die before being with the Queen again. The last I saw of him, as the litter was hauled up to the window, was these bloody hands.

So I was not with my lord when he died. But one of Cleopatra's servants, soon fleeing from the Monument, later told me that he died saying, "She ought to rejoice in the memory of his past happiness rather than bewail his present misfortunes. He had been illustrious in life and was not disgraced in death. He had conquered like a Roman and been vanquished only by a Roman."

Though I have always been inclined to disbelieve anything said by Cleopatra or her servants (even my dear Alexas would often lie to me) I think these words may be authentic. Cleopatra would never have invented that last sentence.

XXX

My lord had been my life, and I would not now have known what to do without him. But I had still one duty to perform. I returned by narrow streets and with great caution to the palace, which I found not yet occupied by Octavian's men – so great was the respect they entertained for Antony that they dared not follow the wounded lion to his lair, but held back still fearful of his renown and power even in such extremity as he had been reduced to. And nothing testifies more surely to his greatness than the timidity his enemies displayed even when they had brought him to the dust.

I sought out young Antyllus, and told him his father was dead, at which we both wept. But there was no time for grief, and I escorted him, leaving the palace by a secret passage which led underground, to the Temple of the Divine Julius, where I had arranged with the priests that he should receive sanctuary. I took with us his tutor Theodorus. Antyllus begged me with many kisses to remain with him, but, having been assured by the priests that the sanctuary was secure, and that it would be sacrilege on their part to surrender one entrusted to their care and to that of the Divine Julius, I told the boy that for his sake I was obliged to leave.

And this was true – whatever stories my enemies may subsequently have put about. When I hastened to the harbour and boarded, as I had arranged, a ship bound for Corinth, I was not thinking of my own safety. My purpose was, believing the boy to be safe for some months, to make my way to Rome, and seek out Octavia and plead with her, as she had loved my lord, to intercede with her brother on the boy's behalf.

And I have no doubt that she would have done so, on account of the nobility of her character, the love she bore Antony, and the esteem in which she had always held me.

But while I tarried at Corinth seeking a ship that would carry me safely to Italy – and this was not easy for I dared not ask openly or offer much gold for my passage – word came that Antyllus had been betrayed by the tutor, who proved a scoundrel, and that the poor boy had been dragged from sanctuary by order of Octavian, who then commanded his execution. This murder is not among the least of the crimes of which the tyrant is guilty.

The world knows that Cleopatra, having tried in vain to bend Octavian to her charms, despaired of success, and rather than walk loaded with chains in his triumph, chose to take her life, by means of an asp which she had smuggled to her in a basket of figs. She pressed it against the breasts which Antony had loved to kiss and fondle, and the poison entered her heart. She died nobly, but I could not weep or pity her, for she had destroyed my lord whose nobility surpassed hers as the sun's light surpasses that of the moon.

As for me, I lurked in Corinth for some months, finding a refuge in the attic of a brothel kept by one whom I had known years before as a tavern-boy in Athens. He had been established in this house by Scribonius Curio who had an affection for him. Curio himself was executed, not the least distinguished victim of the tyrant's blood-lust.

The compilation of this memoir occupied me for some months, for I thought it necessary to make several copies and could not entrust the task to another hand.

I lodged one in the Temple of Dionysos at Corinth, and one in the Temple of Herakles at Tiryns, his birthplace. Then I thought it meet to have one conveyed secretly to the Temple of Vesta in Rome, since it was Octavian's act of sacrilege there in purloining (and altering) my lord's will which had set his tragedy in motion.

In a moment of rashness or bravado I caused another to be conveyed to the tyrant himself. I was certain he could not forbear to read it, and it pleased me to think that he would understand that one man at least knew the full extent of his villainy. Moreover, the knowledge would breed the suspicion that there were other copies extant; and I rejoiced to think how this would disturb his nights.

Finally, since this action rendered my own life precarious, I fled from Corinth, and passed over into Asia, and thence to the lands beyond the Euxine, outwith the Empire. Here, with the gold and treasure I had taken from Cleopatra's palace I established a house. The elegance of the entertainments I offer is much appreciated by the Greek traders who are happy to taste the wares I collect in the slave-markets beyond the frontier. I am happy to say also that I find the barbarians' reputation for virtue and chastity greatly exaggerated.

In fact I may say I prosper; but I would yield all my ease, comfort, and wealth for one of my lord's smiles; and the splendour of the mountains that tower over the city where I live is as nothing to the majesty of his presence.